CW01266650

THE QUARTER YEAR MAN

ELDON CALLAWAY

Sale of this book without a front cover may be unauthorized. If this book is coverless, it may have been reported to the publisher as "unsold or destroyed" and neither the author nor the publisher may have received payment for it.

ISBN 978-1-5323-9449-2

Copyright © 2019

The Quarter Year Man

All rights reserved. Except for use in any review, the reproduction or utilization of this work in whole or in part in any form by any electronic, mechanical or other means, now known or hereinafter invented, including xerography, photocopying and recording, or in any information storage or retrieval system, is forbidden without the written permission of the publisher,

The Quarter Year Man is a work of fiction. Names, characters, places, products, and incidents are either the product of the author's imagination or are used fictitiously, and any resemblance to actual persons, living or dead, business establishments, events, or locales is entirely coincidental.

Cover design and art: Robin Casares

Dedicated with love to my mother, Carolyn Callaway, and to the memory of my father, Eldon Hayden Callaway. You both taught me how to be a better human and infused in me our family's love of history.

CONTENTS

Prologue – Washington D.C. – March 30, 1981 ix
Chapter 1   California – September 24, 2015 1
Chapter 2   Research 27
Chapter 3   Haig Men 42
Chapter 4   City of Orange, 11:48 a.m. 50
Chapter 5   Mister Thomas 62
Chapter 6   Los Angeles, California, 5:35 p.m. 73
Chapter 7   Turn of the Century 87
Chapter 8   City of Orange, 8:00 p.m. 97
Chapter 9   Washington D.C., 1981 118
Chapter 10 Yesterday's Today, 8:30 p.m. 132
Chapter 11 Washington D.C., 7:00 p.m., 12:00 a.m. 142
Chapter 12 France, April 1916 160
Chapter 13 The Hotel Solomons, September 25, 8:00 a.m. 167
Chapter 14 Hotel Solomons, September 25, 4:00 p.m. 182
Chapter 15 Washington D.C., September 25, 8:00 p.m. 190
Chapter 16 San Francisco, September 26, 2:00 a.m. 198
Chapter 17 San Francisco, September 26, 9:00 a.m. 202
Chapter 18 Hillside Cemetery, September 26, 10:15 a.m. 204
Chapter 19 The Hospital, September 26, 11:02 a.m. 215
Chapter 20 St. Michaels Hospital, Ten Days Later 226
Author's Note 239
Acknowledgments 241

PROLOGUE

WASHINGTON D.C. — MARCH 30, 1981

Robert Hunter sat at one of the small, nondescript tables in one of the break rooms of the White House. He was leaning back in the chair, almost recklessly, while stretching his legs out on another. In his left hand, he was reading a folded over newspaper, while in his right, he would take the occasional sip of black coffee from his cup, emblazoned with the nation's seal on its side.

He was enjoying one of those rare moments in a day when he could put aside his job as a Secret Service agent. He preferred waking early so he could spend a few quiet hours relaxing, before the duties of his day took over. The silence of the moment was abruptly interrupted by the entry of two fellow agents.

"I'm serious. Hoopsnakes are a real thing. Saw one once when I was in Death Valley, when I was a kid."

The deep voice entering the room belonged to Ezekiah Stone. Forty years of age, he looked closer to thirty. His body was fit to the extent that he appeared to be cut from black marble. Normally, he would have been sporting a close crop of hair, but his family's early gray curse had hit him hard a few months back. He now sported a clean, bald head. When Stone smiled, as he was now, you wondered how his square chin didn't chip from the effort.

Stone walked over to the double set of coffee pots, picking up his mug where he had left it, sitting upside down on a paper towel to dry from cleaning it the night before.

"Yeah. I'm not catching what you're flinging, Zeke," Hal Henrad said flatly, leaning against the entry doorframe.

Hal Henrad appeared to be fresh out of high school, though that would be an error in judgement, as he was nearly twenty-five. Thin as a rail, though all of it muscle, one might have expected him to be surfing on a beach rather than working at the government's center. His hair was naturally blonde, almost bleached blonde. That, and his age, made most people underestimate him. He had risen through the ranks quickly, managing to gain a post in the Secret Service at the White House, something unheard of.

Stone poured himself a cup of coffee from the full pot, replacing it as he spoke. "The problem with you younger folk is you don't believe anything. You want proof." Glancing over at Hunter, almost noticing him for the first time, Stone pointed his mug in his direction. "Ask him if you don't believe me. Bob lived out west. He'll back me up on this."

With a resigned sigh, Hunter lowered his newspaper, taking his queue. "What do you need proof of now, Wonder Boy?"

Hal pointed an accusing finger at Stone. "Don't need proof when you know someone's blowing smoke up your butt."

"See? No respect for his elders. Just tell him about the hoopsnakes, Bob." Gesturing with his free hand, from Hunter to Henrad, Stone sipped his strong coffee with a satisfied smirk.

Giving up on reading the morning news, Hunter tossed the paper onto the table. Taking a long pull from his coffee cup, he drained the rest of the hot, bitter liquid before answering.

"Hoopsnakes are a close cousin to the sidewinder, belonging to the genus Crotalus. They generally have thick, black leathery scales, resembling the tread on a tire. Part of how they got their name is when they want to move fast, they grab their tail in their mouth, and roll along like a hula hoop."

Henrad stared at Hunter for a moment, then over to Stone, still smugly sipping his coffee. Pulling away from the wall, he walked over to Hunter's table. Slowly, he sat in the empty chair next to him. Staring directly into Hunter's eyes, he asked skeptically. "How is it I never heard of them before?"

"They're on the endangered species list. Only one's left are in California. As far as I know," Hunter said matter-of-factly.

Henrad cocked his head, still with doubt. "Hunted for their skins, venom, or something?" He leaned forward for the answer.

"No, their skins aren't the kind of thing someone would want on their purse or boots. Also, very tough to work with. Venom isn't much to speak of either. Oh, if you were a kid, or someone old like Stone over there," Hunter winked to Henrad, "you could get ill, maybe even die if you have poor health. Their venom is meant just to paralyze its victim long enough so it can wrap around it to squeeze it dead. No, the problem was the invention of the car."

Henrad leaned back in his chair. "Now I know you're pulling my leg."

"I'm serious. They love sunning themselves on roads. Couldn't even begin to tell you the percentage of the species that have died under a car's wheel." Hunter glanced over to Stone enjoying his coffee before he continued. "Of course, cars wouldn't deplete the species that badly. Problem is, they have a natural predator that has just about finished them off."

"Like a mongoose?"

"Kind of. You see, that's the odd part. Their only true predator is also endangered. Think there's only a handful left of them in the country, and they're also only in California now. Tripoderos. Strangest looking thing I've ever seen. Ugly as all get out, but gentle to a human, like a dog. They thrive on hoopsnakes."

Henrad squinted an eye at Hunter, saying the name slowly. "Tri--pod--eros?"

"Yeah, three-legged critters. Metallic grey skin with a bulbous area for the body above. One ugly looking hole for a mouth underneath, with some pretty nasty teeth. Harmless to you and me, but death to a hoopsnake."

Henrad nodded his head up and down, taking this all in, before folding his arms and looking at the two men.

"You guys are so full of shit."

Stone had just begun to take another sip and had to cover his mouth to keep from spitting the liquid out. As he half-choked, half-laughed deeply, Hunter smiled apologetically to Stone.

"Tripodero was a bit much, huh?"

"That's what tripped you up when you tried to pull that story on me, too. Told you to leave it out on Wonder Boy here." Stone laughed before beginning a second bout of coughing.

"Guess people just aren't as gullible as they once were." Hunter said with a shrug.

"Aren't you on Rawhide detail today?" Henrad questioned Hunter.

With a tired sigh, Hunter stood up, and walked to the sink with his cup. "McCarthy is taking care of Reagan. I'm stuck here babysitting Secretary Haig and some others. Appears I am getting too old for the president's detail."

"You and me both, Bob. I've been stuck with Hal here on some errand today. Talk about a living hell." Stone said, recovered from his fit of coughing.

"Oh, ha, ha! You should be glad to bask in my presence all day."

Hunter did a quick rinse on his cup, a lazy smile on his lips, as he listened to his friends banter back and forth. He wasn't completely thrilled about being taken off Rawhide's detail, but he understood. Watching over Haig and a few others in the White House would be a cakewalk. He should be happy for the easy work, but it tugged at a part of him that he was finally aging past doing certain things anymore. *Time eventually catches up to all of us, I guess.* That thought brought another smile to his face.

CHAPTER ONE

CALIFORNIA — SEPTEMBER 24, 2015

The sign on the outside of the small shop simply read *Yesterday's Today* in bold, black, block letters. The front of the building was not large, but did have enough room for two windows displaying various antiques. The window on the left held a few pieces of furniture from the early 1900's, displayed tastefully for anyone passing by to easily see. The window on the right was more of a high boxed area made up to display small items, slightly angled out to the street. Prominently taking up residence there were a variety of pocketwatches, wristwatches, saloon tokens from the 1800's, and an array of pipes set beside metal lighters from various time frame eras.

The interior of the shop was not the usual haphazard display of merchandise strewn about a room, but a well-placed and thought-out formula of time. As one entered the shop, the first items they would see on their left and right were the most recent items in history. Following either wall to the back of the shop led you further into the past, until you came to the glass cases lining the back end of the antique store. In the middle of the shop were rows of tall glass cases, each one leading you further back in time as you moved closer to the rear of the shop, all holding smaller items asking to be bought.

Sitting behind the long glass counter in back, by an old, turn-of-the-century register being used for just that purpose, sat a young man of about thirty years of age on a padded stool. His dirty blonde hair, what some might call a mop top, was neatly combed. He wore a nice pair of tan slacks with a long-sleeved, white shirt rolled up to his elbows. The dirt on his face was an attempt to grow a mustache, something he hadn't yet given up hope on. He was leafing through a *Life* magazine from the 1940's, looking at the pictures. Later, he would take the time to read any article that piqued his interest. He was passing over pictures of Marilyn Monroe at some function when the little brass bell above the entrance chimed, letting him know there was a customer.

Andrew Goulding glanced up from the magazine, seeing the familiar look of sensory overload that crossed the faces of most people who entered the shop. The first thing Andrew noticed was he was wearing a suit. Not that it was out of place, but you just didn't see that very often with the type of people that frequented the shop. The second was that the guy needed a shave. Losing interest, Andrew went back to perusing the magazine, figuring if the guy had any questions, he would ask.

The man entering the shop had been slightly stunned by everything he was seeing. He had never been in an antique store before, nor did he have a reason to ever walk into one. He didn't really understand the reasoning people had to buy up things someone else had once owned. "Antique" was just another word for "used" in his book. Taking a quick survey of the interior of the shop, he decided his best bet might be with the larger furniture that lined the walls. Walking nonchalantly to his right, he perused the various items placed along that wall, trying to figure out which one would be best for what he needed.

As he took his relaxed stroll down the wall of furniture, he would take frequent glances to the back, at the boy behind the counter, to see if he was watching him. He shouldn't have worried as with each glance, he could tell the boy only had interest in the magazine before him. That would help immensely with what he needed to do. He stopped suddenly at a wooden roll-top desk and chair combination with a small cardboard sign stating *New Arrival* in red marker.

Reaching into his coat pocket, he pulled out a small metal case and brush. He glanced once more at the boy to be sure he was still occupied, satisfied, he opened the case, dipping the brush into the powder. Using his body to block what he was doing from the back counter, he began twirling the brush lightly against the back of the chair. Blowing lightly on the powder, he saw what appeared to be a set of fingerprints and smiled.

"Bingo," he whispered to himself.

Putting the case and brush back into his pocket, he took out a few clear fingerprinting cells from his other pocket, and quickly went to work to gather what he could from the back of the chair. That done, he wiped down the dusty mess with the inside of his coat, then continued his walk down the row of furniture to the back counter.

"Excuse me. Are you the owner?" he asked, already knowing the answer.

Andrew looked up from the magazine page showing a picture of Elizabeth Taylor and shifted it out of the way.

"No. That would be Daniel Collum. I'm his assistant."

The man nodded, as if he had expected that answer. Pulling a color photo from his coat, he handed it over to Andrew.

"You wouldn't happen to have this in your shop, would you? It's a one-of-a-kind, and I was informed I might be able to find it here."

Andrew accepted the color photograph, taking a long look at it. The image was of a flag with a green background. On one side was a yellow harp below white clouds, with light shining down out of them. Lighter green shamrocks were below the harp. A golden yellow motto, in a foreign language, was above and below in a banner of red. Below that, and on the other side of the flag, was written a presentation and the locations the regiment had fought in, all in yellow on the green background.

"Civil War flag I believe, correct?"

"Yes, it's the 2nd regimental colors of the 69th. I've been tracking it down for some time now and believe this Mr. Collum may be in possession of it."

Andrew shrugged apologetically, "Well, I know we don't have anything in the shop like this. If we have it, the boss probably has it locked away somewhere."

The man held his hand out for the picture which Andrew returned readily. He then took a pen out of his coat, and wrote something on the back of the photo, before handing it back to Andrew.

"Well, if he finds it, tell him I would be more than ready to offer this price for it."

Andrew whistled slowly, staring at the amount on the back of the photograph.

"My number is there as well. You have a good day now."

With that, the man in the brown suit walked out of the shop, setting off the brass bell over the door again. Andrew looked at the door, and back at the dollar figure on the photograph, then shook his head.

"With a sale like that we could close the place for a month and then some."

The man in the brown suit left the shop and turned right, walking around the corner. He went around back where the parking lot was located, patting his pocket. He had tried for months to get anything close to a fingerprint from this Collum guy, but to no avail. The man had a bad habit of wiping clean anything he touched with his bare hands. He had tried to get into the man's house a few times, but the alarm system was way out of his league. The prints he pulled in the store should finally get him the definitive answer to a big question.

He walked up to a beaten, old silver sedan and unlocked the back door. Upon the door's opening, a couple of empty soda cans spilled out, making a loud, tinny noise. He reached inside, not caring if anyone saw the trash falling out of his car. Grabbing two manila file folders, he placed them under his left arm. Reaching down, he gathered the two Suds Root Beer cans and tossed them back into the car. Closing the door, he locked it again.

Taking the back street of the parking area all the way to Chapman Avenue, he turned right and walked the short distance to his daily destination, *The Ristorante*, an Italian restaurant just before the *Circle of Orange*, a roundabout thoroughfare at the center of the *Old Towne Plaza*. As the hour was still early for the lunch crowd, he seated himself at one of the outside tables, slapping the files down on the black metal surface. In short order, the young waitress he had grown accustomed to seeing, walked up and set down a white porcelain saucer, coffee cup, and four cubes of sugar placed around the edge of the saucer. The coffee's steam sent its lovely bitter aroma to his nose. The waitress walked away without a word, but he knew she would bring him his usual brunch in a little while.

Dropping the four sugars into his coffee, he stirred the contents with his spoon, watching the cubes slowly disintegrate. He was in no hurry, as he knew his mark wouldn't show for another ten minutes or so. Going into the antique store was a bit of a risk, but for months he had been unable to obtain anything even close to a partial print on his mark. He had been forced to go into the store while the owner was away, hoping beyond hope he could lift the man's fingerprints. He once tried going through the high window in back, leading to the restroom, but found it was fixed with a deadbolt from inside the shop. Who does that? Dimico was left with pulling fingerprints from the bathroom. Oh, he managed to get quite a few; patrons and the assistant, but still none from the owner. It was a bit childish of him, but he had been so frustrated about the fingerprint issue that he felt he needed to put a scare in his mark. Now that it was done, he wondered if the whole story about the picture and flag might have been a step too far in his petty, frustrated state.

Morgan Dimico shrugged, taking a sip of his sweetened, hot coffee. It didn't matter now. The damage was done. As he set the cup back on the saucer, he noticed another stray thread on the sleeve of his suit and sighed. There had been a time when the few suits he had owned, while not expensive, were fashionable and well-kept. Now his suit had worn elbows and the occasional thread sticking out here and there. He put his hand to his cheek, rubbing the stubble that had sprouted the last couple of days on his face. A face that had grown much older over the last few years. Even his light brown hair had gone mostly gray and he was only forty-two. Like his clothes, he had become worn with age.

Pulling the fingerprint cells from his pocket, he used his phone to send them to someone he knew in the force. All he had to do was wait for the answer. Taking another long sip of the sweetened hot java, he wondered if his little act at the antique shop had fallen flat. The price he had written on the photo didn't match up to the way he looked at all. Glancing down at the two worn files on the table, he decided not to worry about it any longer. Without noticing the multiple coffee stains on the cover, he opened the faded manila folder labeled Robert Hunter, that was only half as full as the newer one beside it.

He had read through the file dozens of times already, so did not feel a need to do so again. He was looking for anything he might have missed, something that had seemed insignificant at the time, but now might shed some light on his subject.

Robert Hunter had served in the Army during Vietnam, a chopper pilot ferrying the wounded back to the mobile units. Nothing particularly special there until he was shot down on one return run. He managed to safely crash without losing the lives of his passengers, holding off an attack by the enemy long enough for reinforcements to arrive. He had been awarded for that action, and rotated back home, eventually landing a spot for himself in the Secret Service. The rest he had gone over numerous times, but he just could not come up with anything new. To all accounts, Hunter had disappeared during his service at the White House under Reagan's leadership. There were spots in the file that were blacked out. He wished he knew what was there, but knew better than to go digging too deeply, though he was sure that's where the answers were to be found.

Dimico sighed and moved the file aside as his brunch was delivered without comment. He had quickly put a stop to small talk with the young woman, letting her know he wanted to be left alone. It had taken a few days, but she eventually got the message and kept quiet. The place was slightly more expensive than he would have liked, but it was the only place he could sit and watch his prey without standing out in a crowd. Well, that and the food was simply amazing. He closed the file on Robert Hunter, digging into his meat omelet, when he saw his mark stroll up across the street.

Daniel Collum had been taking his usual morning stroll, something he liked to do to get his blood flowing every morning. He would open his shop, spend a little time with Andrew getting things up and running, before taking his long walk through the historic area. Other than the exercise, it calmed him to walk through the history that surrounded him, his joy of life renewed each day. He always began his walk by crossing the street to the post office and spending a few minutes with Victor. Victor was close to eighty and refused to retire from the postal service. His take was that the post office would fall apart without him there to supervise the young whipper-snappers. Daniel loved talking to this just over five-foot, snow white-haired, ball of energy, as he checked his box for any mail -- always junk.

The area around the *Circle of Orange* was a who's who of historical brick shops and Victorian style homes. Even the restaurants looked more like little bistros of another time. The trees lining both sides of the street were still quite green, though some of the leaves were showing the beginning signs of the fall season. Being Southern California, most people were still wearing their summer clothes, though here and there you could see a light jacket or windbreaker.

Crossing Glassell Street, he followed the curve of the sidewalk which would lead him to his destination. Daniel Collum could see that a small number of people were either finishing their breakfasts or beginning their brunch at the restaurant across the street. Not one payed attention to those few pedestrians passing by to unknown locals or errands.

Reaching the finish line of his walk, Daniel sat down at one of the small, black wrought iron tables set up outside his favorite coffee house. He gave a light wave to the young girl inside who smiled and waved back to him. In less than a minute, Chloe came out with a cup of coffee, a plate holding a muffin, and the day's newspaper tucked under her arm. Setting everything on the table, she put her hands on her hips, giving him a motherly look, which might have seemed comical on someone else. She wore a simple uniform of white, with blue trim, the skirt tastefully coming down to her knees. She had her dirty blonde hair up in a bun and Daniel always wondered what it would look like if it was set free.

"One of these days I'm going to get you to try something else. Don't you ever get bored?"

"All the time, but I never tire of this." He blew on his coffee and tried to take a sip of the hot brew, but could tell he would have to wait a moment. "How are your college classes going this semester, Chloe?"

She genuinely smiled at this. "Mostly pretty good. Though I'm having a little trouble with my history class. We're currently going through the early 1900's, turn of the century stuff, and I'm finding it a little hard to keep focus."

Daniel took another tentative sip of his black coffee with no additives and decided it was ready to drink.

"Really? I found that period quite interesting. If you need any help with it, you just ask."

Chloe grinned again, "Thank you, Mr. Collum. That would be great." She glanced inside the coffee shop noticing a small line beginning to form. "I better get back inside and help. I'll be back to check on you a little later."

"I'll be right here." He winked back, unfolding his newspaper to begin his brunch ritual.

●━━•

Across the street where he had set up his surveillance, Morgan Dimico had spread a stack of photographs on the table, over the manila folder they had come in. The faded name on the second folder's label, printed in black ink, was Daniel Collum. The pictures appeared to span over a long period of time; black and white, faded brown, as well as color photos. The viewer kept picking up one picture after another, comparing it with the one he kept in his left hand. With each new photo, he would then look up and gaze across the street to the little coffee shop at the man sitting alone at the small table.

Dimico took another bite of his breakfast, without really noticing, as he gazed at the dark-haired gentleman who had become his own personal Twilight Zone episode. Daniel was neatly groomed, with the appearance of someone between forty and fifty years of age. He wore a light brown jacket, possibly suede, more a fashion statement than an actual need against the current weather. Dimico held up another photo, looking from it to the one in his left hand, then to the man across the street and mumbled, "Normally you might not look twice at that face. You could go your whole life never realizing you'd seen it before, and yet, here you are. How is it you've managed to live for over a century Mr. Collum, or whoever you are?"

As he sat in front of *The Bitter End*, enjoying his sparse meal, Daniel paused from reading about some other horror in the news. He had been having an enjoyable morning and didn't want to ruin it with the bad things going on in the world. He breathed in deeply, having always preferred the fall season and the briskness it would bring in the air. Admittedly, this wouldn't happen for a little while yet here in California, but he could sense it. Having been through so many before, it was almost like an internal clock telling him it was about time to wake up. It wasn't until after Chloe had refilled his cup and he had just about finished the bran muffin, when that feeling came over him. That feeling that makes you think there are eyes on you. Holding his half-folded newspaper low enough to see over, Daniel scanned the street he was sitting in front of. Sipping his bitter coffee, and nibbling on his bran muffin, he took the time to look over the area three times thoroughly before he was sure there was only one individual watching him. He had noticed him right off when the feeling had come up, sitting at the restaurant across the street from himself. As Daniel finished the bran muffin, quite excellent considering the circumstance, he also noticed the watcher holding up two photographs. It was almost as if he was comparing them. Then the watcher did an odd thing. He kept one up in his left hand as he looked across to him.

"Oh great," he thought. "They've managed to find me."

●━━•

Thoughts of the past thirty-four years drifted in and out of his memory as Daniel took the long way around to his shop. He crossed Glassell Street at *Plaza Square*, following the *Circle* to cross East

Chapman, before continuing down this new street. He paused briefly at a store to look in the window before turning right onto South Orange Street, past the *First United Methodist Church*, and turning right again onto East Almond Avenue. He would stop at odd intervals, quickly checking his back to see if he was being followed.

It may have seemed a little excessive, but Daniel figured that, if they were only recently following him, they might not know about his shop yet. Not likely, but it was a hope. All thoughts of the fall season forgotten, Daniel wondered how they could have figured out he was still alive. By the time he reached Almond Avenue, he was satisfied he wasn't being tailed. The frumpy man at the restaurant was not following him, and he had lost that sense of eyes on him as well. That was something at least. He would know how bad it was once he got back to his own shop. Hopefully Andrew had been left alone with no knowledge of what may be happening.

Reaching the corner of Almond and Glassell, Daniel gazed down the street from the direction he had begun his long escape. Looking past the old record store and little post office, he decided it was safe enough, and crossed the street to his own antique shop. He stepped through the door of *Yesterday's Today* and felt over a century of life's smells and visuals assail his senses, and with that, so many memories for a man who should never have lived so long. Allowing himself a moment to gather his senses, he noticed Andrew was not sitting behind the counter in the back, and he grew concerned.

"Andrew?"

No answer. His nerves began to tighten again when Andrew opened the door of the corner restroom and stepped out.

"Hey there, Boss."

Daniel gave a sigh of relief as Andrew closed the door, walking back behind the counter.

"Andrew, how many times have I told you to lock the restroom door."

Rolling his eyes, Andrew walked back to the door, and locked the deadbolt with his key. "Why do we need to lock it when we're here? Why not just wait until the end of the day?"

"In case we forget. Last thing I need is another thief going through the restroom window and entering the store. That's why I put the lock on the door in the first place."

"Seems a little excessive, but okay, I'll try to remember."

Daniel watched him walk back to the stool behind the counter. He was quite slim, gangly really, not in a physically fit kind of way either. He stood about three inches shorter than Daniel's six feet, but had a shine to his personality that had not dimmed in his short number of years. He sat down on the stool, turned the page of the magazine that he apparently had been going through, and smiled. "Hey, Boss. You look like you saw a ghost or something."

"Andrew, how many times have I told you to just call me Danny, Dan or Daniel? There's only the two of us, I doubt 'Boss' really needs to be used between us." Daniel said with a sigh, though the right side of his mouth went up slightly in a smile.

"Sorry, sorry. You just don't seem to fit Danny at all, and Dan just seems too personal. Daniel is a bit formal, but I'll try and remember the next time, Bo . . . next time."

"Anyone been in since I left this morning?" Daniel prodded.

"Only a couple of people. A woman was looking to see if she could sell us something. I told her you'd be in a little later, as I'd never dealt with that kind of item before. The other was a middle-aged guy who was inquiring about a specific Civil War item, the 69th Regimental Colors, I think. He was hoping we might have it. I told him if we did, it was probably locked up somewhere, but I'd never seen it. He gave me a number in case you were interested, along with an offer of what he was willing to pay."

Andrew handed over the photograph to Daniel as he finished his story and whistled. "I looked at the back. Not sure if the guy is some big-time collector or just some crazy dude. That's a lot of green he's offering."

Daniel looked down at the photo showing the flag and his stomach dipped a little. On the back was a phone number hand written below a scrawled amount in blue ink.

"Five hundred thousand dollars for the famous 2nd Irish Colors of the 69th Regiment. Well, he got my attention. Problem is, John F.

Kennedy gave that flag to the government of Ireland. What I have is a copy." In reality, President Kennedy had given them a very good facsimile. Daniel would be the only living person to know that, as he had the original tucked safely away in a metal briefcase, hidden below the bottom drawer of his filing cabinet in the office.

"Forgive me my ignorance, but what's so valuable about this flag?" Andrew said questioningly.

Daniel's gaze drifted away a thousand miles in a moment, going back to December of 1862. He could see the fog that morning just as easily today in his mind. He was then just a boy of fourteen, closing in on fifteen in just a couple short months. Already looking older than his actual age, he was just about as tall as most full-grown men. On this day, though, he was still holding a drum as a weapon instead of a rifle. That same day, he had lost his father, as well as a large majority of his fellow 'Fighting 69th Irish Brigade.' Marye's Heights, consisting of several hills separated by ravines, just forty to fifty feet above the plains themselves, turned into a bed of carnage for his fellow men. "I'm sorry, I lost my train of thought. What was the question?"

"The flag. Why is it so valuable?" Andrew asked again, slightly worried at the harried look on his employer's face.

"The famous 2nd Irish Colors were given to the Fighting 69th the day after the battle at Fredericksburg. So many were wounded or killed that day. The flag stands as a symbol of honor, strength, and heroism. Its motto says it all, "Who never retreated from the clash of spears." Daniel breathed in deeply, letting the air out quietly.

"Didn't know you could read Latin, Boss--umm, Daniel. It was all gibberish to me. Wow, too bad you don't have the original."

"If I did have it I would never part with it. No amount of money would be enough for that symbol of human sacrifice."

Andrew nodded, and Daniel came to a decision. "Why don't you go ahead and go home for the day, full pay. I think we could afford to close down on a slow day like today."

"Something wrong?"

"No, no, nothing wrong. That photo just reminded me of something and I'm going to need to take some time, uninterrupted, to go over the research books."

"Something about that flag?" Andrew's voice hinted of hope.

"No, another flag that I'd been hearing about that might bring us a pretty penny, but I'm going to have to research it first." Daniel hated to lie to his assistant, but he needed him out of the shop, so he could do what was needed.

Andrew stared at Daniel for just a moment, then grabbed his backpack and headed out through the door, the bell ringing his departure. "Thanks, Daniel. You have a good day."

Daniel went over to the door and locked the three deadbolts, then turned the green OPEN sign to the red CLOSED. Turning around, he took inventory of all the items he'd built up over the years. Many were his own, but most were those bought specifically for the shop. Letting out a full breath, he scanned the room for hiding places a bugging device might be. He was convinced that even if he had not been followed to the shop, there was a good chance they already knew of the place and had hidden listening devices, possibly even surveillance cameras in his store without his knowing.

Fredericksburg. The talk of that flag brought the place to the forefront of his mind. Had not thought about that in some time, but it hadn't started there, had it?

You could start at the beginning when he was born, but to Daniel, the start of his life had been the Civil War. His family had left a ravaged Ireland, coming to America in 1848 with dreams of prosperity. It only took one year living in the Land of the Free to realize that dream could be harsh and fleeting. Daniel's father, Sean, had gone from farming in Killimor, to working whatever jobs he could find in New York City. His mother, Mary Kate, had built up a little business of her own washing clothes. Daniel himself had done what he could, taking clean clothes back to their owners, helping take groceries to homes, any menial job a boy could get.

Then the Southern states began leaving Congress, like rats on a sinking ship, in early 1861. His father made the decision to sign up in the Federal army, figuring he'd be able to make enough to send back home. Daniel had gone with him, and at the age of thirteen, became one of the many 'Drummer Boys' of the Civil War. They found themselves in the 69th Regiment, Irish Brigade, what was later known as "The Fighting 69th." Daniel spent most of his time beside the troops, keeping time for their marches, but soon learned there would be other jobs a drummer was required to do. Manassas was supposed to be the beginning and end of the war. As it turned out, the Battle of Bull Run turned into a terrible route for the Union troops, with the Fire Zouaves and the 69th forming the rear guard for the retreat. What was to have been the one and only battle of the Civil War turned into just the first of many in a war that would last four years. Daniel found himself working as stretcher bearer throughout most of the battle. He and the rest of the drummers would go onto the field, where they could, bringing the many wounded back to safety.

●—— •

Daniel came out of his trance with a blink of his eyes. *Yup, we made it back to the Capital with our tails between our legs and licking our wounds.* Pushing those thoughts away, Daniel went behind the glass countertop and bent down to a small drawer. Pulling out an old key, he inserted and turned it, opening the drawer. Inside, among the dust, was a much more modern device than the cabinet it was housed in. Taking hold of the metal box, Daniel began the process of moving it around the room, paying attention to the needle in the window. Slowly and methodically, he completed a full sweep, customer and employee sections of the entire shop. Pursing his lips in a questioning manner, he shook his head disbelievingly.

"No bugs at all, and no cameras. That's a pleasant surprise I'm sure won't last long once they decide I'm who they think I am."

Daniel placed the device back in the drawer, relocking it, then moved to the back office to think. His thoughts jumped from one memory to another as he shuffled his way to the leather chair behind the old walnut desk, but they all came back to his beginning. The

Civil War seemed like yesterday to him but so long ago at the same time. Thirteen years old when it all started, yet I'm no older than fifty-three now. Yeah, fifty-three. Not bad for a man one hundred and sixty-seven years old. Daniel opened the long pencil drawer in the desk, pulling out two very old and worn wooden drum sticks. Thirteen years old. 1861, Manassas Virginia, then 1862 Yorktown Virginia, and after that Antietam Maryland and the worst fighting to date, and he just a boy of fourteen by then. Years later they would say it was the bloodiest, single day battle in American history. To Daniel, it was just a nightmare that would never go away, hiding itself from time to time, only to return when he'd least expect it in his dreams.

September 17[h], 1862, the first major battle fought on Union soil. General McClellan's army of 75,500 met General Robert E. Lee's army of 38,000. You would have thought with those numbers it would have been a complete victory with minor losses, for McClellan's men, but Daniel knew otherwise. The battle was touted as a strategic victory for the Union, though inconclusive tactically. Inconclusive? Disaster more like it. By the end of the battle, McClellan's army had suffered 12,400 casualties, while Lee had only suffered 10,316. Luckily, Daniel and his father were not on the casualty list that day. How, he would never know, but his father survived unscathed through the attack against Lee's center at Sunken Hill. Of all the bad that happened that day, one good thing did come of it. It was enough of a victory for President Lincoln to confidently announce the Emancipation Proclamation. With that one proclamation, the Confederacy's hope of being recognized by the British and French governments were dashed to the ground.

Shaking his head to clear the memories, Daniel lightly placed one old drumstick to his cheek. "I don't know who that man was, but he apparently knows something of me. No bugging devices or cameras hidden in the store. So, what does that tell you? That either this man has just found you and they haven't had time to stake out the shop, or they have no intention of taking you . . . alive." The drumstick tapped a slow beat with each point on his right cheek.

"Scenario two. The man with the photos has nothing to do with the cover up. He might have figured out what I was." That could be almost as dangerous in the long term, but much easier to deal with than the Haig Men, as he had come to call them. Worse yet, what if the man was involved in all of it? "Bad enough to be one or the other, but if it was the Haig Men, and they also have knowledge of my long and multiple lives, that would be a definite problem."

Placing both sticks back into the drawer, Daniel stood up slowly, feeling all one hundred sixty-seven years of his life. *I won't be able to pull any money from the bank.* Well, not the bank he was using under his real name anyway. "Now that was stupid, Daniel. You'd think after living as long as you have, that you wouldn't have become so complacent as to use your real name, even after all this time." A sudden thought struck him so hard he lost the breath he was taking in. Sucking in air, he unconsciously combed his hair with his right hand, stopping at the back of his head.

"Veronica Jenkins. That must be the tie-in to all this." Still holding the back of his head with his right hand, he bent his head back, shaking it from side to side. "Let's see, it's been just about a year ago that she interviewed me for the magazine. Chances are she finished all her research and got her story published." Putting his hand down and moving across the room to the corkboard, Daniel unpinned a business card he had placed there last year. The white of the card was faded and a little browned from the sunlight coming in through the high window into the room, but it was still quite legible.

Veronica Jenkins
Freelance Writer of History

It was that second line on the card that had made him decide to do the interview in the first place. "Freelance Writer of History," not "Freelance History Writer" which he would have expected. He had liked the look of Veronica from the first moment he saw her on his doorstep. Flaming, curly red hair, allowed to run wild and free without the touch of a brush. It flowed down just past her neck, skin just barely hinting the touch of sunlight. Tall, with her retro-vintage black heels and green dress that accentuated the whole ensemble. That she just showed up at his home showed him a woman who wasn't afraid to take chances. Slightly odd for someone who's business was dealing in history.

Veronica had taken an interest in every detail of his home as he showed her in. Offering her a seat in his living room, not one thing in his house escaped her scrutiny. She noticed every knickknack, every photo, and even some of his furniture which he'd kept throughout his life. She never said a word, taking it all in as she sat down, though Daniel felt she wanted to. Being a proper host, he offered her a cup of coffee or tea. She declined, though asked for just a glass of water, if it was not any trouble. While pouring the water into two glasses, Daniel finally broke the awkwardness.

"So, what brings you to see me, Ms. Jenkins?"

"Please, just call me Veronica. I'm sorry for just showing up on your doorstep, but I feel it's sometimes best to surprise those I need to speak to, rather than setting up an appointment to meet. It makes the conversations much more interesting and less sterile, Mr. Collum."

"Daniel, please. Well, what exactly would you like from me, Veronica?" Daniel's mind was turning over a multitude of reasons she could be here. So many things he may have forgotten to cover up or change. Things he may have thought were harmless, but somehow told exactly who he was. He kept an interested, though somewhat bored look on his face, difficult considering what might be at stake.

Veronica took a sip of water, then took to examining the glass itself. Tapping the side with a manicured finger, she commented, "Anglo/Irish thumb cut crystal tumbler." She sounded a bit surprised and impressed. She also noticed he was taken aback by her response. "I'm pretty sure 19th century?"

"On the nose. How . . ?"

"Oh, the history of people is not my only interest, Daniel. If I'm not mistaken, those candlesticks on the fireplace are Georgian Anglo/Irish cut crystal as well, also 19th century." She nonchalantly pointed over her shoulder with her thumb.

Slowly regaining his composure, Daniel replied "Yes, handed down in the family since the 1800's. I'm guessing you've also noticed other items as well. I keep almost all of the family antiques here, none for sale, unlike what I have in my shop."

"Too bad." Slightly pouting as she set the tumbler down, "The price of the candlesticks alone would catch over four thousand dollars."

"Over four thousand five hundred, but priceless as sentimental family heirlooms." Daniel responded taking a sip of his own water.

"Of course. Well, why I'm here. I'm doing a story for a Civil War magazine. I try to find stories in history that don't get touched on as often and write them up with a slight twist. In this case, I'm doing a piece on the true boys of the Civil War, drummer boys to be exact. The twist on the story is finding descendants of the boys in blue and gray, getting their part of the story. What they may or may not know of their ancestors, how they feel about it, what value it may or may not have had in shaping their own lives. That sort of thing." She took another sip of water.

"What makes you believe that I may have anything to do with a story like that?" Daniel decided to see where she might be going with this before revealing anything on his own. This could be a touchy area to get into without him getting into trouble.

Smiling that 'please don't waste my time' sort of smile, Veronica flatly stated, "Well, to start, your name for one. Daniel Collum. The name of one of the boys in blue was also named Daniel Collum. I researched quite a bit on family history, and though there were some odd missing spots, I'm pretty sure I have the right person. Seeing the picture on the mantle just verified my suspicion that you are a descendant of the young Collum. The resemblance is actually pretty uncanny if you just add years to that boyish face." She took another sip of water, and set the glass down, still looking directly at Daniel.

"You could be a detective with that kind of attention to detail, Veronica. Yes, I am directly related to the boy in the picture." What a fool, Daniel thought. First, leaving the picture where someone might put two and two together. And using his real name was another mistake. Sure, it had been almost one hundred fifty years, but it apparently had not been long enough for someone as bright as Miss Jenkins to figure out. It was almost funny to him that by using his real name, he had unwittingly made noticeable holes in his history. Ever since computers had become a household necessity, his job had become much more difficult when forging his past.

All this flashed in his mind in a second. "Really, it's no secret that I'm related. I was just curious as to how you managed to piece it all together." *Yeah, no secret, that was rich.*

"I'm very good at what I do, Daniel. May I also ask if that old photo is an original? I would love to get a copy if that's at all possible, if it is. Antietam, correct?"

Daniel smiled genuinely, "Yes, it's an original photo. From what I recall, it was taken before the 69th charged on Sunken Hill. Everyone in the picture were the drummers, except for the man in the back. He was the 69th's chaplain. I believe the picture was taken after he prayed over the boys before the battle. Yes, you may get a copy if you like, and yes, you are definitely good at what you do."

Daniel had spent the better part of that afternoon going over his feelings about his younger self. What he thought of a boy who had fought in the War Between the States. If he thought knowing any of it had shaped his own life, etcetera. He had found Veronica very easy to talk to, too easy in fact. Daniel found himself needing to be extra careful he did not let anything slip he did not want her to know, present or past.

They also spent a good deal of time just talking about whatever hit their fancy. He commented on her style of clothes which were a throwback to the 1940's and 50's. He had made them a lunch and shown her around his house while they talked about the architecture's history. He had a feeling she was extending her visit well past what was needed for her article, but he hadn't cared. Eventually she packed her old recorder away, closed her notebook, and thanked him for taking so much of his time to chat with her.

A shock suddenly coursed through Daniel as he remembered something locked somewhere in the back of his mind. As he had been cleaning up, taking the plates and tumblers to the kitchen, he remembered a quick flash of light. He had not thought anything of it back then. Now he wondered. Veronica had been taking a picture of the Antietam photo with her phone. He assumed she had taken a few extra shots for insurance, just in case the first had not come out. Now a flash came to him but this time it was an epiphany. "I told her I'd prefer not having my picture taken for the magazine." Now it was all making sense. While he had been distracted with dishes, she managed somehow to snap off a shot of his face. He needed to find a copy of that magazine, but first things first. Turning the faded card over in his hand, the still crisp phone number was easily visible. Picking up the receiver of the old charcoal rotary phone on his desk, he began the long process of dialing Veronica's number, the sound of the rotary spinning back with each digit pleasing to his ears.

●——•

Veronica Jenkins had not answered the phone when he called, so he left a message to have her call him at her earliest convenience. A feeling came over him after hanging up. Something told him he should not wait to see if she called him back, so he decided to go to her. Through the years with some of the lives he had led, he was able to get hold of an "old friend" who was able to give him her current address. Luckily, she was living in California, a place called Cambria. The drive would only take a few hours by car, as her home was somewhere just south of *Hearst Castle*, of all places.

His contact took very little time in gathering the information needed. Daniel found himself sitting at his desk, drumming his fingers, just waiting. Veronica's call still had not come by the time he decided it did not matter if he was overthinking his worry. Pushing his chair back with determination, he made up his mind.

Daniel went home first, only long enough to grab a stash of rainy-day money he kept hidden inside a false brick in the fireplace border. He did not waste time checking to see if his house had been compromised. No telling when he might be able to come back, but he decided he could do without most of his personal belongings until he could figure a few things out first.

He settled on a circuitous route through Solvang to get to his destination. He turned down the radio in his silver Austin Healey, so he could think while he drove. None of this would have happened had he been more careful. That was the funny thing, really. He had been so incredibly careful, for years. It took about a century before he started to get lax, taking chances. That too was also funny, since he had spent most of that century trying to get himself killed. Being a soldier for most of his life, you would have thought the odds would have taken care of that for him.

The Austin Healey found its way into Solvang. He pulled into one of the very few parking spaces available, across from the *Old World Bakery & Coffee Shop*. Daniel stepped out of the car slowly, a mite creaky, stretching his long legs. "Oh yeah, I'm feeling the full one hundred sixty-seven years now."

His coffee from the morning had caught up with him. He ordered a blueberry kringle for the drive, picking it up on his way out. He felt grateful for the brief stop, but he needed to see Veronica Jenkins and find out if she was the connection.

•———•

Morgan Dimico managed to inspect a plethora of photographs, matching them all to the one he had been given, but still could not believe what he saw. It just wasn't possible, but the evidence in front of him, and the man across the street told him differently. He glanced up again in time to see his prey getting up from his seat across the street. He watched him leave a tip and walk off down the sidewalk. Dimico wasn't worried about following him yet. Daniel Collum would be headed back to his antique shop. There would be more than enough time before he would have to decide whether to follow him. See where else and what else he might show of his past. There was also the phone call from his employer he was expecting today. He could finally tell him they had found the right man.

Morgan Dimico had been a good cop, nothing all that spectacular to speak of in his career, but still he was good at his job. With no promotions coming his way, he decided to leave after hitting his twenty years, and go into business as a private detective. He read a lot of Mike Hammer, and the idea of being a gumshoe carried a bit of nostalgic justice to it. Turned out he was completely wrong, and it had cost him. He had no family other than his wife, and he lost her and his house. He had his car, not that his ex would have wanted it, even back then. Any money he managed to make as an investigator went back into his private business. There was hardly anything left to him after paying rent on his small office, feeding himself, and maintaining enough technology needed to keep the circle going. It could be worse - one bill he no longer had to pay was alimony. A couple of years back, his ex-wife, Anne, had been killed by a drunk driver. That was the one bill, out of the bunch, he would have wished to still pay.

That's when he was visited by a new client. Nothing as Hammer-like as a gorgeous blonde in a tight-fitting outfit or anything of the kind. His new client was a man of about five foot-nine inches. He carried about him the look of someone who might once have been trouble for those he took a dislike to. The years gave the appearance he might have calmed that storm a bit, just a bit. He looked and probably was about mid-sixties, hair gone completely white, thinned with age. His face held a sourness to it, as if he couldn't hide his disdain for the world. Dimico pictured someone who just took a bite out of a lemon.

His visitor entered his office without knocking. That was unusual, as no one ever just entered into his office. He wore a confidence bred from many years of knowing what to do and having his words acted on without question. He had been dressed in an expensive dark blue suit, tailor made just for the wearer. In his left hand, he held an intricately designed dark crimson leather briefcase. The fingers holding the briefcase were immaculately groomed and seemed strong, even though they were gnarled and wrinkled with the signs of age. Dimico had felt both envy and hatred for this individual at first glance. His caller had taken no more than a glimpse around the office before settling in on the private investigator. Dimico was sure that if his visitor had closed his eyes, he could have described the entire room without error. Dimico decided to stay seated in his uncomfortably squeaky wood swivel chair, his legs still propped up on the stained desk. He wished he was a drinker, as a stiff drink would have looked the part better than the Captain Cola can he was holding.

"May I help you?" Dimico attempted to ask nonchalantly.

His visitor gave a small grin, moving to one of the two wooden chairs on the opposite side of the desk. Sitting with purpose, he placed the briefcase lightly on the floor.

"I have need of your services, Mr. Dimico. There is someone I wish to have found, if it is the same person I believe him to be." He pulled a silver cigarette case out of his jacket pocket, and without asking, opened it. Taking a custom-made cigarette out, he tapped it on the case. Staring directly at Dimico, he placed it confidently in his mouth.

Sitting up in his chair, Dimico stated, "No smoking please."

The blue suited man smiled, took a gold lighter out of his pocket, lighting the death stick. Dimico began to say something, thought better of it under the circumstances, and instead said "Finding things is my business."

"This particular lost item may be an impossible task. I wish to be sure before I lay the matter to rest." The visitor gave that little grin again. It had the look of a snake about to devour a mouse. Taking a long pull from the cigarette, he savored the nicotine a moment, then blew the smoke directly across the desk at Dimico.

"Well, finding the unfindable is what I do best." Dimico managed to maintain a smile, and keep his cool, as the death cloud rolled across the desk to him. He just could not get the image of this man stretched out like a huge snake, taking him down in one gulp, out of his mind.

"Good." Lifting the crimson briefcase to his lap, his visitor opened it loudly, pulling out an old photograph. Holding it out, Dimico took it, his interest peaked.

"The man in this picture is Robert Hunter. He was a Secret Service agent working at the White House in 1981. Shortly after the assassination attempt on Reagan, Hunter disappeared without a trace. The two situations are unrelated. No full investigation into Hunter's whereabouts were ever begun due to the issue with the President. Hunter became just another picture on the milk carton."

Dimico scrutinized the black-and-white picture of a man in his mid-thirties to forties. Did he detect a bit of malice in that last sentence? He glanced back to the cold gray eyes of the speaker to confirm that question, but received no indication either way from his expression.

Pulling a manila folder from the briefcase, the suited man handed it over to Dimico. Dimico took the folder, opening the file to a small stack of pages inside. What he found himself looking at was a dossier of a man named Daniel Collum. The picture attached to the first page was Robert Hunter's.

"Appears you don't need me. You already found him."

Dimico was about to close the folder when something caught his eye. The birthdate and age of Daniel Collum was decades off if he was also Robert Hunter. Something wasn't right here.

"Yes, I see you noticed the problem as well." Cigarette in hand, he leaned forward deliberately, gazing directly into Dimico's eyes. "I need you to find out if Daniel Collum really is Robert Hunter."

Dimico's eyes were hypnotized by the intensity of those gray, cold orbs for a few seconds until the trail of smoke reached him, irritating his eyes. The moment broken, he let out an uncontrolled laugh.

"You can't be serious. Robert Hunter looks to be, say forty in this picture. That would make him seventy-three years old now. Daniel Collum's file says he's fifty-three."

Leaning back in his chair, his smoking visitor crossed his left leg over his right in a casual way that did not fit the man. "Actually, Mr. Hunter was forty-seven years old when he disappeared. Still, I have a gut feeling that both men are one and the same. I just need you to prove or disprove it."

Dimico jerked his head to the left, raising his eyebrows. "Who am I to deny a client what he wants." *Especially if it puts food on the table tonight,* he thought. "This could take some time, as I don't see how you could be right. But it's your money." *And hopefully he could stretch this out enough to pay this and last month's rent on the office.*

His visitor pursed his lips for an instant and nodded. "I knew I had picked the right man for the job. So there won't be any time wasted, you have everything on Daniel Collum I was able to gather." Pulling a thick folder from the briefcase, his new client dropped it on the desk. The cover was stenciled diagonally with the word CLASSIFIED. "I've taken the liberty to procure Robert Hunter's files as well."

Dimico stared at the thick, red word covering the folder. He opened his mouth to inquire about the file, but was interrupted by his client.

"Also, to save time, I will give you one thousand a day, plus expenses. On completion of your task, whatever the outcome, you will receive a bonus of fifty thousand."

Dimico just stared blankly, his mouth still open.

"I see that will suffice. To get things rolling in the right direction," he pulled a stack of green bills neatly wrapped with a paper band, tossing it onto the desk, "a start-up fund of ten thousand, just in case there's anything you need to get things moving. You will not be able to reach me. I will reach you when I want an update." Taking another item from the briefcase, he placed it more gently on the desk. Dimico could see it was a new, shiny, black cell phone.

"When this rings," he emphasized by pointing to the phone, "you answer. I believe that should take care of everything."

The mystery man then closed the intricate leather case and stood up. "We have a deal then?" Dimico looked from the files, to the money, to the phone, then at the proffered hand from his new client. Without thinking, he reached across and shook that cold, manicured hand. His benefactor then walked out of the office just the way he had come. Dimico stared at the door for a moment before he realized he still had his arm outstretched. He looked at his hand for a second, as if it was soiled, and slowly wiped it on his right pant leg. Sitting back into his creaky chair, Dimico quickly took the money and dropped it into a desk drawer. Staring at the manila folders on his desk, he opened the first of the two files, the one labeled "Daniel Collum."

CHAPTER TWO

RESEARCH

And so, it had started. That long journey down the rabbit hole and into the nightmare he now found himself in. He should never have accepted the money, let alone shaken that hand. He had felt it was wrong, but he really needed the money. The amount he found himself looking at on his desk had been too good to pass up. But even that paled to shaking that hand. Dimico couldn't get rid of the feeling he had just given away his soul, by shaking that hand. But there was no way to stop it now. It was done.

Dimico commenced by reading through the files. The men in both files were very similar: same height, weight, dominant hand, etc. The detail in the files was a bit disturbing. Dimico theorized the best way to work this was by going backward from Mr. Collum to Mr. Hunter. If Hunter was trying to hide himself from the world, it would be much easier to backtrack from Daniel Collum. He would see if there was any salt to what his new boss believed.

Daniel Collum was an antique shop owner living in Southern California. Fifty-three years old, good health, a man of few actual habits though he did like a drink from time to time. Mr. Collum's home was just a few blocks from his shop in the historical district of Orange. From the papers in the file, the home had been handed down to him through the generations. Regular life growing up, nothing abnormal in school from grade school all the way through college. Collum had majored in Business, but then who hadn't in the 70's and 80's. His life seemed quite boring really, until Dimico decided to go all the way back to Daniel Collum's birth. It was there he finally found a discrepancy that made Dimico sit up and take notice. His sixth sense kicked in like it always did, raising the hairs on his neck, when he knew he was on the right track.

Daniel Collum had supposedly been born in *St. Mary's Hospital* in New York in 1962. The problem arose when Dimico had checked the hospital's records. He found out *St. Mary's Hospital* in New York, the one whose stamp was on Collum's birth certificate, had burned down in 1947. It seemed the cause had been due to a gas leak, resulting in a fire. This was when Dimico plunged more deeply into Mr. Collum's past. Going back through his life history with a fine-tooth comb, Dimico saw minute discrepancies here and there. Little things no one would have noticed had they not actually been specifically looking for it.

Well, what do you know, he thought to himself. His benefactor may be crazy, but there might be something to all this after all. Oh, no chance Hunter was Collum, of course, but possibly father and son? Time and research would tell. "I have to admit, Mr. Collum, you are good, very good, but I'm just a little bit better at this than you are," Dimico stated to himself with satisfaction.

Time, it would appear, was exactly what it took, and it did tell. Every couple of weeks that phone would ring, and Dimico would answer it. It got to where Dimico hated when the two weeks was up from the last phone call. He knew he would hear that old rotary phone ringtone he had been unable to change on the phone, and he would then hear the one word: "Well?"

Dimico had given him updates at first, but as he dug deeper and deeper down that hole, he had begun to hold things back. He held back not just to milk his client for money, but because things that didn't, and shouldn't, make sense were there no matter how many ways he looked at them. Dimico knew he'd eventually have to tell the blue-suited man everything, but before he did, he wanted all his ducks in a row. Well, that and the extra money that would keep flowing in as long as he could string this guy along. A dangerous proposition, but one he felt he was going to have to go through with all the same.

Finding the discrepancy on Daniel Collum's birth certificate had only taken a short time. Picking through his history and catching the inconsistencies had taken a little longer, about a week all told. The problem had been with trying to figure out who he had been before becoming Collum and after he had decided to stop being Hunter. That turned out to be a brick wall, ten feet thick, and him with only a toothpick of an idea to break through it.

Dimico tried one avenue after another. After about a month of continuous failures and dead ends, Dimico changed gears. When Collum had forged his birth certificate, he had it forged so his age would be correct currently, at least currently for when he appeared as Collum. With this avenue of thought, all he would have to do is go back to Hunter for a moment. Hunter had been forty-seven years of age when he disappeared. So now he just had to find someone about that age who suddenly appeared from nowhere, then go back and check the birth certificates of those people who fit the same criteria. Easy-peasy.

Well, it had seemed easy enough at first, but again he had hit that damned brick wall. No one with the same features as Collum or Hunter came up in his search. He spent days mulling over that, wondering where he might have gone wrong, until he realized something. Every single easy search engine, and even some of the harder ones, had been used by his employer. This was easily proven through the dossiers given to him. They were such a treasure trove of information - so detailed it scared Dimico. No, his epiphany came when he off-handedly wondered what he would have done had he been Hunter.

Why make yourself the same age you were, especially when you had the fortune to look younger than your years? If Collum truly was Hunter, he certainly wouldn't have used his real age, but the age he looked. As far-flung a thought as that was, wouldn't Hunter have also done the same? The real question was exactly how much younger would you go? Hunter had been forty-seven when he disappeared, Collum fifty when he appeared. If there was a connection between the two men, where was it? They could easily have been father and son, yet why would Collum have changed his surname and falsified his records? There were no records Dimico, or his employer, could find that proved Hunter ever had a son, or daughter for that matter. So Dimico found himself circled back to the idea of Hunter and Collum being the same person, as much as he didn't believe it. He decided to set his parameters at the age of forty and work older until he found anyone that fit his formula.

You had to love computers and what they could do. Before the advent of these machines, he would have had to go through old microfiche files and paper filled filing cabinets. A painful chore which would have taken him years to find the information he needed, if he ever found it. As it was, Dimico had spent over a month going over all the possible suspects. He first cut out anyone who did not match the very basic criteria of what a man could not change about himself. From that list, Dimico decided to search the same hospital Collum had used to forge his birth, but nothing had panned out.

That's when another idea struck him. Take the list and run a search engine on the father's names. Again, nothing conclusive to help him narrow his search down, until he thought to go one step further. He took Collum's birth certificate and matched the signature of the father to that of the fathers of the other births, and BINGO!

Michael Pierce had been born at the Brooks Cottage Building of the Wyoming State Hospital in 1936. There was no information on Mr. Pierce at all, until he just seemed to appear out of the mist, claiming to own a ranch in Wyoming. No paper trail on the ranch itself, which had been bought with cash. A dozen or so each of sheep and cattle, along with three horses, had also been bought with cash. Nothing on anyone specifically living in the home until Pierce just showed up, taking residence a couple months later.

No wife, no children, not even ranch workers. No job to speak of either, and the sheep and cattle never left the property, though it seemed there was a diminished number of each as the years wore on. Mr. Pierce had also set aside part of the ranch, turning it into a small greenhouse farm. By all appearances, Michael Pierce was a retired gentleman of some money, living out the rest of his life without the rat-race world around him, alone and in peace. To Dimico, it smelled of someone attempting to disappear from society. Someone who hoped he could erase himself from the world and any prying eyes that may be looking for him.

Well, it had worked. It had taken Dimico over two months to find Mr. Pierce. Using a mental hospital for the birthplace of his new persona had been a stroke of brilliance. Who in their right mind, no pun intended, would ever have thought to check the women's ward in such a place for a child's birth? Dimico hadn't. It was only due to the point of comparison he set up in his search engine that he'd even had this one name on his list. Daniel Collum had even done a turn around by not giving Michael Pierce any real history as well, making it even harder to find the man. As a final jab, the location of Pierce's ranch in Wyoming was in Daniel County. It was like Collum was daring anyone to find him.

It was shortly after Dimico hit upon this link in the chain that his private phone began ringing. He almost jumped from his chair at that sound. Over time he learned to hate that phone, answering it was becoming harder to do with each call. Yet, he grabbed the cold thing up, waiting for the unmistakable, "Well?"

"I found a lead," Dimico said excitedly, "I may be on track to connect the dots. It may take some time to go through everything, but I should definitely have more information for you the next time you call."

"Good. We were beginning to wonder if I'd made an error in using you, Mr. Dimico." That cold, calculating voice just as quickly ended with the disconnect buzz on the phone.

Dimico gave a sigh of relief as he put the cell phone away. Over time, his body had built up a condition of the shakes, with a tightness in his chest every time the phone rang. He had been so excited over his find that his body forgot to be afraid of the caller. Then something his client said sent his heart into his throat, giving his body a sinking feeling. The exact same feeling when he had sealed the deal with a handshake from this man.

"What did he mean by "we?" A cold sweat suddenly covered his body, his heart dropped from his throat into his stomach. It had been a casual enough statement, a mistake for sure, but Dimico realized with growing fear that he was in even more trouble with this man in a blue suit than he originally thought. "Who else is with you? And why do you want to find this Hunter so badly?"

The hairs on the back of Dimico's neck stuck straight up. He now knew, instead of just felt, that he had made a huge mistake in taking this job. But he was in too deep now. He must find the connection to Hunter. If he didn't have any information for these people, he feared what they might do. He was going to have to be careful.

"Oh, sure, be careful now. Didn't listen to yourself the first time. Just saw the money sitting on the table. Now look at the trouble you've gotten yourself into." He wiped the sweat from his cold forehead. "Nothing you can do about it now but finish the job, and hope that's where it all ends." He wiped his hand on his pants, let out a deep sigh, and turned back to his computer.

The house in the wooded hills overlooking the Pacific Ocean was simple in its design. The architecture portrayed more of a two-story log cabin feel, rather than the cookie-cutter modern home models that had been built recently over the past few years. Even the grounds surrounding the cabin were simple in the same Pioneer style. Wildflowers surrounded the cabin in redwood planters, spaced uniformly one after the other. The walkway leading to the front double doors were lined with more wood planters, this time maple, filled with a variety of daisies. As the Austin Healey crunched slowly up the gray gravel drive, the double doors opened, and the quizzical look from the owner made Daniel Collum smile.

Slowly extricating himself from the vehicle, Daniel stretched with satisfaction as he heard, and felt, his back make a few popping noises.

"Daniel?" Her voice surprised, but just as lovely to hear as a year ago.

"You are not the only one who likes to surprise people, Veronica." Daniel grinned as he made the slow trek up the daisy walkway. "I am glad you remembered who I was."

Veronica walked down the path to meet him halfway, dressed in a simple white blouse and knee-length black skirt. She was wearing a pair of well-worn, white yachting sneakers, her hair as free as it was the last time they met, and just as vibrant in the sunlight that touched it now.

"You're not an easy man to forget, Daniel. More so when you leave a message just a few hours before you show up."

"Well, my mother always said it was the gentlemanly thing to do. To announce yourself before calling on a girl." Daniel met Veronica the last few feet at the middle of the walkway.

"Interesting turn of phrase, 'calling on a girl.' Were you planning on starting the courting process, Mr. Collum?" she said playfully. "You're a bit frumpy looking, and without gift, if that's the case."

Daniel looked down at himself, noticing his black pants were quite wrinkled from the drive. His dark blue dress shirt and tie didn't look much better, though the light brown suede jacket he was wearing still looked in good shape. Even his black dress shoes looked as if they needed shining.

"I apologize for my appearance, but it has been a bit of a long drive. As for a gift--" He looked around and noticed one daisy broken partway down the stem. Gently reaching down, he snapped the flower from the broken end, lifting it as a prize to Veronica, "--would this suffice?"

Veronica smiled again as she took the yellow daisy. "A daisy in greeting mayhap have much meaning." She nodded, raising an eyebrow to him. "Please, come in and tell me why you took such a long drive to see me."

The two made it up the colorful walkway and into the cabin, where Daniel immediately felt at home. Her style was so much like his own, though not so spread out in time with the items she had accumulated. Her style of clothes carried over to her style of furniture and knick-knacks. Everything appeared to have the flavor of the 1940's and 50's. What most would have called a simpler time, though from Daniel's perspective, no time was ever really any simpler than another.

Veronica showed him to the living room, gesturing to a sitting chair opposite the couch she herself stood by. "May I offer you anything?" Daniel shook his head in the negative. She sat down on the end of the couch closest to his chair and Daniel followed suit.

Turning the daisy in her fingers absently, Veronica said "You're a very interesting man, Daniel. I knew it from the moment I first met you, but more recently I'm beginning to believe it even more so." She waited for any reaction but only received a blank look back.

"Did you know that after the story you were in was published, I received a call asking about you?" She stared at him again for a reaction.

"Did you? Someone I knew from grade school or some such?" Daniel asked quite calmly back.

Veronica shifted her head to one side, staring back at him. "No, actually it was someone more interesting than that. They said they had read the publication and that you looked so much like someone else they had known. They were wondering if there was a chance you might be related."

Daniel swallowed hard. He had been correct in his assumption that Veronica was the connection. She had no idea what she had done by taking his photo, and with that, no idea what kind of trouble she may have put herself in.

"Um, may I trouble you for a glass of water? My mouth is suddenly dry." He tried to appear calm, though he felt he was failing miserably.

Veronica watched him briefly, then with the hint of a smile at the corner of her mouth, she stood up gracefully. Still twirling the daisy in her hands, she went to the adjoining kitchen. "I hope tap water is okay?"

"Absolutely. Would it be possible to add a couple of cubes from the icebox?" Daniel felt himself calming a little, now that she was not sitting across from him, scrutinizing his every move.

"No problem at all." Her voice carried back from the other room. She returned with two glasses, one filled with ice, the other with the daisy. She handed him the ice-filled glass and he thanked her.

"You know, Daniel, one of the things I always found interesting about you is your way with words. You often say things no one else would normally think to say."

"Thank you, I think," Daniel said defensively.

"No, really, it's very endearing. 'Calling on someone' for one, or using the word 'icebox' instead of freezer, for another. Very quaint and refreshing, not to mention old fashioned." With this last statement, she stared directly into his eyes.

Daniel could not tell if she was fishing for something or just genuinely complimenting him. He had always found women something of a mystery. Never completely sure if they were flirting with him, stating a fact, or digging for information. He considered himself a bit dense when it came to that sort of thing. A long life of experiences had not helped him in the least. Men were much easier to read as far as he was concerned.

"Just something my -- grandmother used to say. Kind of stuck with me, I guess." He forced a smile at her as he sipped his water.

Veronica set the glass with the yellow daisy on the coffee table between them and gazed back at Daniel. "It might also interest you, just a few months ago I received another call about that same publication, and about you. I considered calling you up myself, but I thought it best not to get myself involved at the time. Since you've contacted me though, I'm quite curious to know what's going on."

Someone else had reached out to her? Daniel knew the Haig Men would probably have been looking for him, but who else could be tracking him? This was unexpected to say the least.

"Do you know who these people were that reached out to you?"

"Well, the first didn't actually say. Come to think of it, I never got his name, though he sounded like a much older gentleman. He did mention that he and a few of his friends have tried to locate someone who looked like you for quite some years. They were hoping I might have information that would help them. Something to do with a very large sum of money left to their friend. I didn't believe it for one minute, so I didn't give out anything but the bare minimum information to get him off the phone." Daniel sighed with relief at that.

"Now the second caller was quite interesting in that he said his name was Morgan Dimico, a private investigator. Mr. Dimico said he was attempting to locate information on a Daniel Collum to see if he might be connected to a lost person from the 1980's by the name of... Oh, hell. Now what was that name again? It was something simple. Robert something, had to do with animals, I think." She creased her forehead trying to get the right word that just wouldn't come to her. "Robert Scout, Robert Ranger, Robert . . ."

"Hunter." Daniel said flatly.

"Yes, that's it." Veronica said with satisfaction. Then a look came across her features as she stared at Daniel. His expression was set in his face, almost resigned. "How did you know?"

Daniel took a long drink of water, welcoming the burning cold as it went down his throat. He allowed the ice cubes to hit his upper lip. How much do you give away without being sent away yourself? How much can you trust before you find yourself someone's guinea pig? There had to be a happy medium here somewhere, but where?

Setting the near empty glass down on the etched top of the coffee table, Daniel coughed once to clear his throat and his mind. Leaning forward on his elbows, he looked straight into Veronica's eyes.

"Robert Hunter was a relation of mine from my mother's side of the family. He worked for the government, but seems to have disappeared in the early 1980's. We were never able to find him, and we never had any information come in that has helped us know if he might still be alive, dead, or disappeared on purpose."

"Daniel, that's horrible. You haven't had any information for thirty years?"

He noticed real concern in her voice, which both warmed and hurt him, as he continued his lie. "Nothing that has given us any answer as to what happened. It would seem your picture of me has stirred up some new interest. My mother always said I looked exactly like him."

"Is there anything I can do to help? Is that why you've come by?"

"I came by to see if you were contacted, as I was, due to your story. Veronica, my uncle worked for the government. No one knows in what capacity he was serving, though if he disappeared without a trace for so many years, I would assume it was something important. We were never able to find out. If there are people looking for him now, I worry there could be a level of danger I am not willing to have you connected with. If you get my meaning." Bit of a huge hole he just opened, but hopefully convincing enough to get her to safety, and away from the Haig Men.

Veronica leaned back against the couch taking this all in. Daniel could see in her eyes she knew he wasn't telling her something. He could only hope she would believe her involvement put her in danger.

"I understand, but I don't have the kind of funds to just go off willy-nilly. I also have work that I just can't drop. I have a deadline to meet."

"I am not asking you to disappear, just not be where people would normally expect you to be. For just a little while. You are a freelance writer. Can't you work from anywhere?"

"True, I can take my laptop and work from a hotel or something, but this all just sounds so ridiculous."

"I would not ask you to do this if I didn't think you might be in trouble." Pulling a wad of bills from his coat pocket, he recklessly removed a sizeable stack. "Here, take this and find yourself a safe place to stay for a few weeks. Leave a message with Victor at the post office across the street from my shop with your location. I'll meet you there if I am able. If not, I will leave a message for you with him, with instructions on what to do."

Veronica looked at the money he was holding out to her. "I can make do, Daniel. I don't need your money."

"Yes, you do. You don't know the kind of people who could be involved in this. Cash is not traceable, and if you take a large withdrawal out yourself, they might get suspicious. This way you can just disappear for a little time while I try to figure out what it's all about."

Shaking her head slowly for a moment, as if she did not believe any of this was happening, Veronica reached out her hand, gingerly taking the money from Daniel. "This is only a loan."

"No interest, of course." Daniel responded lightly.

Looking at the denominations on the bills he'd given her, Veronica just stared for a moment at them, before looking up at Daniel. "A retirement fund? Or shouldn't I ask?"

"Let's just say that I like to keep something aside for a rainy day. They say it's supposed to rain within the next week or so." Daniel stood up.

"Make sure you get far enough away from here before you settle someplace. Take everything you think you may need. Under no circumstances do you come back here until I make sure everything is safe."

Veronica took a moment to look around the room as she stood up. Shoving the bills inside a pocket of her skirt, she then walked around the coffee table to Daniel, giving him a big hug. "Thank you. Whatever this turns out to be, it might be a better story than the one I'm writing right now."

"Don't thank me yet, you might regret it later. Just promise me you will do as I ask."

She smiled and nodded, but the serious look on his face instantly removed it. Gazing directly into his eyes she responded. "I promise."

●—•

Daniel had told her he was going to head directly back to his shop to get a few things himself. He asked her to book adjoining rooms in whatever place she decided to hole up. He needed to get in touch with his one employee to tell him to take care of things for him while he was away. That was another odd quirk of his that she found refreshing. He carried no cell phone, said he didn't have a need for one. Problem was, he couldn't remember Andrew's phone number to give all the instructions over the phone. She'd offered to look his info up on her computer, but he refused. He didn't want to take a chance on her computer being tracked. She had begun to joke about him being paranoid, but when she saw the look on his face, she had stopped and agreed not to look it up.

Veronica had decided where she could go by the time she had packed a few things. Some place she'd been to before would be a bonus for her, and this place was also quite a distance from where she was now. It wouldn't take Daniel as long to get to her once she'd left the message with Victor. That was another thing. She was not to take her phone, but to buy a prepaid one. Once she'd made the call to the post office and Daniel returned the call, she was to destroy it. She had a funny feeling Daniel had seen one too many spy movies, but she consented to his wishes.

She had collected enough clothes to last for a week, bagged all her research papers, computer, and necessaries for the trip. One stop at the bank to pull a few things from her safety deposit box which she felt she might need. Well, one item she didn't really need, but she just wanted it with her all the same. She'd been mulling over doing a story on the journal she'd acquired, but she just hadn't found the time to really go over the thing. That could change if she finished the story she was currently working on and still found herself in hiding. That word still seemed odd to her even now, "hiding." She decided to change it to "leave of absence." It sounded less ominous. Anyway, she was sure she wouldn't have to worry about her stop at the bank going through the system.

With everything tucked away in her vintage 1942 Chevrolet Fleetline Aerosedan, a parting gift from her father when he passed away, Veronica took the scenic route down Pacific Coast Highway. She felt anxious, excited, and free all at the same time. She sensed the sea foam green car purr as it stretched its legs on the long trip down to San Diego. She ran her right hand over the cloth bench seat she sat on, thankful it was comfortable. Her father had loved this car with every ounce of his being. He had shown her how to take care of it with the same devotion he himself had for it. She knew she'd have to stow the car away eventually, as it stood out a bit from the norm, but she couldn't leave it behind either.

Daniel Collum would have a lot of explaining to do once he showed up after running his own errands. Enough time had gone by for her to mull over what he had told her while she was on the drive. There wasn't much else she could do since the radio had gone out on her again. Her dad had fixed the thing a few times through the years and she herself had fixed it once.

Veronica knew Daniel may have been telling the truth, to some extent, about Robert Hunter and his relation to him, but there was much more hiding under the surface there. She could feel it. There was a huge hole in his story once you had a chance to go back over and look at it. She could not be sure why he had lied to her, but she planned to confront Daniel and get it all in the open, once they'd settled down in their new hideaway digs.

That was another thing too. Daniel's namesake from the Civil War. When they talked that one day, she had told him the stories of that young boy. Laying out his ancestor's life in front of him, Daniel had only seemed slightly interested. Compared to all the other men and women whom she had talked to about their own ancestors, she found his reaction confusing. Even the least caring of those people had shown some interest after looking at the pictures and history of someone they were related to, but never known. Not Daniel. When she had shown him all her hard work, he had just given disinterested grunts. It was as if he was only confirming she had succeeded in getting her research right. Almost as if he knew more than what she had uncovered.

She thought she would get some reaction when she laid down her ace in the hole, showing Daniel that his namesake had enlisted in the same brigade as his father. The kicker being that this young Daniel had even seen his father die at the Battle of Fredericksburg, but nothing. Well, not nothing she reflected, but something she had not expected - grief. She had looked across the table at him when he did not respond to the information, only to see his eyes welling up as he looked through the pictures and material. She could swear his far-off gaze was to another time.

Veronica was about to ask if he was all right, when he suddenly stood up from his seat, and headed to the kitchen. He asked if she would like a refill of her glass, but she knew he was covering. She had let it go; sometimes the emotions of a bloodline ran deep. Daniel's family had certainly kept very detailed records of their ancestors, from what she could gather. It must have held much importance for them.

"Well, there will be more than enough time to talk with Mr. Collum about a few things once he shows up. I should really put my mind on the story at hand." She shook her head, her red hair moving from side to side with the motion, to clear her thoughts, and began the process of going over the recent article she needed to finish if she wanted to be paid.

CHAPTER THREE

HAIG MEN

The office room was lit only by a couple of lamps, one tortoiseshell floor lamp near the door, and the other, a green-hooded banker's lamp sitting on the mahogany desk. The desk itself was immaculate, with nothing out of place, no dust that could be seen. Point of fact, the entire room mirrored the desk in its cleanliness. The walls were lined with floor to ceiling rich mahogany shelves. Those shelves were filled with a potpourri of books on U.S. law, various state's laws, American history, Presidential biographies, and the like.

The left of the heavy mahogany double doors opened, admitting a man wearing a tailored, dark blue suit. Closing the door behind him, he walked with purpose over to the weighted chocolate brown drapes blocking the window near the desk. Pulling the drapes aside roughly, he let in a wash of drab light. Outside, the early fall weather had set in with an uncommon freezing rain and sleet storm. In the distance, through the maelstrom, the Capital Building could just be made out.

The man's reflection looked back at him from the window; a face lined with many years of use. His hair as snow white as a winter flurry, his mouth was set in a near grimace. From the lines on his face, this appeared to be its normal state. The gray eyes reflecting in the pane were as cold as the stormy afternoon outside. Those eyes stared icicles of hate to the world it saw.

He stood there, staring out for long minutes. Lost in his own dark thoughts, he was jarred back to the present when his desk phone's speaker spoke.

"Mr. Bennett? Mr. Royston is here to see you." The bored feminine voice on the other side was all business.

Without looking away from the window, Bennett flatly stated "Let him in."

The left door to the room opened again, this time admitting a man still in good shape for someone in his mid-sixties. His body had been in peak physical condition when he was a younger man, but there was very little indication this man sat doing nothing with his time. His salt and pepper hair, cut short and styled cleanly, was appealing in contrast with his naturally tan skin. Other than deep crow's feet around his eyes, he showed very few marks of age in his face. Walking over to one of the Radcliffe tufted leather armchairs, he sat down uninvited, straightening the dark grey pant legs of his suit.

"Hello, John." His voice calm, but still as strong from his football days in college, so many years ago.

Turning from the window, John Bennett stared briefly at his visitor before speaking. "Well?"

The invitation now given, Mark Royston relaxed in the chair. "It's all taken care of, just as you expected."

Showing no outward signs other than a slight nod and gleam in his eyes, Bennett replied, "I knew we made the right choice for our presidential candidate. All that was needed was a little push in the right direction."

"I have to admit, I was a little hesitant to tell them everything, but you were right. Fame, money, and power was all it took to bring them onboard."

Turning back to the marred view of the Capital Building, John Bennett smiled to himself. "I realized the mistake we made before in not using someone who had our own sensibilities. This way uses much less money and energy overall. Not to mention fewer people we'll have to worry about."

Bennett turned back to face Royston, seeing something he wasn't sure he liked on the man's face.

"Something else on your mind?"

"First, you could speak with Frank."

Rolling his eyes unconsciously, Bennett walked over to his leather desk chair and sat down. "And what is worrying our Mr. Thomas this time?"

"What doesn't worry Frank anymore? Currently, it's the Hunter issue -- again."

Bennett shook his head. He took a moment, so as not to let his blood pressure rise, before answering. "If Frank had done his job properly in the first place, he would have nothing to worry about now. Locating a dead man takes time and money. My money. Frank needs to calm down or he'll end up with another bleeding ulcer."

Royston nodded in full agreement. "That's what I told him, but you know Frank. Hunter put a fear like no other in him thirty years ago. Now that Frank thinks he might still be alive, well, it's difficult to bring him back to reason."

A silence fell over the two for a moment before Royston spoke again.

"Look, you know Frank's always been a bit edgy. Even when we thought he was dead, Frank was convinced Hunter would come out of a dark closet like the boogeyman to get him. Hell, it took years for him to get back to normal. Well, normal for him."

"Frank has always worried a bit too much for my liking. That kind of mindset leads to mistakes," Bennett said sternly.

Putting his hand up as if to calm his conspirator, Royston said, "Yes, he has always been quick to jump, but he is also stable. Sure, we've had to talk him down a few times. The Hunter situation was bad, but manageable back then. The Alexander Haig thing? Now that took a bit to keep him from bursting a blood vessel."

"Haig was old, eighty-five years. He had no idea what we tried to do back in 1981, and still had no idea when he was bedridden in 2010," Bennett stated.

"Of course, but you know Frank," Royston sighed. "He was sure when Haig was on his deathbed, he'd want to clear his conscience before meeting his maker."

"Oh, for God's sake!" His blood began boiling. "Haig knew nothing of our plans. How many times did I tell Frank that? There was no way he would have gone along with us. We needed for him to believe that what he was doing was the right thing, which was the beauty of it. He would have been sworn in as President, and we would have had someone in a position where we could pull strings when we needed without his ever knowing."

Royston stood up and walked to the opposite side of the room, to one of the bookshelves storing a selection of U.S. law books.

"Yes, it would have worked. Could have worked had everything gone as planned. The real question though is should it have ever worked?" His fingers brushed gently across a few of the law books.

Bennett stared at the back of his conspirator, his lips pursed. "Et tu, Mark?"

Turning from the law books, Royston shrugged. "What's done is done. I knew what I was getting into then, so did Frank. I'm older now, and I would like to think wiser. But it won't change the course I decided to make, if that's what you are worried about."

"No, no, of course not." Bennett reassured. "It's Frank. He has a way of bringing out the worst in my moods."

Royston smiled knowingly, returning to his chair.

"You have to admit that after Haig passed away, Frank calmed down a lot. One less skeleton to clutter his mind's closet, if you like." He faltered for a moment before speaking again, not wanting to bring up another point. "Of course, there's always the non-ending issue about Hinckley."

Bennett sat back, closed his eyes, and used his right hand to rub the slowly growing headache behind his right eye.

"Hinckley knows what he thinks he knows, nothing more."

"You know that, and I know that." Royston said matter-of-factly. "But every time Hinckley comes up in the news, or his case is reopened and looked at, Frank gets edgy all over again."

Bennett breathed in deeply to calm his blood pressure and his headache. Letting his breath out slowly while still rubbing his right eye, he remarked, "I knew I should never have given Frank the job of seeding Hinckley's mind with the idea to kill the president. I should have done that myself. But I doubt Hinckley would have taken to me like he did Frank."

"Look, John. We knew Frank was the only one Hinckley would click with. One deranged mind to another, so to speak. Seriously, it was a stroke of brilliance you had. Take a man whose mind was already a bit sketchy, who lived and breathed for Jody Foster. A man who wanted nothing more than to prove his love for her. Befriend this person, make him believe the only real way for him to show his love, and have her love him, was to do something aggressive. Oh, say assassinate President Reagan. He kills Reagan, the Secret Service kills him, or takes him down. It doesn't really make a difference, as anything he'd say would just be the blathering of a madman. Genius."

Bennett's only response was by continuing to rub his right eye. Royston tried to lighten the mood. "Personally, I have no idea what he saw in Foster. Raquel Welch, Sophia Loren, now that I could definitely have seen." A snort of laughter from the other side of the desk reassured him it had worked.

"Who could have foreseen Hinckley was such a bad shot?" Bennett said offhandedly. "Even so, it might still have all worked, had it not been for Hunter getting in the way."

"Speaking of, how could you be so sure that this Collum guy actually is Hunter? I mean Hunter was forty-seven when he disappeared. That would make him close to eighty now. If that picture of Collum in the magazine is recent, I just can't see how a man who looks to be in his mid-to-late forties could be the same man?" Royston asked.

Taking his hand away from his eye, Bennett opened the center drawer of his desk. Pulling out a magazine, he dropped it on the desktop. He opened the magazine to a well-worn crease and folded the pages over to show Royston. "I was thumbing through this magazine to see what story might hit my interest. Imagine my concern when I came across this picture." He pointed to Collum's photo, "Thought I'd seen a ghost. I immediately read the story, looking for anything to tell me this wasn't the same man." Setting the magazine back down on the desk, "There was nothing in the article indicating Collum was Hunter. Problem was, something kept pricking the hairs at the back of my neck. Those same hairs kept us from getting caught all those years ago for treason."

"But come on John, the same guy?"

"We've had this argument before. That's why it's my money being spent to alleviate my worries. My logical mind tells me he can't be Hunter. The illogical part just isn't so sure." Bennett noticed Royston sit up straighter at this. The trust built over so many years allowed him to say this without pause.

Mark Royston looked across to his co-conspirator. "Are you thinking plastic surgery or some such? That would have to be some pretty good work for him to look no older than when he disappeared."

Bennett shook his head "That's what I originally thought. Trouble is, all my inquiries into surgeons who could do that kind of work proved to go nowhere, as you already know. Even the resources at our disposal failed to come up with anything tangible to prove he still exists, but that annoying scratch at the back of my neck just won't go away. That's why I hired an outsider to do our work for us. A fresh perspective."

Royston nodded "I know, I know. Still, do you think that was wise? What if he comes up with information we wouldn't want him to know? To what extent are we willing to go?"

"We'll bridge that gap when we come to it."

"Why a private investigator? Morgan Dimico was it? It's been a few months and nothing."

Bennett leaned back in his chair gloating. "Now that's the perfection of it. I chose a man who has his own business. Has no ties to anyone, including family. He was in desperate need of money and he has a special knack for finding things, at least, from all the records I read on him of his past cases." Bennett spread his hands out away from his body. "If nothing comes of it, we're no worse off than we were before, and I'm only out some chump money . . . but if he comes up with anything . . ."

At that moment, Bennett's wristwatch beeped, and he looked down to check the face of it. "Speak of the devil. Give me one moment."

Bennett picked up the receiver of his phone, punched the speaker button, and dialed a number from memory. The sound of the ring filled the room, and when they heard the connection on the speaker, Bennett asked flatly, "Well?"

The voice on the other side, Dimico's, responded. "Sorry it took so long, but it's confirmed. I was finally able to get a good fingerprint of Collum's. I sent it in to someone I know at the department and it came back a match to Robert Hunter's fingerprint. I've also managed to finally connect a trail from Collum back to Hunter as well."

Both Bennett and Royston glanced at each other with this confirmation. Bennett held up his index finger to Royston for silence. "Thank you, Mr. Dimico."

The voice on the other side of the country spoke up, "Um, there's something else though. There's more to this Collum guy than you might know. It may be hard to believe, but the information I've picked up is undeniable."

Royston shot Bennett an "I told you so" look.

Bennett interrupted Dimico "I'm sure your work was impeccable, Mr. Dimico. I will have someone come to you with your final payment and a bonus for all your hard work. You may hand all your notes over to him as you will not be hearing from me again." He hit the disconnect button on the phone and turned off the speaker.

Royston just stared at Bennett for a few minutes, the silence thick between them, then he mimicked Bennett's voice "Well?"

Bennett glanced over, giving a disapproving smirk. "Call Mr. Smith and have him take care of Mr. Dimico for us. Then call Frank. Have him get together what men he thinks he may need, and head to California. We'll have Mr. Smith meet him after his business with Dimico is done. Just a little insurance to keep Frank in line."

Royston nodded "You know Frank will raise a fit about this."

Bennett's face turned rock solid and his eyes went very cold. "You tell Frank, from me, this is his mess to clean up. He made the mistake, and now it's time for him to correct that mistake. No one else."

Royston nodded confirmation again. "Good enough. What are you and Valerie doing tonight?"

Bennett slid right into the change of conversation, as if the topic of killing a man was nothing more than small talk. "Nothing as far as I know, why?"

"Brittany wanted to know if you two would like to go out for dinner. I think you and I could use a little celebration after this information anyway."

Bennett smiled uncharacteristically. "Why not? Some expensive champagne over our final victory sounds quite good right now. And within another forty-eight hours, we should be free of Hunter forever."

CHAPTER FOUR

CITY OF ORANGE, 11:48 A.M.

Morgan Dimico stared at the phone in his hand for a moment before tossing it back on the passenger seat of his car. He hadn't liked the sound of the voice on the other end of the phone, especially the part about a final payment. He also suspected someone else had been listening to their conversation, as the sounds from the other side of the phone seemed more hollow than normal. Something you might expect if someone turned the speaker on. Best thing to do would be stay on guard, especially when his payment showed up.

Dimico started his aged silver Ford Focus sedan. He had given Daniel Collum enough time to get to his shop and settle in. His job was done with his anonymous benefactor, but what he was up to now was on his own time, and with his newfound funds. Cutting through a well-smoked paper trail, he managed to prove Collum was Hunter, yet he still had reservations. But after sending the fingerprint via phone to his buddy at the precinct, and receiving confirmation, he was forced to admit the impossible. Collum and Hunter were the same man.

Problem was he still didn't want to believe it. He'd built up much more information than was necessary to prove what his employer had wanted. Dimico wasn't sure what had made him think to do it, but he had gone to Robert Hunter's birth certificate to alleviate an itch he had. What he found was both satisfying to his investigative mentality and a shock to his belief system. The father's signature was a spot-on match to the other birth certificates.

At first, Dimico assumed Robert Hunter had been someone else before changing his name, just a younger man, though he noticed Hunter/Collum hadn't seemed to have aged much in thirty years. Good genetics or just good surgery? Possibly both he told himself. He used the same method he'd used before to search backwards and found a man who moved to Texas to retire from a very humdrum life of door-to-door vacuum sales. It took a bit of looking around, but he finally found a picture of the man, a William Kinney.

Just as Michael Pierce's life story had been somewhat vague, so too had William Kinney's. Something else had also been similar about the two men -- the picture was a spitting image of Daniel Collum. William Kinney had supposedly retired at the early age of forty-two back in 1968, passing away in 1978. The picture was taken when Kinney would have been about forty-five years old, according to the handwritten date on the back of the picture. And here was the conundrum: if Kinney was forty-five in the picture, how could he possibly be Hunter who was forty-seven when he went missing in 1981, or even Daniel Collum who was fifty-three? Now that he thought of it, Collum looked like he could be between forty-five and fifty-five. With that thought, Dimico nearly jumped out of his skin.

It couldn't be possible, yet it was staring him straight in the face. Every ounce of his body told him to stop looking. He should just close the books on the case, but he went back yet again, this time to a Benjamin Richter. Benjamin Richter had been a flying instructor in the United States Army Air Force. Captain Richter had been stationed at Wheeler Field in central Oahu at the time the United States entered World War II. Richter had been thirty-five years old in 1940, disappearing somewhere in the Bermuda Triangle in 1968 when he took a private, single-engine plane on a joy ride over the Atlantic Ocean.

Before Benjamin Richter there had been Hayden McClellan, a decorated World War I flying ace. Later, during Prohibition, Hayden McClellan served under Elliot Ness as one of his Untouchables. Eventually they took down Chicago's kingpin, Al Capone, with the charge of tax evasion. Dimico felt like he was losing his mind, even picking up a nervous twitch in one eye. For his sanity, he was unsure if he should go back any further, and yet his curiosity would not allow him to stop. He knew if he did not go back to the beginning he would never be able to sleep. He would never stop thinking about this man with multiple lives.

And just as quickly, Morgan Dimico found his finish line. Strange that the end would be exactly where he started, with Daniel Collum. He found the last thread staring him in the face the entire time. The magazine article in Collum's file given to him at the start, point of fact, what had caused his employment from the beginning, had been the answer to all their questions about Daniel Collum. The two photographs on the first page of the article, staring back at him like bookends. The one on the left the beginning of the journey, and the one on the right the end.

Dimico began to laugh uncontrollably. So much time had been spent trying to figure out who Collum might once have been. With each new persona, Dimico went further back, until he remembered the magazine article and the two photos. Looking back at those photos he had seen a drummer boy, and an antique's businessman, both Daniel Collum. The man hadn't even deigned to hide who he was anymore, giving himself his own name again. At first, Dimico had thought it reckless and ballsy. As he read through the article multiple times, staring at all the photos he'd accumulated through this man's history, he realized the genius of it all.

Daniel Collum had been born in 1848, at least from what records he was able to find from Ireland. One hundred and sixty-seven years had passed since Collum's birth. What easier way could there be to explain any similarities than to set yourself up as your own descendant? This realization, the release of all that pressure through an almost maniacal laugh, he believed, saved his sanity. It took nearly ten minutes of uncontrolled laughter to do it. Dimico's lungs and stomach had hurt from that release, but as he wiped away the tears streaming down his face, he had felt so much better.

Dimico pulled the car up to one of the parking slots behind the shop as the few on the street itself were all filled. Picking up his folder with years of evidence, he stepped out of the car. Closing the door, he took a deep breath to steady his nerves. Walking slowly, but with purpose, He went around the corner to the front of the shop to confront this man of history.

So deep in thought was Dimico, going through possible ways to open his end of the conversation, that it had taken two attempts at opening the door before he realized the front door to the shop was locked. Clearing his mind back to the present, Dimico stared at the sign hanging right in front of him through the glass front door. In bold red letters, it simply said CLOSED. Holding one hand up to the glass of the door, he could see the lights were off, and there appeared to be no one inside. This was not good, not good at all. Collum always kept his shop open until six in the evening, every work evening. Something had caused him to close early.

Dimico stared at the old brick and mortar of the darkened shop for another minute before walking briskly back to his car. He needed to get to Collum's house in a hurry. He knew without a doubt he had been good at staying far enough back, not showing himself to the man he followed. Something must have changed that. Dimico went back over the morning in his head. He had pulled up and parked his car out of the way, as he always did, and walked the small distance it took to get a seat across the street from where Collum always ate his late breakfast. Dimico never sat in the same seat two days in a row, and always made sure to change up his clothes to look different from each day. Collum himself had not changed his routine that morning or shown any signs he had known someone was following him. So, what could have given it away?

As Dimico reached for the car door, he suddenly pulled back, as if shocked by the handle. His eyes shifted over to the hand holding the evidence folders of Collum's long life.

"Damn me to Hell!"

The files. Those damn files. He realized he had still been holding on to a shred of false hope that he had been wrong, and Collum had not been this centuries-old man. He never paid any mind to what he had been doing when he held up each photo to the current one of Collum. Never thought what it looked like as he compared each photo with it, then to the man across the street.

"Damn, damn, damn. You stupid fool!" he exclaimed to himself.

Throwing the files to the passenger side of the car, Dimico jumped in. Violently, he started the engine and burned rubber to get to Daniel Collum's house, hoping against all hope he hadn't just fucked up everything.

⚫━━･

The same train of thought went through Daniel Collum's brain on the drive back to Orange. He had been going back in his mind to see where he had messed things up. Truthfully, all he could really come up with was it was partly due to his becoming complacent through the years, but mostly it had been his desire not to see another world figure shot. If he had stayed under the radar, just lived his life, he could have been retired, out of the way, not in the trouble he was now.

That had always been his one failing in life, keeping other people safe from harm. He knew it stemmed from the death of his father on the battlefield. He had been unable to do anything but watch from a distance as so many sons and fathers fell. But he also knew it had grown out of so many other factors and people in his life.

As the Austin Healey took the long drive back home, memories intruded back into Daniel's mind. He kept trying to fight them back, worried about how much time had gone by since he left the shop that morning. He was worried about Andrew and cursed himself for forgetting his black book of phone numbers. Cursed that, and his laziness in never memorizing them. He never particularly cared for phones, ever since Alexander Graham Bell started the whole business with the noisy things. He could not be particularly angry over never carrying a cell phone, knowing how easily you could be tracked by one. He also worried about Veronica and how he inadvertently managed to get her involved. He hoped against all hope he would be able to pick up what he needed and disappear before the Haig Men found him, and whoever else it was who was tailing him. The problem for Daniel Collum, though, was his past always seemed to come back to him.

•———•

The shock and pain of Abraham Lincoln's death lingered deeply for Daniel; hell, for an entire nation. As divided as the country had been, somehow the assassination of the President helped close the wound to some degree, healing the nation as a whole. For Daniel, Lincoln's death brought home to him how fleeting life was, and how short it could be. Taking a plunge, he began courting a young woman he had been infatuated with for some time, but had been too self-conscious before to do anything about.

He felt he needed stability in his life if he ever wished to marry and have a family. Reenlisting in the service, Daniel transferred to the 7th Cavalry Division, under a man named George Custer. The Indian Wars were going on and Daniel felt it his duty to help clear the way for settlers in the West. He asked Kathryn McAllister to accompany him, much to the dismay of her parents. Without hesitation, she had said yes. Daniel had fallen in love with her even more at that moment, as she left everything she knew to be with him. Taking only her clothes and what few items she could easily travel with, Kathryn followed her heart, and Daniel, to the West with those few other wives and girlfriends of officers.

That was something else Daniel had been proud of, gaining his status as an officer, 2nd Lieutenant. With his new status, and his fiancée on his arm, he felt he could conquer anything. This could just have been the wild oats of an eighteen-year old man seeing his future open ahead of him, but Daniel felt there was something more to it. Felt that what he was doing was right. All that came shattering down two years later in 1868 with the Battle of Washita River.

Washita Massacre was more like it. He had been in shock that day, and all his dreams had come crashing down in a moment. Daniel Collum had thought himself a man when he was given the rank of an officer, but the events that occurred on the Washita River left him feeling like a small boy, ashamed and naked to the world.

Custer's 7th Cavalry had been tracking down a war party. This eventually led them to Chief Black Kettle's village on the Washita River in Oklahoma. Unbeknownst to Custer, many villages were scattered down the length of the river. Black Kettle's village was just the farthest of them. Had Custer taken the time to reconnoiter the area, he would have discovered a much larger population than what he thought he was up against. Lieutenant Colonel Custer ordered his force split into four parts that evening, with each set up so they could converge on the encampment when the charge was called the following morning.

The first shot fired that morning along the milk chocolate-colored mud river, lined with green brush grass, came from Kettle's own village. Double Wolf, one of the Cheyenne warriors, awoke early to see the forces prepared to attack his village. To warn the village of the impending attack, he fired a shot from his rifle into the air. Double Wolf's warning shot would be his last as he became one of the first to die. The charge had gone as planned at the start. The orders were to kill the hostile Cheyenne and capture any others. There would be time to sort things out later.

In very short order, the supposedly sound plan turned into a living nightmare. In stunned shock, Daniel had pulled his horse to an abrupt halt. He stared in horror as he watched his fellow soldiers plow through the women and children, shooting them from behind as they ran in fear for their lives. As these innocents desperately tried to get away, many were trampled under the horses of the soldiers. Frozen in his saddle, Daniel observed Black Kettle and his wife attempting to flee the carnage of their village on the back of a pony. Paralyzed, he watched as both were shot in the back. They fell to the ground holding each other for mutual protection, even in death.

But the bloodbath had not ended there. Once the initial carnage had ended, many of the wounded on the ground were shot in the head. Due to the wounds received in the surprise attack, they were unable to defend themselves. Not only were the warriors killed outright, the women and children were treated with the same disregard. Making matters worse was the order from Custer to use fifty or so women and children as human shields. Custer realized too late the encampment they had decimated was only the first in a long chain of villages along the river. As these forces were gathering to aid their fallen brethren, the invading cavalry with hostages in tow, were ordered back to the supply train.

Custer's forces had been about five hundred strong going into the charge. Coming out of the battle, he had twenty-one men killed and thirteen wounded. The casualty list of the Cheyenne was worse, having been a camp of about two hundred and fifty families, one hundred and fifty of those possibly warriors. Daniel heard around two hundred men, women and children had been killed that day. Many decades later, he would learn the numbers had been falsified. The true losses had been somewhere between thirteen to one hundred fifty Cheyenne killed, and fifty-three women and children captured.

Daniel had felt numb for weeks after that nightmare day. Worse yet, Major Joel Elliot, a man Daniel had spent much time with, died that day. It seemed Elliot decided to take a small detachment, against orders, all to gain fame and fortune. Elliot's detachment found themselves surrounded and Custer had refused to send aid. All twenty men died waiting for help which would never arrive. This was but one of many acts by Custer against his men. Daniel's respect for the man dwindled with each passing day. While the officers ate well, the enlisted were left with hardtack and water. Desertion was a problem solved by maiming the offenders and carting them in wagons. Daniel's hate for Custer grew steadily, and his concern for his chosen career weighed heavily on him.

To erase the horrors of that one day, Daniel and Kathryn were married just a few short weeks later in December. It helped to dull the pain of his memories and brought life back into him. Kathryn's flaming red hair, a beacon in contrast to her white wedding gown, proved to help Daniel forget for a short time the horrors of his new career.

Less than two years later, in 1870, Daniel's wife gave birth to their first child, a boy. Nathaniel Collum was not only a welcome addition to the family but gave Daniel a sense of purpose all over again. Then again, in 1873, Kathryn gave birth to another child.

Their daughter Mary was as beautiful as her mother, the same red hair and milky white skin. Daniel could spend hours gazing at his daughter, who seemed to hold the wonder of the world in her eyes. A perspective he himself had lost but was able to live vicariously through his newborn child.

Around this time, Daniel's wife and long-time friends began commenting on how he never appeared to age. The mild kidding had first come from those few men he still knew from when they fought together at Gettysburg, back when Daniel had been sixteen years of age. But with repeated comments about his youthful appearance, Kathryn also took notice. He had brushed it off until she produced the few photographs taken of him since then as evidence. Admittedly, Daniel had always looked older for his age and taller than most. But when he gazed at his reflection in the mirror, scrutinizing the photographs, he started to believe what they were saying. He was twenty-five now, but still looked only about eighteen to himself. He had gone from looking older than his years to looking very much younger than he was.

His family and career took up most of his time, and he soon forgot about this little youthful quirk of good fortune. There were much heavier matters to think about. Now that he had two young children and a wife, he began to consider leaving the service. His thoughts wandered for a career which would keep him in one place, with a much higher ratio of survival. Daniel did not have long to wait. In 1874, Custer discovered gold in Black Hills, South Dakota. This was the moment Daniel had been waiting for. Turning in his resignation gladly, he became one of the first to join in the Gold Rush, finally removing himself from a commander he no longer respected.

Daniel found the life of a prospector grueling. Life in the Cavalry had been hard, but the days of sweat and toil it took to bring enough gold in to feed his family, let alone set some small amount aside, took its toll. Still, a couple of years of back-breaking work produced a sizable nest egg of gold. When the town of Deadwood opened in 1876, he sold his claim, suspicious it might play out within the next year, and moved the family there. He hoped the move into a town would be better for his family, but he learned far too quickly of the lawless nature of Deadwood and some of its citizens.

More a mining camp than an actual town at its beginning, Deadwood grew quickly on land given to the Lakota Sioux in a treaty in 1868. Thousands of people, mostly men, swarmed to the territory in search of gold. By the time Daniel's family arrived into this illegal settlement into Sioux territory, the shacks and tents filling the area were just beginning to be replaced by buildings. Still, Daniel had made his choice and was set to make it work. With the money accumulated from his gold stake, and connections he had with some fellow soldiers who had also left the service, Daniel was able to open *Collum's General Store and Supplies*. He anticipated this type of business would be greatly needed out in the wilds of South Dakota.

Collum's General Store and Supplies prospered better than Daniel could ever have hoped. In so doing, it drew attention from the predators in Deadwood, who would try to take whatever grew prosperous in the town. Daniel held his ground against these few without bloodshed, though guns were needed to emphasize his point on more than one occasion.

On August 2nd, 1876, Daniel had heard a commotion from down the street. Coming out to see what trouble was brewing this time, he quickly learned from the verbal grapevine that it involved Wild Bill Hickok. A casual acquaintance who had helped him in a situation regarding the ownership of his general store, Hickok had just been shot in the back of the head while playing poker in a saloon he frequented. The coward, Jack McCall, had escaped in broad daylight. Daniel donned his guns once more to join the posse setting out to catch Jack McCall and bring him to justice. Just a few days after returning with McCall, Daniel was sitting at the table in his home for breakfast. He had been reading one of the papers that filtered their way into Deadwood when Daniel received another shock. General Custer and his entire 7th Cavalry had been defeated at Little Big Horn - with no survivors - on the 25th of June.

Daniel had spent so much time staring at the column, not moving or making a sound, that Kathryn had become worried about his health. Without a word, Daniel handed the paper over to her, pointing to the article. Once she had finished, the two of them just sat and held each other. So many friends had been lost, but what stood out to them was the good fortune Daniel had in leaving the service when he did; otherwise he would also have been one of the casualties.

Life continued, and business thrived in Deadwood. Men lived, and men died, almost daily at times, but it wasn't until Deadwood was bathed in a smallpox epidemic that Daniel feared for his family. The virus spread so fast that tents were erected in the streets outside. Just as quickly, they were filled to overflowing with people showing the symptoms: fever, rashes, blisters, muscle pains, headaches, and others. The smell of vomit, and the general stench of the sick, was overwhelming. Daniel's entire family were not exempt. It had been touch-and-go for both his wife and son. They developed sores and blisters that oozed sickening pus, but they both eventually managed to recover, though Kathryn's health never seemed to be the same after that. Daniel alone came through unscathed, showing no signs of the smallpox virus himself.

The last straw came on September 26th, 1879 when a fire swept through Deadwood like a herd of stampeding cattle. By the time the fires were put out, over three hundred buildings had been destroyed, including *Collum's General Store and Supplies*. Never one to leave all his money in one place, Daniel had not been ruined, but it convinced him Deadwood was no longer where his family should call home.

Pulling up what stakes were left, Daniel and his family loaded the wagon, moving to Dodge City, Kansas. Dodge City was a place Daniel could feel safe moving his family. The city had its own problems in the past, but the lawmen currently running the town had shown they would not sit still for any unlawful activity within its borders. Using the money stowed away and recovered in Deadwood, Daniel could just afford to purchase a hotel. The original owner had decided the business was not to his liking after all and was glad to get it off his hands. Daniel had bought the place, partly to try his hand at a different venture, and partly for its name -*The Occidental Hotel*. Something about that name spoke to him.

A flash of headlights from the opposite direction yanked Daniel back into the present. He had driven the entire trip from Cambria on a mental autopilot, finding himself just a few exits from where he would need to get off the freeway. His first stop would be Anthony's apartment. He would give some excuse about needing to travel for business to look at some new inventory. So Anthony wouldn't have to hold the fort, he should take some vacation time for a few weeks, all paid by his humble employer. Anthony had talked, in depth, about wanting to visit the Boston area. He wanted to see many of the American Revolution historical sites. That would make sure Anthony would be safe and out of harm's way from the storm clouds Daniel knew would be coming.

Then he would have to make the trip back to his house for a few things. He couldn't believe he hadn't thought to take them with him the first time, but it could not be avoided now. He had to admit to himself that he had grown rusty over the last thirty years. He was slow to do things he would not have missed doing the first time when he had been Robert Hunter, all those years ago. The last stop would be to his shop. There was a good chance, by the time he arrived at the shop, it would be under watch. Worse, a trap could be waiting for him. He should just go across the street to the post office where Victor would have left any message from Veronica in his post office box. Problem with that was he just couldn't leave without the items hidden in his office. Come hell or high water, he wanted the pictures hidden away there with the flag of the 69th. If it put him in danger, so be it. Once he had those items in hand, they could disappear for a while until he could figure out what to do next.

CHAPTER FIVE

MISTER THOMAS

Frank Thomas had never liked to fly. In fact, he detested flying so much that it took a couple of Valium chased with a good stiff whiskey or three to calm him before boarding a plane. This flight, though, had been different. He had just calmly walked up, handed over his boarding pass, and gotten on the plane. There were very few things that scared Frank more than flying, but one of them was Robert Hunter.

Frank had been having nightmares of that day in 1981 for decades, though he would never have told his compatriots that. He realized early on anything he said to them would fall on deaf ears, especially the ears of John Bennett. Mark Royston called him with the news that Robert Hunter was still alive after all this time, and Bennett had specifically said it was Frank's job to take care of it. He had attempted to argue with Royston at first. Royston had let him run on for a few minutes before giving him the message from Bennett, and it was then Frank knew he would have no choice but to fly to California and deal with this demon from his past himself. He had made a couple of calls and six men would be waiting for him at the airport. Six might have seemed a bit of an overkill, but Frank was not going to take any chances this time.

His limousine drive to the airport had been quiet as he spent the entire time thinking about Hunter, and how that one encounter with him all those years ago had changed the course of his own life.

These thoughts were swimming in his head as he stepped out of the limousine and into the airport terminal without a word. These same images made him forget to take his Valium and forget to stop for a few drinks.

Frank Thomas had once been a man worried by little in his life. He was not all that good looking and was also a little bit on the shorter side. He could have gone into many different professions, but there were three good reasons he decided on the world of politics: money, power, and women. With money came power, and with either of the first two, a man of even his unlikely looks and size could get attractive women. Women had always been Frank's downfall. Early in his career, he had very little power, and he did not have the kind of money that would attract the kind of women he wanted to further his career. His only recourse had been paying for escorts to play the part. They would walk on his arm as a beautiful trophy in public, and if they were a little less than scrupulous, end the evening in his bed, where he could order them to do anything and everything he ever wanted.

This lifestyle had gone on for some time and worked for him up to a point. His involvement with John Bennett had stemmed from this addiction to women as well. Frank had found a service where, for the right fee, you could have some of the most gorgeous, up-and-coming young models and actresses fawn over you. They were hungry to make it big at whatever cost, mostly due to a lack of any talent. They would gladly go to dinner, or a function with you, ending the evening having your way with them in any way imaginable. The rate was somewhat high, but the service was very discreet, and Frank had paid more for much less. The bonus of a night being a sure thing made it worth it. He would have the girl in his bed, shower, on the kitchen counter, or anywhere else he could think of for that evening.

He had meticulously gone over the list of choices mailed to him in a nondescript manila envelope, which conveniently gave the pictures of the available starlets in many poses, some graphic. Included for his benefit, was a dossier of each woman, almost a hardcore version of the centerfold profile. Last on the list was the price for one day with these women. Far too many were way out of his price range, but some, fresh from the Midwest, were well within his wallet. Some were even near enough to Washington D.C. to make his choices easier. Frank decided upon a nineteen-year old, blonde-haired girl's dossier. She wanted to become a big film star, but found herself better suited for the pornography industry, and its own brand of stardom. Perfect for what he wanted. Her lush hair, full figure, and the swelling curves of her body, were exactly what he had been looking for.

His day with her was everything he could have hoped for, beginning the moment he opened the door and welcomed her in. Holly Huntress, her stage name, looked like a younger version of Marilyn Monroe, yet more approachable. Her white dress almost seemed to have been painted on her, and the matching white high heels she wore made her much taller than him, though he could not have cared less. Frank had taken her out on his arm to a few functions that day, the envy of every man, as heads turned wherever they went. He was positive many wondered how he rated a woman such as Holly, knowing they would all think he was a man of power, and he felt the stirring between his legs at the thought. He had planned to take her to other events that day, but could not wait any longer to get her back to his hotel room to quench the thirst of his growing member. With a whispered comment in her ear, and his hand firmly placed along the curve of her left buttock, they retired to his suite. Behind the secrecy of the walls of those rooms, he had been pleasured by her in ways he could never have imagined, before or since.

It was then, after the sex in the shower, and then on the bed, that everything had gone wrong. It had started somewhat innocently, as she asked him if he had wanted a real sexual dynamo experience. Her mention of this as she stood over the bed, her body glistening lightly with sweat, only increased his arousal. He had agreed immediately. Playfully stepping from the bed over to her small bag on the hotel table, she returned with a pouch of cocaine. Applying a light amount of it across her lips, she then powdered her nipples in a circular motion, causing them to grow harder with each pass of her fingertips.

Working her tongue over her lips, Holly worked her way seductively across the bed on her knees. She lifted her swelled breasts, motioning him to take his dessert.

Frank was in heaven as his tongue flicked over her erect nipples, the tingle of the drug working its way into his system. He could feel himself quickly rising to her game and thought he might explode then and there, but she was in control this time. They spent time sprinkling the drug over parts of their bodies for each to consume as she intermittently snorted small amounts of the substance. Frank had never had such a prolonged experience in his life, all due to the drug. His mind exploded with the overload of senses, right up to the moment she was riding him hard and fast, each downward thrust of her body taking his engorged shaft fully into her. He thought he would lose his mind. Her body stiffened, shaking uncontrollably, gripping him to her between her legs as she had what he thought was a mind-blowing orgasm. She had suddenly fallen off him, rolled onto the floor, off the bed and lay still. Frank playfully moved over to the side of the bed, laughing, until he saw her. Her eyes were partly open and glazed over, and her body was unmoving. His erection disappeared in a heartbeat. He sobered up enough to jump off the bed and check her non-existent pulse. He ran to the table, grabbing up the small mirror she had been using for her snack tray. Wiping the powder from it as he returned to her side, he placed it under her nose and confirmed she wasn't breathing.

He tried for almost a half hour to bring Holly back to life, but to no avail. Frank panicked. He kept moving from the bed, to the bathroom, to the living area, and back to the body of this young woman who had either overdosed or had a heart attack during their sexual encounter. The scandal over something like this would ruin his career.

Not knowing what else to do, Frank called the one friend he had. It took some time for Mark Royston to piece together everything that had happened, as Frank babbled nonsensically over the phone, but eventually he had summed up the trouble Frank was in. Royston told him not to worry, he thought he knew someone who could help, and to let no one in until Frank heard Royston's voice at the door.

When the knock finally came, Frank quickly let Royston and another man in. This was the first meeting Frank would have with John Bennett. Apparently, Bennett had taken care of a problem or two for some other men who were climbing the power ladder as well. He had known exactly what to do, telling Frank to clean the room as best he could to remove any evidence of the girl ever having been there. After that, he was to leave and to let Bennett take care of the rest.

Frank had argued with Royston at first about this, but Royston had calmed him down enough to tell him he had seen Bennett do this before, and everything had worked out perfectly in the past. He would call Frank at his home when it was all finished. Frank had done everything Bennett told him to do without question, then went home to pace back and forth for the next several hours. When the call finally came, he was told not to worry and watch the news the next few days.

Those few days had been a nightmare for Frank. He couldn't sleep, could not eat, and he could do no work as his mind raced. He had called in sick, spending hours in front of the television set, not knowing what he was looking for. Then three days later, a news story appeared of a young woman's body having been found in a flop house, along with the body of a young man. It seemed the two of them had been high on cocaine when the situation became ugly. By all appearances, it was a case of murder/suicide. The police had found a bevy of photographs of the girl in possession of the man. Adding to this were many handwritten letters which proved, without a doubt, his plans to kill her after making love to her, so they could be together for eternity.

Old mugshots of both showed up on the news screen and Frank immediately recognized Holly's face. He had never seen the man before. Then his phone rang. He answered it without thinking, all the while staring at the image of Holly's beautiful face on the screen.

"Everything has been taken care of, as you can see. Never speak of it again. There may come a time I will need you in the future. Please remember this moment when that comes."

The phone suddenly lost its connection, and Frank just looked blankly at it for a moment. He had not really thought much about it at the time as he had been so elated over his current stroke of luck. But later, in less than a year, he would realize just what he had signed himself up for with this John Bennett.

●—•

"Excuse me?" Frank asked, pulled from his thoughts.

"Would you like a drink, sir?" the flight attendant asked, holding a pen and small pad in her hands. "We have a selection of wines, champagnes, or other beverages if you like."

"No, no thank you, nothing for me." He said absently, going back to his thoughts. He had already forgotten the attendant as she quietly went to the next seat in first class.

Frank gazed at his reflection in the window of the plane, not really noticing the puffy clouds in the blue sky outside. The face that looked back at him was now a man he hardly recognized. His hair, which had only started to thin a little thirty years ago, was now nearly gone, and what was left was all a very lackluster shade of grey. What few strands of hair remained on top were combed across to give the appearance he wasn't bald there now, but all it did was show how vain he was about going bald. He felt the paunch around his waist, as if for the first time, as his stomach hung over his belt, and realized how round he had become. He had never been a physically fit man, but the years of drinking case after case of beer had given him the "gut." Not that it mattered. He had power and money thanks to Bennett, and a trophy wife who was half his age. She was willing to please his every want, as long as the money kept coming in.

As his vision shifted to a larger patch of clouds darker from the rest, a thought struck him, *If there is a Heaven, and God out there, then there most definitely must be a Hell, and I have met the Devil himself.* Frank's eventual meeting with Royston, Samuel Phillips, Donald Worth, and finally the Devil himself, John Bennett, had been the start of his current state, good and bad. Yes, he had finally reached the pinnacle of what he wanted, but at the cost of becoming a fraction of the man he once was. The constant drinking, ulcers, the pills to ease his sleep and his mind. The nervous nature that had grown, all out of that meeting. All of it slowly eroded away whatever strength of character he might once have had.

⚬―――•

Not knowing what to expect, Frank entered the room of the hotel chosen for their meeting. The room was bigger and swankier than most rooms he had frequented himself. Unlike some of the places he had been, where the colors exploded your senses, this suite was arranged to calm your nerves. Solid colors of blue, dark for the bedspread and curtains, and lighter shades for the walls, all made the room feel pleasant. He guessed the view from the windows was spectacular, not that he could know, as the curtains were pulled closed for complete privacy from prying eyes.

Sitting on a couch were two men he had not met. He guessed they must have had the same look on their faces as he had on his. Sitting on the right side of the couch, fidgeting with his hands, was a man of about average height. Thinner than would be normal but not outwardly noticeable, he sat on the edge of the couch with nervous energy. His light brown hair was neatly cut, giving his face an almost boyish appearance. The kind of face you wouldn't think twice about trusting with your back turned. Sitting next to him with his legs tightly crossed, was a man smoking a cigarette vigorously, as if it was his last. The ashtray next to him on the maple end table already contained the stubs of several previous victims. The air around his slicked back, black hair held a halo of his habit. He had the face of a movie star, with deep blue eyes that knew and used those looks to his advantage. Even his physique was a poster of athleticism. Everything about the man oozed perfection and Frank immediately disliked him for it.

The last man in the room was sitting casually in a plush brown lounge chair, sipping a cocktail without a care in the world. Frank walked over to Mark Royston to ask him what was going on when the door to the room opened, admitting John Bennett. Frank noticed he was wearing a dark blue suit, the same color as the one he had first met the man in, but of a different designer. Through the years, Frank would come to realize dark blue was Bennett's signature. He would never wear anything but that one color for any, and all, suits he owned. John Bennett smiled that smile no one would ever want to see. He looked around the room at each of them, nodding approval.

"I'm glad you are all here on time. It shows you took me seriously. I'm in charge, and you have a debt to pay to me, and as long as you remember that, everything should run smoothly."

Walking to the middle of the room where he could see everyone easily, Bennett took center stage and began his pitch.

"You are all here for one of a number of reasons. First and foremost, you all feel the same as I do about the coming election. If it goes as we all feel it inevitably will, we will be at the front line to cause a change in our country's history that has not happened since Lincoln and Kennedy."

The two men sitting on the couch cast sidelong glances at each other uncomfortably. Frank turned to look at Royston, but he just nodded, pointing with his drink back to Bennett.

"That is correct. If Ronald Reagan becomes our next president, you my friends, will be at the center of his assassination." Bennett let that sink in briefly in the stunned silence. "I can say this as I have complete confidence that none of you will leave this room without agreeing to what I have planned. I have spent the last couple of years picking a very small number of men who would fit the skillset I deemed vital, and you, the chosen few, are all in this room now. For some, it may have been no more than a mutual feeling of what needs to be done. For others, I hold over you your livelihood. The secrets that you hold dear are in my hand, ready for me to crush them to dust if need be. Now, I don't mean to make this sound like a threat, but I want you all to know exactly what I am capable of if you choose to go against me in any way. I have resources you could not begin to fathom, and I am more than willing to use them for what I know must be done." He paused a moment to let this take hold in their minds.

"You can't seriously be considering killing a man who could be our next president!" the blue-eyed athlete stated, bewildered.

He stood up for emphasis, holding each of the others in his eyes individually as he spoke. "You can't all think this will end well. What he's proposing is a death sentence for each of us."

Bennett allowed the silence to continue for a moment, just long enough to know this was the one person he would have to deal with, the only one to stand up to him. Bennett stepped slowly over to his target, speaking as if he was reading from a page, "Donald Worth. A man with a very select taste in young boys. The evidence built up against you would have put you away for the rest of your life. From my understanding, pedophiles don't do very well in prison. I made it all go away, and don't think for one moment that I cannot bring it all back in an instant." Worth slowly sat back down on the couch, drawing a long pull on his nearly spent cigarette. The brown-haired man shifted away from him.

"Oh, don't be so reviled by Mr. Worth's habits, Mr. Phillips." Bennett turned to look down at the boyish-faced man. "Samuel Phillips. A rising star, soon to be the new district attorney. What would they say if they found out about your secret Cayman accounts, your two other wives, and seven children?" Phillips just sat and stared at his feet, his hands fidgeting vigorously. "So as not to be left out, though I doubt I need to remind him, Frank Thomas has a body in his closet as well. Mr. Thomas has a long list of prostitutes, paid escorts, and the dead body of a young woman on his hands. Yes, you each have strings with which I can pull at any moment if you choose to go against me."

The three men who just had their garbage thrown into the center of the room for all to see, just glanced from one to the other before Phillips finally spoke up.

"What about him? What have you got on him?" He pointed an accusing finger behind Bennett at Mark Royston, still seated, casually drinking as if none of this was out of the ordinary.

Bennett glanced back to Royston, who turned his attention to each of the three men, before nodding his assent to Bennett. Bennett nodded back, giving that smile again. "Oh, did you not all realize? Mark Royston is a patriot. His sole reason for being here is the same as mine. The United States of America should not be led by a man who has built himself up through play acting his way on the screen and on television. That our government should not be allowed as a dumping ground for women taking roles they should leave to men who know better. This *actor*," his voice held contempt, his face wrinkled as if it caught the whiff of something that reviled him, "thinks he can pull the wool over the eyes of the intelligent members of this country. He smiles that smile of his, exuding his charisma through years of playing make-believe, and expects that when he's sworn into office we will accept the eventuality of a woman on the Supreme Court. No, my friends, I do not trust this man. Can you look at him and truthfully say that you did not once think he would push the button to end our world? Every time he smiles and his eyes flash, I have the feeling he would, just to see what would happen."

Bennett looked around the room again, gave a sigh as if to say he understood, before he continued. "I know you all have reservations. Killing someone is not easy." He turned his attention to Frank as he finished, "for most of us." Without waiting for a response, he swiveled his soapbox stance back to the others.

"Let me assure you all that I have not come into this lightly. I have a plan that will make sure none of us will ever see the inside of a cold cell or the hangman's noose. How could any of us be implicated if none of us actually holds the smoking gun?"

Donald Worth blurted out what the others were thinking, "You plan to poison him? Set up an accident of some kind? How can you expect that to work? He has men taking care of him day and night, watching his every move."

Bennett closed his eyes and nodded, as if he had been waiting for that very question, before opening those lifeless gray eyes again.

"Oh, don't you worry, Donald. May I call you Donald?" He didn't wait for permission. "What I have in mind is something so special, so out of the box, that even his men would not expect it. It's only in the early stages, so I don't want to spoil the surprise yet." That smile again that just sent shivers up Frank's back. That smile which made him think of a writhing mass of snakes, venomous snakes, just waiting to bite.

Frank sat back in his seat. He waved to the flight attendants who were talking at the other end of the aisle at their station. One left her conversation without showing any disgust for having to do her job. She even smiled and patted his hand when he apologized and asked if he could have a drink of water. After she handed the small drink to him, Frank had come out of his thoughts long enough to watch the sway of her butt as she walked away down the aisle. He noticed how her uniform fit snuggly against those curves, her legs extending down from that lovely show, muscles well-formed and accentuated by the heels she was wearing. He wondered what it would take to get her in the bathroom stall, face against the mirror, skirt up high enough so he could join the Mile-High Club.

Frank shook his head to clear it, took a drink of the cool water which did little to help his thirst, then remembered how the conversation that fateful day had gone - more arguments, more accusations, all the while Bennett's smile and calming tone, laced with warning. Eventually they all agreed to do as he asked. What choice did any of them really have? He had them by their testicles and they all knew it. What none of them knew was that Bennett's plan was much larger than what he initially told them, but by then there was no going back, even if they thought they could. Frank gulped the rest of his water, rubbed his tired eyes, and fell asleep for the first time in his life on a flight.

CHAPTER SIX

LOS ANGELES, CALIFORNIA, 5:35 P.M.

The 767 landed uneventfully at LAX airport, taxied in, and stopped. Through the whole event, Frank Thomas never woke from his sleep. It had taken his favorite flight attendant a few minutes to bring him out of his exhausted slumber. She had been a little worried at first when she had shaken him hard and his eyes still wouldn't open, but with one last grab of his shoulders and a stiff shake, he finally woke up. He had looked around as if expecting someone else, fear in his eyes, until he focused on the full breasts hinting out of the uniform near his face. Glancing up, he saw the concern in the blue eyes of his dream attendant and calmed immediately.

"I'm sorry, I must have passed out there," he smiled, a little embarrassed.

She smiled back with relief. "Flying can really knock some people out. We've landed at LAX, sir."

Frank turned his head, staring out the window for a moment, to verify her statement. Sure enough, he was on the tarmac. He slowly got up, opened the overhead, and pulled down his one black bag. Turning back to his blue-eyed beauty, he shot her a knowing smile.

"If only you were going to be on my flight back." He brushed up against her as he passed, making sure her breasts touched his body as he moved to the exit. He grinned as he went past her without looking back, never seeing her smile move down, her face turning to sudden surprised contempt.

Frank had forgotten to set up a meeting place at the airport for his men to find him. He was confident enough they would show up without him having to look around for them. By the time he collected his one suitcase from baggage claim, no one had come to meet him. He began to wonder if a call would need to be made. He was still making up his mind as he exited the building, only to have a black sedan pull up. An imposing man in a black suit and sunglasses got out, came around, and opened the front passenger door for him.

"Everything set?"

Sunglasses nodded. "Yes, sir. I was told there was a small issue with Mr. Smith, but he will meet you at the location you requested. The others are just waiting on your orders."

Frank shot a glance at Sunglasses, but waited for him to settle into the driver's seat before asking hesitantly, "Small issue?"

Putting the sedan in motion, the driver kept his attention on the bustle of the airport road with all its taxis, shuttles, civilian drivers, and pedestrians. Weaving his way through the bustling crowds, he waited to answer after he swerved around a group of tired travelers crossing the pick-up area.

"Mr. Smith said he would explain when he reported directly to you. What are your orders for the rest of the men, sir?"

"Have four of them go to Collum's house and wait for him if he shows up there. Have the last man meet you at his place of business and keep watch there. I'll meet up with you at that location once Smith and I are finished."

"Yes, sir." Sunglasses replied, then immediately touched something in his right ear. Speaking in low tones, he gave Frank's directions to the rest of the men.

They managed to escape the rat race of the Los Angeles Airport, and as the black sedan merged into traffic on the 405 freeway, his driver asked "Any particular reason you need so many men for this job, if you don't mind my asking? It's just one man."

Frank stared out the passenger window, watching the urban scenery go by. He did not answer right away, and his driver was about to ask again when he said bluntly, "Robert Hunter caused the death of four secret service agents and put me in the hospital for six months. I am not going to take any chances with this man. Fool me once, shame on me."

The trip to Orange County was uneventful and quiet, something Frank's nerves appreciated. His driver had not said another word the whole way, and he was happy not to speak himself. All Frank kept thinking about was Hunter. Six months in the hospital and he had been unsure if he would ever have made it out of there. After that, it had been a year of physical therapy as his arm and legs took the slow road to recovery. He still suffered from back issues; the back brace he could wear would have eased the pressure on his spine, but he hated the damned thing. The way the pills made him feel when he took them for the pain was a pleasurable bonus, though.

The black sedan made the connection from the 405 freeway to the 22 freeway before exiting the Glassell/Grand offramp. Sunglasses made the left turn at the light, taking them onto Glassell toward their destination. Frank watched the older buildings go by, almost wishing he could disappear into this kind of life himself. The 1930's style street lamps lent a nostalgic ear to the buildings and trees lining the road. Their leaves, still green in the California weather, caused him to sigh without knowing it. He read the street signs as they passed, with names like Orange and Grand, until they took a left turn at South Center Street. Frank took a deep breath in, letting it out slowly to steel himself. He could never have imagined thirty years ago he would have done the kinds of things he had by now. The sedan pulled up on the opposite side of the street to the single-story, beige and brown apartment homes. What did they say? "Be careful what you wish for?"

Standing across the street waiting for him was Mister Smith. He stood there like one of the 1930 street lamps, unmoving, looking straight out to the street. Smith was much taller than Frank Thomas, but then, who wasn't? He stood at six feet exactly and carried himself in a way that would make most think a military background. They would have been correct. Problem was, if you could have looked up his military records, Smith would have shown as KIA, Killed-In-Action. Well, you could, if you knew what his real name was. He was one of those individuals who had chosen the mercenary life and enjoyed it. His psych profile, if there was one, would show he reveled in it. He worked the jobs he wanted, had no scruples, and never failed to deliver.

His sandy blonde hair was cut tight in the military fashion. His suit fit him well, but you could tell there was a great deal of muscle underneath. The one thing that moved constantly on this human statue were his eyes. Those chocolate brown orbs shifted back and forth, constantly surveying their surroundings, taking in every detail.

Frank got out of the car and watched the black sedan drive off. Smith's demeanor did not change the entire time. Frank began to wonder if he was a robot, or android, or something. It wasn't until he walked across the street, and onto the sidewalk near him, that Smith finally moved.

"Welcome to California, Mr. Thomas." He did not offer his hand but stood there with his arms behind him at military rest.

"Thank you. Dryer and warmer than what we're having in D.C. right now. I understand you had a problem?"

"A small issue really. One I will take care of after the business at hand has been completed. The private investigator got away from me, but nothing I can't rectify."

Frank stared at Mr. Smith briefly. "I hope so. Failure is not something Bennett takes lightly. Believe me, I would know. Make that your top priority once we're through here. After that, if there's still an issue with Hunter, meet up so we can deal with him and be done with it."

"Yes sir."

Frank had Smith lead the way to the one level apartment that was their target. The one they wanted was last in the small batch, and at the back of the lot, which would be good. The only real problem at this point were all the cars in the lot. That would mean most of the tenants had returned home from work. Frank's plane had come in during the worst of the gridlock, and the 405 freeway had been a nightmare to drive down. He was still having an issue with the time change. When he left the east coast, it was around three in the afternoon. His arrival on the west coast was just two hours later, California time. His mind always boggled at things like that.

They walked up to the beige door labeled **8**, and Frank knocked lightly on the door. Smith noticed a momentary change of light from the peephole, as someone from the other side took a look to see who was outside. They heard a deadbolt slide back, then the door opened as far as the chain would allow.

"Yes?"

"Mr. Andrew Goulding?" Frank asked neutrally.

Andrew's eyes looked directly at Frank, then shifted to Mr. Smith, causing him to step back slightly behind the door and safety. Focusing back on Frank, he raised his eyebrows.

"Yes?" Andrew responded.

"Hello Mr. Goulding. We are here on some urgent business having to do with your employer, Mr. Collum. We believe he may be in some danger."

Concern immediately crossed his brow, "The Boss? What's happened? Who are you guys?"

"We're with the government." Frank pulled out the badge he'd been given just for this occasion, showing it to Andrew through the narrow slit allowed by the chain on the door.

"The government? I don't understand. What would Mr. Collum have to do with the government?"

Frank looked up and back, as if he was making sure no one else could hear. "Could we come in Mr. Goulding? It's a sensitive matter that would be best discussed privately."

Andrew's face gave a V-8 expression, causing Frank to bite his tongue to keep from laughing out loud. The door closed quickly, but briefly, as he heard the chain being removed. When the door opened again, it was wide and inviting. Andrew moved aside, motioning for them to come in. His gestures were almost in a frantic, hurry motion. Frank crossed the threshold, with Smith at his heels, before the door closed behind them.

"Looks like we interrupted your meal."

Andrew turned to see Frank looking down at the plate on the kitchen table. Dipping down, Frank sniffed at the chicken and rice on the plate.

"Mmmm. Lemon pepper?"

"Uh, yeah. Leftovers." Andrew said, nonplussed. "Is Mr. Collum in trouble with the government or something?"

Frank turned from the food, walking the few steps back into the living area, smiling. "Or something."

As Frank walked further into the small living room, turning Andrew's attention to him, Smith silently took the few steps to the kitchen to pick up the spare chair.

Andrew waited as the balding man walked past his entertainment center to sit on the brown couch, opposite the kitchen area. "If he's not in trouble, what's the problem?"

"I didn't say that. I just said he wasn't in trouble with the government."

"I don't understand." Andrew's confusion was plain on his face.

"Your Mr. Collum has been living a double life. The man I knew, and with whom we have business, used to go by the name Robert Hunter."

Andrew stared at the man sitting on his couch without noticing the other moving up behind him with the chair. "I'm sorry. I still don't understand. I think you have the wrong person."

"I wish you were right. I really do. I won't go into details, as it doesn't matter. I just need to know where Hunter – Mr. Collum is right now and what he's told you about us."

Smith moved forward with ease, set the chair down, and pulled Andrew down into the seat.

Initially surprised from being pulled down into the chair, Andrew quickly grew angry. "Hey, look. I don't have any idea what you're talking about. I don't know anyone named Hunter, and the Boss is off researching something. Now get out of my apartment!"

Still holding Andrew down with his right hand, Smith reached behind his back, coming back with a gun he lightly tossed to Frank.

"I'll run a bath for Andrew here." Smith first stepped over, locking the door and setting the chain. "Shouldn't take but a moment, Mr.

Thomas." Smith walked past the entertainment center, disappearing down the hall to the right.

Frank managed to point the gun at Andrew in what he thought was a menacing gesture. "Hunter. Mr. Collum. Whatever you want to call him. Boss?" Frank said that as if it was a funny joke, "Let's go over where you think he might be, before Smith gets back."

Andrew glanced at the hall entry, to the gun in Frank's hand pointed at him, and to the door, his eyes longing for escape. Frank smiled.

●———•

Morgan Dimico had spent the better part of five minutes cussing himself out in front of Daniel Collum's home. The house was only a short distance from the antique shop, and Dimico just happened to catch the time before he walked across the street to the two-story Folk Victorian house Collum called his home. The jigsaw shingles, trim, and fret work appealed to Dimico, as well as the steeply-pitched roof. There was a nostalgic feel to this house, with its decorative barge boards along the gables, the vertical windows, ornamental brackets, and the brick chimney with its own patterned overtures. From everything he now knew of Daniel Collum, this would have been the only home he could picture the man in. Even the exterior colors worked for him, what Dimico thought of as a burnt green with an orange-red trim.

That feeling of nostalgia ended once he walked up to the porch and noticed that the house appeared dark and empty. Moving around and peeking through a few windows confirmed his suspicions, along with the absence of the Austin Healey that was almost always parked in the driveway. It was in this driveway that his tantrum had occurred. Luckily, only one or two passersby caught the comical tirade of this crazy person spewing profanity. What they saw was a middle-aged man degrading himself, as he stomped up and down the empty driveway, flailing his arms around.

"Morgan, you're a fool," he stated, still a bit out of breath. "Nothing for it now but to head back to the office and see if there's any leads I can find. Oh yeah and wait for my payment." That brought another feeling to him, a sick-in-the-stomach feeling. He had better get back to the office and make sure he was ready for when his guest showed up. He didn't trust his ex-client any more than he knew his name, which of course he did not. Best to take a step back from Mr. Collum for a moment and make sure of his own longevity. Collum could wait a bit longer.

Dimico took another moment to appreciate the home in front of him, wishing he could have seen the inside under better circumstances than through darkened windows. He could feel at home in one of these places, not that he could ever pull that kind of money to buy one. He walked back across the street to his car, stealing one last look at the Victorian home, before opening the driver's door with a heavy sigh. Maybe another time and place. Sliding behind the wheel of his beat-up Ford Focus, he considered what he needed to do once he was back at his office in Pasadena.

Dimico took the 57/210 freeway connection to Pasadena to avoid traffic. Even so, it still took him well over an hour to get there, and then what seemed an age for him to find parking. By the time he climbed the one flight of stairs to his office, almost two hours had passed. Shaking his head, he pulled his keys from his pocket, then noticed the door was just slightly ajar already. His sense of danger heightened. Problem was, his gun was still in the desk drawer. He hadn't seen a need to bring it with him.

Opening the door as slowly and quietly as he could, Dimico immediately noticed the disarray. Papers were thrown haphazardly on the floor, his filing cabinet drawers open, and files tossed here and there. Then he noticed the man sitting in his chair, with his feet propped on his desk.

"Bad bit of luck you had here. Looks like you were robbed, though I can't see what anyone would want. It would appear I got here just a little late to stop them."

"Who are you?"

"Merely a messenger. You may call me Mr. Smith if you like. I'll make the obvious assumption that you are Mr. Dimico. I was sent here with your final payment for services rendered, but first, I was to ask for any and all information you have on this Collum person. I hope it wasn't in here where one might have taken it." Smith looked around the room with mock concern.

Dimico stared at his uninvited guest with veiled anger, "Get your feet off my desk, and no, the files were not in the office." He had wanted to say, "as you well know," but he held it on the tip of his tongue. That sinking feeling had him full in the stomach now, and he felt naked with this man sitting behind his desk.

Mr. Smith slowly pulled his feet off the desk and said, "I'm sorry, that was rude of me. Glad to hear the files are still in a safe place, as my employer would greatly wish to have them back."

Dimico may not have been the best cop in his time, but he could see the military composure of the man opposite him. He could also see that his desk drawers were open, even the locked one in front which held his revolver. He noticed a manila envelope sitting on the desk which had not been there before, and piles of papers tossed carelessly about his desktop, cluttering what would normally be his one tidy area. Those papers suddenly gave him pause when he caught what might be a lump under a small pile situated near the manila envelope.

"I'll hand them over once I have my payment. I spent a lot of time gathering it all together, so I hope you understand." Dimico picked up one of the chairs on his side of the desk, setting it down on its legs opposite Mr. Smith, and the lump under the pile on the desk.

Waving his left hand dismissively, Mr. Smith then placed both of his hands, palm down, on top of the desk. His left hand just behind the lump, Dimico noted. "Oh, I fully understand Mr. Dimico. In our line of business, it does one well to be cautious, doesn't it."

Dimico really was beginning to dislike the condescending tone of the man sitting in his chair, but he held back a few choice words as he glanced at the hand by the lump. Instead, he chose a different course. "Truthfully, I don't understand why Mister . . . you know, I don't even know his name, why he would want the files. He has the acknowledgement that Daniel Collum is Robert Hunter, as unbelievable as that may seem. The files will do no more than show the same thing."

Smith did not take the bait. He seemed a little put out by it, about the only real emotion he had shown since Dimico entered the room. "Our employer would like the files back as there is a sensitivity to the subject matter which he gave you. Anything you have accumulated since then would also fall within that realm of sensitivity." He motioned with his right hand to the manila envelope in front of him on the desk, next to the lump which was still dangerously close to his left hand, "All you need to do in order to get your last payment, and may I say that there's quite a bonus added in, is to hand over all your files on the subject."

Dimico was pretty sure what the bonus was as he shot another quick glance at the lump. He knew those files were the only thing keeping him alive right now, and he was running out of ways to stall that outcome. The only card he really held was that this Mr. Smith had no idea where the files were. His employer apparently wanted them back in the worst way. A sudden realization, and plan, hit him at the same moment: the desk, the open drawers, and the lump on the desk itself. Leaning forward to put his weight on his end of the desk, Dimico steadied himself.

"All right, they're downstairs. But first, may I take a quick look at the envelope?" Dimico tried to make himself sound genuinely interested only in that bulky manila package.

Smith smiled, "Absolutely, if that is what it will take to end this exchange." He leaned forward with his right hand to push the envelope to the other side of the desk, while at the same time, moving his left hand under the lump of papers.

As Smith's movements put him slightly off balance in the chair, Dimico quickly stood, shoving upward on the desk. The drawers which were already slightly open, shot out, adding weight to the desk, which turned over and onto Smith. His chair rolled away with the weight, sending him to the floor. Tossed as well were the manila envelope and Dimico's revolver, which was the lump on the desk. If he hadn't been fighting for his life, Dimico may have laughed at the surprised look that came over Smith as he disappeared under the heavy wooden desk and shower of paperwork.

Dimico immediately bolted for the door, managed to open it on his first try, and was almost out of his office when a shot rang out. He felt an impact close to his right shoulder as part of the door frame splintered, sending wooden shards through his coat and shirt, embedding themselves into his shoulder. That shot had not come from his own weapon - must have been from Smith's. He was fast! Dimico raced down the end of the hall, hoping he would make the staircase before he heard another register from that pistol. His body tensed as he threw his full weight against the stairwell door and his escape. He flung himself down the stairs to his car, all the while waiting for another bullet to zero in on him, but nothing ever came. His chest pounding - he got to his car, opened the door, and jumped in without hearing another shot. Starting the car, he raced off, all the while looking in his rearview mirror for any indication Smith might be following him.

Smith had never made it out from under the desk, as one leg was pinned under the heavy furniture. The drawers and chair kept getting in his way each time he tried to gain leverage. All the papers, pencils, paperclips, and what-not that had spilled onto him made matters worse. He had taken a blind shot at Dimico with his own Glock, and if the chair hadn't shifted his aim, he might have hit the man in the shoulder. All he could do now was get out of this room quickly, in case anyone had called for the police. He would need to inform Mr. Thomas of this setback when they connected at the meeting place he was to go to next. After that was taken care of, he would then have to find Mr. Dimico and pay him off for the last time. Grabbing the manila envelope on the floor next to him, he threw it across the room, where it exploded in a shower of white and black print newspaper, cut to look like money.

⁕

Daniel slowed his Austin Healey to a crawl, parking across the street from Andrew's apartment. He rubbed his eyes for a couple of minutes to try and clear them. It was eight in the evening, and he had spent half his day on the road. Pulling himself out of the car was a tedious process as most of his muscles screamed at him to leave them alone. Turning a deaf ear to his body, he staggered across the street, working to stretch out the angered muscles on the way. Daniel was not happy with how he had handled the surprise of being found out. Had he been thinking clearly, he would have done this before he had driven off to Cambria. Unfortunately, his flight instinct had kicked in, taking over any rational thought. He hadn't felt that ugly instinct in some thirty years, and it would seem he had grown rusty over the course of time.

Knocking on the door, Daniel worked his neck a little, attempting to massage the stiff muscles there. He had been standing there for almost a full minute before he knocked again, a little louder, but still no answer. Trying the doorknob, the door opened easily. Daniel's adrenaline quickly kicked in, causing any aches he had to disappear from his mind. He sensed something was wrong immediately, almost felt as if he'd known that before getting out of the car. Unconsciously, he reached into his coat for a weapon that wasn't there. He balked for only a fraction, before slipping into the apartment, closing the door behind him. Luckily, as it was already dark outside, he did not need time for his vision to adjust to the inside of Andrew's apartment. He scanned the interior quickly with eyes that had once been trained for such work, taking in every detail.

The living area on the left side of the door was clean. A futon with faded blue cushions took up the front door wall, and a small camel brown couch took up part of the wall adjacent. In the corner between was a tall wooden lamp, and in front of both couches was a low, dark stained wooden coffee table with a few personal items on display. The opposite wall from the door held a large entertainment center with a darkened TV staring back at him, his reflection just a hint in its face. The shelves were filled with a variety of DVD movies, DVD player, and sound system. The last wall held two tall wooden bookcases, full to brimming with books Daniel assumed were mostly biographies, autobiographies, and books pertaining to antiques of various kinds. Such was the life of his assistant.

To Daniel's right was the kitchen and small dining section. The dining area held a small, round wooden table with two chairs around it, the one closest to the kitchen pulled out, an unfinished meal at the place setting. The kitchen was small and cramped. Stove/oven, cabinets, and refrigerator against the connecting living room wall. The microwave, cabinets, knife rack, and dishwasher against the outside wall on the other side. A calendar, displaying an old Model T Ford in all its glory for the month of September, was tacked on the end wall.

The apartment was small enough that Daniel hardly needed to move to be sure Andrew was not in either location. The wall with the entertainment center also led to the bedroom. A small hall to the right of that behind the bookshelves and kitchen, which would logically lead to the bathroom. The bedroom door was closed and just stared back at Daniel. He moved to the kitchen, pulling the chef knife from the wooden block. Softly walking to the bedroom door, he surveyed the short hall to the bathroom, noticing the door was open. He would check that last if he had to. Putting his ear to the bedroom door, he could hear nothing from the other side. Holding the knife firmly in his right hand, he gently turned the knob with his left. The door creaked minutely, but in the deafening silence, it sounded more like a scream. Daniel's nerves tensed as he waited, but no other sound came from within. He entered, taking inventory of the super twin bed. It was a simple box spring and mattress combination, made with care. Covering it nicely was a brown, cross-hatch patterned comforter. Next to this, a small wooden nightstand with small wood lamp on top. Both sides of the closet were partially opened, showing neat rows of clothes and shoes, but nothing out of the ordinary. A small dresser on the same wall as the bedroom door, as clean and tidy as its owner, finished the room's décor. Still no sign of Andrew.

Daniel swallowed hard, taking a deep breath, before slowly making his way to the bathroom at the end of the small hall. Opposite the open door on the left was the linen closet, and at the end, the water heater door. Peering into the bathroom, Daniel's body went numb. The knife dropped from his fingers to the brown carpet floor, forgotten. Andrew's body was bent over the bathtub full of water, his head immersed in the tub, the water slightly murky from blood. Daniel rushed over, pulling Andrew's lifeless body from the bathtub to the cold tile floor. There was a cut over his left eye which had barely begun to bruise and swell. His skin had that pale, almost yellow pallor to it, which immediately told Daniel there was nothing he could do. He slid to the floor, tears flowing freely from his eyes. All he could think to say was, "I'm sorry, I'm so sorry."

CHAPTER SEVEN

TURN OF THE CENTURY

Daniel had no idea how much time had passed when he regained his senses. Wiping the tears from his eyes, he looked down at the unwavering stare of his assistant. An anger and sorrow built up in him which he had not felt in about a hundred years. Memories came flooding back to him. Memories he had tried to suppress for a very long time, and whose doors all opened at once, blinding him in their light.

That light had been strong, just as strong now in its emotions as it had been back in 1900. He and Kathryn had been enjoying their life in Dodge City. *The Occidental Hotel* was working out quite well for them and they prospered. Just a few years earlier, Daniel had decided to take on a business partner who would take over all the work necessary to run the *Occidental*, so he could stay back as a silent partner with controlling interest. One of the main reasons for doing this was he had grown tired of the work and wished to relax with his wife. The other, more pressing reason to stay out of the limelight, was his age. All the talk, the light gossip about how young he appeared through the years, were finally catching up. He began to realize it was not just politeness on their part. He was now fifty-two years of age, his wife just a few years younger, and yet, while she looked to be in her late forties, he could easily still pass for someone in his mid-twenties.

Kathryn had been worried and wanted him to see a doctor. They discussed the matter on many occasions, but Daniel had been adamant with Kathryn about keeping this to themselves. He knew what the general populace would do if they found something drastically different from themselves. He had seen what that kind of thinking caused, time and again during the war, and he preferred keeping his neck attached to his body. Kathryn had laughed at that once, years before, but now at the *Occidental*, they could both see he had been correct. The stares, the whispering around town, and eventually the avoidance, reminded them of the smallpox epidemic. It was enough for the two of them to grasp the gravity of the situation.

Daniel did not have to worry as far as Kathryn was concerned. Her love for him far surpassed any worry she might have had about his lack of aging. Luckily, both of their children had moved away. There would be no need for stories or subterfuge. Their son Nathaniel and his wife had moved to Galveston, Texas, and become successful in the trade of exporting cotton. They had two boys, which Daniel and Kathryn had a picture of, the whole family happy in the portrait. Their daughter Mary married and moved to Massachusetts with her husband. They prospered in Boston, giving birth to a daughter of their own, another picture Kathryn and Daniel were proud of.

With Kathryn's help, Daniel began the task of using makeup to age himself when in public. Nothing more drastic than adding white to his temples gradually, to slowly age him, it had helped. Keeping himself out of the public eye for weeks at a time assisted in the process, and eventually life had gone on as it should have, until the hurricane in 1900.

There were rumors of the devastation from the storm that hit Galveston on September 8th with little warning. Unable to reach Nathaniel, they waited for any scrap of information from the newspapers - it finally came. Of the 38,000 residents, a staggering list of 8,000 appeared in the paper. The two collapsed to the floor on reading the names of Nathaniel's entire family on the list of deceased. Their grandchildren still under the age of ten when they drowned.

They sold everything to the partner, left *The Occidental Hotel* behind, and moved to California. They settled in San Francisco to retire from the world and spend their time together. The move seemed to help Kathryn physically and mentally. She grew more active than she had since the year she contracted smallpox. Daniel, on the other hand, was still dealing with depression over the loss of his namesake. He had not only lost a son who would carry on his name, but two grandsons who would have carried it on further. His wife had joked once to him while they were relaxing in their sitting room, that he was much more emotional a person than even she was. He had chuckled lightly at the joke, but had then stated without really thinking about it, "I just might be." Kathryn smiled at first, but dropped the subject altogether. At her urging, Daniel wrote to his daughter, to see how Mary and her husband were doing in Boston with his granddaughter. The correspondence seemed to have helped. A small spark of life returned to Daniel's eyes.

The only real worry that crossed Daniel's mind during his emotional fog at that time, was something he kept seeing in the *San Francisco Call* newspaper. It had been hidden on page thirteen for weeks, just a small blurb in the paper. But as weeks turned into months, and as 1900 gave up the year to 1901, this news story inched forward in the pages, creeping larger and larger in size. The Bubonic Plague was in Chinatown, spreading throughout the populace there. Daniel worried that they may have made a poor choice of location to move to, but he kept his worries away from Kathryn, as the rest of San Francisco was not infected yet. The containment to Chinatown seemed to be working. If the news changed, and he saw it spread further out, he was prepared to have them move again. They were unprepared for the fire that had destroyed so much of their lives in Deadwood, and were lucky they had squirreled away what was needed to restart in Dodge City. Daniel had made sure something like that would never happen again, peppering his money into various banks and holdings, not only in San Francisco, but in neighboring cities as well. As a final measure, he hid a few nest eggs here and there in their home for emergencies. He wanted to be sure that if anything were to happen again, they would be ready for it.

One year would leave and another would come. Chinatown's plague did not spill further out, though the situation there was not any better. It was during one of these days, checking on the news of the plague on page 5 in 1903, that Daniel came across another article that peaked his interest.

AIRSHIP'S FLIGHT IS A SUCCESS
Craft Sails Skyward Without Aid of a Balloon

Apparently, the Wright Brothers attempt at a flying machine had taken to the air. Despite all the negative comments, it stayed aloft for an astounding three miles at Kitty Hawk. The headline on the front page grabbed Daniel with such fervor that he found himself reading the article repeatedly. His mind wandered as he imagined what it would be like to soar above the ground like a bird in flight. The advances that could be made in travel alone would be astonishing, though there were still many naysayers denouncing how it was a quaint schoolboy project. They were positive it would go no further than to prove we could slip the bonds of earth for just a moment, but Daniel was positive it would be so much more somewhere in the future.

He searched for anything in the papers on the subject of air travel from that point on, never realizing this was helping him heal. Eventually, the plague threat from Chinatown also waned. Exhausting the supply of viable hosts, it had run its course in Chinatown, seeming to fizzle out in 1904. Life returned to normal in the Collum home, and Daniel was able to breathe deeply and relax for the first time since the death of their son.

In 1906, on the morning of April 18th, Daniel was rudely awakened by someone shaking him. Springing up, he found no one else in the room except Kathryn. She was lying next to him, her eyes as big as saucers, the covers gripped in her fingers by her neck. Grabbing his pocketwatch on the nightstand, he could just make out the time, 5:12, in the dark morning hour. It was then that he felt the shaking increase, the room moving as it should never have, with the roll of the earth below them. Throwing the sheets and comforter off his body, Daniel jumped out of bed, snatched up his pants, yelling to Kathryn to get up and run downstairs. Grabbing his shirt and shoes, he attempted to make his way down the stairs as they shifted first this way, then that. Hearing a shout of surprise from Kathryn at the top of the balcony, Daniel turned hastily, causing him to stumble and fall the rest of the way down the stairs, landing heavily on his back in the parlor room entry. His vision, blurred from hitting his head on the floor, could just make out Kathryn holding onto the guardrail with one hand, carefully moving down the stairs. With a horrifying scream, the overstressed wood of their home gave out, splintered, and everything went black.

Daniel woke to the warmth of daylight shining onto his face. His head felt as if someone had split it in two. Tightly closing his eyes, he felt the back of his head gingerly, causing him to cry out in pain. He laid there for a few minutes, just trying to get his body to work, before he realized he could see open sky above him. Swiveling his head slowly around, he took in his surroundings and saw what was left of his home. The parlor room was a mess, the ceiling half caved in, walls partially destroyed, and everything broken. He coughed from the dust which filled the room, sending shooting pains through his head again. He stood, turning to face the stairwell. None of the walls still existed on this side of the house, and if he had not known where he was, he would not have been able to tell he was even looking at the stairwell.

That's when he remembered Kathryn had been at the top of the stairs. There was no sign of her, and every shout of her name brought another shock of pain to his head. With each unanswered shout, Daniel grew more frantic.

"Kathryn! Kathryn, where are you?! KATHRYN!"

Coughing, eyes filled with dust and tears, Daniel tore into the pile that was once the stairwell, throwing anything and everything he could out of his way. His every muscle screamed, and his head began to pound more and more with each item he savagely removed from the rubble. He lost sight in his right eye. Wiping at it with the back of his hand, he came away with blood from some cut bleeding from his forehead. He thought his lungs and heart might burst, when he threw a section of plaster wall aside and saw a woman's hand, still holding a framed picture. With renewed energy, he dug in, eventually uncovering the upper half of Kathryn's still form.

"Kathryn?" No response.

Daniel carefully reached out, gently touching her cheek with the back of his bloodied hand, leaving a red blotch on her white skin. She seemed cold to the touch. "Please Kathryn, wake up." Her eyes refused to open, no answer came back to his pleading. He noticed a piece of wood as big as his arm lodged in her side, a pool of blood nestled around her body in the wreckage. With no gentleness left in him, Daniel grabbed Kathryn's shoulders and pulled her to him. He cradled her in his arms, sobbing as he had never done before in his life. He tried to clean her face, but the blood covering the back of his hand kept leaving small crimson streaks. Eventually he gave up. Gazing down at her lifeless face, he kissed her now cold lips softly, one last time. Tenderly, he laid her head back down on the rubble. Grabbing a torn sheet from the debris, he carefully laid it over her upper body, covering her face from the elements. He heard something past his right shoulder, and saw a framed picture sliding out from Kathryn's fingers, the muscles no longer capable of holding it in her grasp. Daniel reached down, picked up the picture, and turned it over. It was the portrait of the two of them and their children, all smiling. Kathryn had insisted on them having a family photograph taken, looking their best, right after the move to Dodge City. Nathaniel would have been ten years old, Mary all of seven.

That photograph by the still body of his wife, inside the wreckage that had once been their home, was the last thing he could remember for some time. He assumed he had wandered aimlessly through the debris of the city. San Francisco had been ravaged. Over eighty percent of the city had been wiped out. The earthquake had lasted for a long forty-two seconds, the fires that followed swept through to cleanse the wounds, finishing what the earthquake could not. It seemed, to those who survived, that the end of the world had come. Mission District lay in ruins from a fire. Over twenty-five thousand buildings on four hundred ninety city blocks were destroyed. The loss of life was something over three thousand people dead, some five hundred of those assumed to have been in the initial earthquake. Looters were being shot in the streets by enforcement and civilians alike, and the smell of death lingered in the air. Everywhere you could see, the walking wounded moved about in need of care.

Daniel's Angel of Mercy came in the form of Father Dunne. Dunne, with the help of his surviving parish, had managed to clear out an area that, before the quake, had been their church. Setting up mattresses, blankets, and a fire pit with a food station, Dunne and his followers established a haven for the survivors. Father Dunne had found Daniel only two blocks away from this sanctuary. Daniel wore no shoes or socks, his pants torn, his unbuttoned dress shirt covered in soot, dirt, and blood. He was clinging to a framed photo which the Father was unable to remove from his grasp. Nonresponsive, seeming to stare miles past the Father as he stepped directly in front of him, Daniel did not acknowledge the world at all. Father Dunne had led him by the arm back to his church, the steeple still standing as a beacon to those in need. Giving him a mattress, Dunne cleaned his mud caked face, hand-fed him a hot meal, and handed him a shot of something to drink, then laid him down. Covering him with a blanket, Daniel collapsed into sleep.

Two days later, Daniel woke to the smell of coffee and stew. He never gave his name, but helped Father Dunne for a few days, before leaving to find his home. What he found were three-quarters of his house collapsed. Near the property were the bodies of a couple of looters shot dead and left as a warning. He had been able to dig out enough of the rubble to collect some of their hidden funds to buy a horse and cart. This he filled with what valuables he could salvage from the wreckage. With that done, Daniel carefully dug Kathryn out from where he had left her. Gently, he placed her broken body on the now legless kitchen table where they had shared meals for many years. Using one of the curtains from the dining room windows, he covered her body, posting a wooden sign with black letters by her, written with a burned stick:

Please bury the body of Kathryn Collum
Daniel Collum missing, presumed dead.

With this fire-blackened message, Daniel Collum ceased to exist. Like the rising of a phoenix, Hayden McClellan would come out of the ashes, eventually appearing in Norfolk, Virginia.

•⎯•

Daniel covered Andrew's body with the comforter from his bed, returned the knife back to its place, and sat at the table with the unfinished meal in front of him. Daniel stared at the food that would never be consumed, his thoughts drifting again.

Yes, it had been the birth of a new man back in 1906, but it had taken years before he would become Hayden McClellan. He spent a few years traveling back east in that horse-and-cart which carried all his belongings. He moved from one location to another, extricating a large portion of his money from various banks. He had been lucky enough to remember to retrieve what identification he would need from the rubble. He eventually settled in Virginia in 1914, when war erupted across the ocean in Europe. By 1915, the world was engulfed in conflict. A conflict begun by the death of Archduke Ferdinand and his wife by a lone Serbian assassin. This same year, the news ran stories that peaked Daniel's interest, all revolving around battles that took place in the air. Initially used for reconnaissance purposes only, as it was thought it would be good for not much else, the aeroplane had blown into another type of warfare altogether. Warplanes, the terrors of the skies, and the knights that flew them, carried a mystique which called to Daniel. He began to formulate the plan that would give him his new identity.

Finding a pilot in the United States willing to teach took money, something Daniel had more than enough of. In short order, he had taken to the skies. As it turned out, he was a natural in the cockpit. Every time he left the ground below, soaring over the fields, he felt alive as he had not felt since the earthquake. By the end of 1915, Daniel, now Hayden McClellan, had become an accomplished pilot. By luck, he befriended a young man who would head up the first of many American flyers leaving for the European war effort. Travelling from Great Britain to France, Daniel found himself among boys in their late teens and early twenties. Full of piss and vinegar, these young British and French men were jumping out of their skins to join in the war. There was some fear, but with youth came invincibility and immortality. Daniel had no illusions of what he was about to do. He was almost seventy years old now, yet still looked to be in his twenties. He found it funny that when he was thirteen, he looked to be in his twenties. Now that he was a much, much older man, he still looked to be that same age. Collum, now McClellan, had passed himself off as twenty-eight years old in 1915. By the time he entered Europe and joined the Lafayette Escadrille, everyone believed him to be twenty-nine years old. His fellow flyers took to calling him by the nickname Pops, not because he was the oldest of them, he was not, but because he carried himself like a man twice his age. If they had only really known, Daniel thought with a smile.

Ever since leaving San Francisco, Daniel's psyche had been horribly damaged. He felt alone and forgotten. The mental scars were taking their toll on the man. There had been many attempts to end his life by his own hands: drowning, pills, jumping from a great height, even shooting, or stabbing himself to death. Each time, he had stopped before the act could not be reversed. Daniel eventually came to the realization that his will to live was just too great. He also concluded that he just did not believe in suicide as an option. World War I had become the exception. Even if he was unable to kill himself to find the peace he so wanted from the pain he felt, the war would obviously have men who would gladly take his life. He had found a loophole by removing the killing stroke from his own hands.

The experiences he had from the Civil War had taught him war took a man's choice of life out of his hands, putting it into the weapon of the opposition. Luck was all there was for a man to survive war, and there had been six hundred twenty thousand unlucky men in the Civil War. Daniel had not escaped that war unscathed, receiving his own calling card at Gettysburg, in the form of a .58 caliber musket ball from an 1853 Enfield muzzle-loading rifle. He had been one of the lucky that day. Had he been just slightly taller, and not turned to hear an order given just at the right moment, that musket ball could have ended his life. Instead, it had taken him out of service for a time, giving him a badge of honor in the form of a nice scar on his right shoulder.

That scar became less of an honor and more of a curse to him in the years that followed. That same year, Daniel had turned sixteen years of age. From what he could gather, it had also been the year his altered aging begun. He often wondered whether that shot had caused his current state. As each year passed, and more information became available to him, he found that thought ludicrous. Truth be told, he kept coming back to puberty and hormones. Why that would make him a quarter year man, he might never know, but that was who he was. He had come to terms with it in his own way, until Mother Earth's cruelty ripped away two-thirds of his family from him.

So, he found himself on a boat headed for Great Britain, then France after that. It was only the second time in his life to cross the Atlantic Ocean. The first time was as a young boy when his family left Killimor, in Ireland. He now gazed at the Statue of Liberty, as his boat sailed to England from the United States. Daniel took in every detail of that monument to freedom, whose gaze seemed close to tears for all the sons who might never return. Something inside him felt it would be the last thing he would see of the country he called his home.

CHAPTER EIGHT

CITY OF ORANGE, 8:00 P.M.

Daniel pulled himself back to the present with difficulty. He needed to get out of Andrew's apartment before it became a problem. He hated to leave his friend where he had found him, but the less evidence they could find of him the better. Now more than ever, he needed to get to his house and grab what was needed before the Haig Men found him.

Quickly cleaning everything he thought might hold any print evidence of himself, he left quietly. As he drove the few blocks from Andrew's apartment to his own home, he mentally kicked himself in the ass for having no weapon with him. In fact, that was the main reason for returning home. He had left his guns in a safe in his bedroom, never once thinking to take one with him. Had he really been out of the killing game for so long that it never once occurred to him to take them? He sighed, realizing how much he had grown tired of death.

He pulled his car up to the curb around the corner from his home and moved from shadow to shadow in the dark of night to gain a good view of his house. I may be rusty, he thought, but I'm most definitely not stupid. Surveying his home, he found he had been correct in his assumption. He counted four men total staking out the house. The first was easy enough, as he was on the front porch, walking back and forth from one end to the other. He was not paying much attention, except for the occasional glance at the street from time to time. The second was inside his home on the first floor. He would walk past the windows in front, disappearing for a few minutes, before coming back into view.

Daniel carefully snuck around his neighbor's home for a better vantage of the back of his house. On taking up a position in the bushes there, he realized the second individual was walking from front to back, probably moving through each room on the first floor. The third man had been at the back of his home, leaning against the wall, smoking a cigarette.

"Where did they get these guys anyway?" Daniel thought to himself.

They seemed lax in their job. That would help him with what he would need to do. He had almost missed the fourth man, as that one stayed in the shadows of the upstairs windows. Daniel just happened to be looking at his bedroom window in back, when the third man moved his right foot against the wall, making a slight noise. That was when man number four appeared in the window, pulling one curtain aside to look out. Daniel could see his hand move to his ear and the man by the door respond in kind. Great, they had earwig communication devices. What happened to the good old days and walkie-talkies? Daniel did notice the one thing that seemed to be missing -- weapons. Oh, they had them, he was positive about that. Chances were they had hand guns, probably with silencers attached.

"You wouldn't want to wake the neighbors, now would you?" Daniel quipped. "Now, how do I go about getting my own weapons, since they're in the bedroom with number four man?"

He spent a good ten minutes thinking, running things over in his mind. During his time in the service, well, multiple services, he had learned a variety of hand-to-hand fighting styles. The problem with that was it had been years since he'd practiced any of them. He also admitted to himself that he was much older now. That brought a chuckle to his lips. These men all looked to be in peak physical shape, probably in their mid-twenties, and in their prime. Even if they were a bit lax in their guard techniques, he would have to be smart.

As these thoughts rolled around inside his head, he kept watch on the house. Every once-in-awhile he would look over at his small garage. Really, it was more of a glorified work shed. The small building was almost behind the house, at the end of the long driveway. A lightbulb finally went off in his head. Slowly moving through the shadows of his neighbor's property, he made his way to the shed from the back side. The problem now was how to get in. The third man had a view from the back porch to the shed, if he looked in that direction. The shed only had the one door, and the hinges would loudly creak from the rust accumulated over years of his neglect. One problem with living such a long time, you found yourself letting things wait another day. Another day . . . needs fixing . . . something else about the shed itched at his brain . . . his brow furrowed in thought as he stared at the back of the shed. He felt it had something to do with where he was but didn't know why. Scanning the top, then down the length of the back wall, he could not think what it was. As his eyes made it down to the overgrown, knee-high weeds at the bottom of the shed wall, he was about to give up when it finally struck him. Moving the weeds aside from the shack wall revealed what he had been trying to remember. The bottom few boards were only somewhat stacked atop each other. Daniel had been storing a few boxes from his other life for safekeeping, and accidentally pushed the boxes back with such force that the boards had given way from their rusty nails, popping them out the back side. Figuring he would eventually get around to fixing it, he had just propped them up and left them. At this moment, Daniel could not have been happier at his ability to procrastinate. Now the question was whether he could fit himself through the opening, once the boards were moved out of the way.

As quietly as he could, he removed both boards, setting them aside out of view from the back porch. He then spent what felt like a decade trying to slide the boxes left under the workbench years before, without raising too much noise. There were a couple of moments when his nerves jumped at the sound of a box scraping over loose gravel, but the very loud noise to his ear was too minor to draw the attention of the backdoor guard. Once that was done, he turned over onto his back to slither over the weeds and into the small shed.

The interior was darker than the half-moon lighting from outside, and it took a few seconds for his eyes to adjust enough to see what was inside. Unfortunately, he had moved all the tools from the shed to one of the rooms in the house. He had turned the shed into storage, for boxes of items you never knew what to do with, but never wanted to let go of. He spied where he had put the old 'L' hand-sized green flashlight. Taking it up in his hands, he pointed it at the back wall, flipping the small switch - nothing.

"Well, it has been over forty years. No doubt the batteries have eaten away the inside of this thing by now." He whispered to himself putting the item back. Not even useful as a weapon, unless you wanted to give someone a small bump on the head.

He tried to read the faded writing on the boxes left there so many years before. In what little lighting he had, he was just able to make out something that appeared to say **Odds and Ends**. Making the slow trek back out of the shed through his makeshift hole with the box, Daniel could see better with the help of the moonlight. Moving through the parted hedges, box in hand, he found a spot in the next-door neighbor's back yard.

The aged box held a treasure trove of American Nostalgia, among them an old cookie tin from some Christmas past, a baseball glove still well-oiled after all these years, a cigar box from Cuba which stored stacks of baseball cards up through 1950, an engine with a couple cars to a train set, a metal wind-up motion toy, and an old wooden wind-up plane.

He pulled out the red cookie tin. Gritting his teeth, Daniel carefully applied pressure to the lid so as not to make any noise, and with a sigh of relief, pulled the lid off. The seal on the tin was just as strong as when he first opened it, during his tour in Hawaii, when he enjoyed the Christmas cookies. Inside now was a jumble of old rubber bands, most having adhered themselves to the inside of the box, a small book of *Moana Hotel and Bungalows* matches which, when opened, proved to still have about half the matchbox still full, and an array of old firecrackers: Gee Whizz, Big Bang, and Buster brands. Taking the firecrackers, he stuffed them in his outside jacket pockets, put the matchbox in his pants' pocket, and as an afterthought, took the few good rubber bands, shoving those in his pants' pocket as well.

Daniel then detached the faded red and black engine from the cars, hefting the cold metal in his right hand, making a fist. Yes, this could work nicely to send someone to dreamland if hit just right. He put everything back in the box and hid it in the shrubs of his neighbor's yard. Putting the engine in his coat and gathering up the two toys, he made a last check of his four home intruders to be sure they had not moved from their positions.

Back in his hiding place in the hedges between the two properties, Daniel set the toys on the ground, formulating a plan of action. First, he grabbed the metal oddity and very slowly wound it up. The gears inside only made the slightest noise, so Daniel didn't worry. Pushing the button on the toy to pause its movement, he then looked to the wooden plane. Best not to take a chance that the plane might still actually fly. Not that he could think of a way for that to benefit him in this situation, but the noise the propeller would make should be sufficient. Taking one of the rubber bands from his pocket, he attached it to the toy plane, turning the propeller to wind it up. He had only made two revolutions when the rubber band broke.

"Damn it."

Taking one of the only two rubber bands he had left, he worked a little more carefully to wind up the toy. Tensing with each turn of the propeller, he breathed a sigh of satisfaction when he felt the torque of resistance telling him it was ready. Holding his toy prizes in his hands, he studied the man on his porch one last time to be sure his pattern had not changed. When the time was right, he made a low crouch run across the short span of lawn, slipping between the shrubs on the side of the house. It would have been so much easier if there had been no moon at all. The porch had a long front, which took a ninety-degree turn around the side of the house. This area held a small love seat swing. There was only one small window on this side of the porch, and the curtains were drawn, making it impossible for the man downstairs inside to see. The shrubs lining the front and side of the porch made it easier for Daniel to hide. At the end of the short side of the porch, by the building, was a much taller bush. Adding to the pleasing nature of the architecture, it also lent Daniel a good place to hide.

Setting the toy plane upside down in the low shrubbery, he released his hold on the propeller. Moving quickly, he ducked between the tall bush and the side of the house. Taking the train engine out of his pocket, he held it in his right fist, and waited. Sure enough, he heard the footsteps of the porch guard as he returned. The sound of his steps continued to the bend of the porch. Daniel could just make out his face in the half moon's light as the guard tried to figure out what the noise could be. Moving toward the odd sound, he closed the distance carefully. He reached the end of the porch near Daniel's hiding spot, shifting his eyes back and forth, attempting to gauge where the noise was coming from. Setting his sights on the small shrub below him, he finally made up his mind. Without taking his weapon out, he used both hands to lean over the railing, trying to get a better view. Daniel swiftly reached out with his left hand, pulling on the guard's shirt collar, flipping him over the railing and into the shrubs. Before he had a chance to recover from his surprise, Daniel hit him in the jaw, then shifted his hold on the engine to give the man a hard strike to the temple. The guard immediately went limp. Daniel took a moment to make sure that the brief struggle had not been heard, then pulled the porch guard's body across the lawn, and into the wall of foliage separating the properties.

A quick search of his body produced a Glock 9mm pistol, complete with silencer, just as expected. Daniel also took the earwig the man wore, placing it in his own ear. Just as he had hoped, there was no sound. It seemed they were maintaining radio silence. That was a good thing, as it meant no one would have heard the recent scuffle. Something else Daniel had expected, the absence of anything on the man to identify who he was, or who he might work for. Still, Daniel was positive they worked for the Haig Men.

Placing the pistol in his pants at the small of his back, Daniel moved back across the lawn to the side of the house. Gathering up the metal toy he had left there, he moved along the short 'L' section of the side porch. Raising his body enough to reach the bottom of the porch floor, Daniel set the contraption down and turned it on. It immediately began to make a winding-up noise, then the back half of the toy flipped over to the front, connecting with the wooden floorboards. The sound on the porch as it hit was loud. It threw itself forward another step. With that in place, Daniel moved back to the dividing hedges, and worked his way to the back end of the properties.

"What the hell is that?" he heard through his earpiece.

"I don't know. I can't see anything out the window I'm at." The voice of the ground floor guard responded from inside.

"Abel, what are you doing out there?" No response came back.

"Son of a bitch. I'm going to rip you a new asshole if you're messing around out there. Charlie, go around front and see what that moron is doing now."

"You want me to check it out, Dutch?" The ground floor guard asked.

"No! You stay put, Charlie can handle it. And Charlie, if he's fucking around out there again, you have my permission to beat the shit out of him. I'm going to have a serious talk with Thomas about him once this is all over and done with. Fucking asshole."

"I'm on it Dutch. With pleasure." Charlie responded.

Thomas! Could it be? Daniel had assumed Frank Thomas would have died years ago from a heart attack or some such. That was if the wounds Daniel had given him the last time they met hadn't done the job first. Storing that information away for a later time, he watched Charlie move down the length of the left side of the house to the front. Maneuvering the rest of the way to the back of the property line, Daniel crossed into his own yard. He hugged the corner to reach the porch, and the back door. Testing the doorknob, he found it unlocked.

Closing the French door as quietly as he could behind him, Daniel took a quick survey of his surroundings. The breakfast area to the left of the back door was empty, and through the archway to his right, the family room was also dark and void of guests. Making his way through the breakfast nook and into the kitchen, he could see through to the dining room, just as empty of people as everything else so far. He soundlessly worked his way into the dining room, past the table and chairs. Giving his eyes a moment to adjust, he could make out the parlor beyond, well enough to see someone peeking out the window to the front of the house. All this was done in under a minute, all the while with the play-by-play going on in his ear.

"All right, I'm almost to the front side of the porch. Bender, you see anything from where you're at?" Charlie whispered through the earwig device.

Bender hugged the wall in the parlor, moving the curtains further to one side, trying to obtain a good view of the front porch area. "I can hear someone thumping around out there real slow, but I just can't see anyone."

"Abel? Abel, you better respond or I'm just going to shoot you when I get around the corner."

"Damn it, Charlie. Whoever is out there, is right in front of the window I'm at, but I can't see them. How is that possible?!"

"Dutch, Bender, I'm moving around the corner of the house to the front..." A moment of silence took over before a response came back, "... What in hell?! There's no one there but I hear it too." Charlie's voice had gone from a whisper to an octave higher than conversation level.

"Charlie, stay frosty. What do you see." The calm voice of Dutch came through.

"You stay frosty, Dutch. You're not out here!" Charlie snapped back. "Wait a minute, I think I see something."

During this back-and-forth banter, Daniel had slipped into the parlor, crouching down to give less of a target. He inched his way, closing on Bender's back, as his opponent moved the curtains back as far as he could to get a better look. Daniel could have grabbed one of the knives from the block in the kitchen as a better weapon, but he just didn't want to go to that extent if he didn't have to. There would also be the problem with cleaning up the blood spatter afterward. He may procrastinate on fixing things around the house occasionally, but one thing he wasn't was a slob. Yes, there was the silencer on the gun he acquired, but using it would require that cleanup.

The sound of someone climbing over the railing and onto the porch out front could be heard, then tentative steps towards the window Bender was watching from. Mixed in with this, every few seconds, was the heavy thump of the metal toy Daniel had set in motion. It shouldn't be long before this guard, Charlie, would reach the window from where Bender was looking out. Daniel would need to move soon.

"I don't see anything. Whoever it is just passed my window, headed for the front door." Bender was beginning to lose his composure.

"Charlie, you see Abel? What the fuck is going on out there?" Irritation was creeping into Dutch's voice.

"It's a goddamn fucking toy!" The sound of Charlie's voice echoed through Daniel's earpiece, and through the front wall near Bender's position.

"Say again? Did you say a toy?"

A few quick steps on the porch, and a brief shadow moved past Bender's window. The thumping sound suddenly stopped.

"A toy! A fucking, metal toy!" Anger rose in Charlie's voice.

Bender took a step back from the window, allowing the curtain to fall back in place as he heard this bit of news. With swift reflexes, Daniel reached out, grabbing Bender around the throat in a chokehold. There was a second of inactivity from Bender, that quickly turned into an attempt to elbow Daniel in his stomach, as his other hand tried to pull the headlock away from his neck.

While the two were in close combat, Dutch's voice could be heard through the earpiece. "A toy? Charlie, where's Abel?"

"How the fuck should I know. I haven't seen him at all. If that bastard is playing a joke…"

"Charlie get your ass around back. I think Hunter is here. Forget Abel. Bender, keep your eyes open. We have a visitor."

"Roger."

Daniel struggled with Bender, trying to keep out of the reach of his arms and legs, while endeavoring to apply more pressure on his windpipe. The two of them moved around the parlor in a strange, macabre dance. Bender attempting to get enough leverage to gain the upper hand before he blacked out, Daniel fighting against time to put his opponent under before the other two found them.

Daniel heard Dutch's voice in his ear. "Bender, did you copy? Bender, do you copy?"

In their struggle, Bender's foot kicked out to gain some purchase, and in so doing, hit a small table by one of the sitting chairs. The glass bowl of sour ball candies, and the table they were sitting on, tipped over. As Daniel watched, the bowl shattered into a million pieces, a rainbow of candy flying across the floor. He could hear the French door to the breakfast nook open. At the same moment, he heard Dutch's voice in his ear.

"Son of a Bitch is in the house! Charlie, watch your six, Hunter's in the house. Bender! Bender! Shit, I'm coming down!"

With only a brief second to make up his mind, Daniel applied pressure to Bender's head and twisted. He heard the crack of his opponent's neck, and Bender's body went limp. A brief surge of remorse hit Daniel in the stomach before he let loose of the body. He could hear the hurried steps of Charlie, already in the dining room, and the heavy footsteps of Dutch above, almost to the stairs. He noted the soft pop from a silencer, the bullet whizzing just above his head, as he dropped prone next to Bender's inanimate form. Without thinking, he pulled the Glock from its place at the crook of his back waistband, firing blindly at the dining room entry. Without waiting, he rolled away, then sprinted in a low crouch toward the foyer. As he reached the bottom of the steps leading to the upstairs, and Dutch, he subconsciously registered the sound of a shot from above, which hit the wall near the front door. Scrambling past the stairs, Daniel could hear the falling of chairs in the dining room, followed by the sound of Charlie hitting the floor.

"You're a dead man, Hunter," Dutch's voice called from the landing on the stairs. "Charlie, circle around, we've got him."

The only response was a weak groan from Charlie in the dining room. I must have hit him, Daniel thought, as he did his best to move silently past the study, heading for the family room in back. He heard Dutch's steps creak on the stairs which meant he was almost to the foyer. Changing course, Daniel turned right, just before the family room, entering the small wet bar opposite the bathroom. Quietly closing the split-level door, he hunched down and waited. He didn't have to wait very long before he heard Dutch's footfalls moving in his direction.

As silently as he could, Daniel slid closed the latch on the bottom half of the wet bar's door, just as he heard the handle jiggle. Seconds ticked off, then the upper handle turned, and the top half of the door swung in enough for someone to look inside. Daniel hugged the lower half of the door, willing himself as small as he could in the dark area. After an eternity of seconds, he heard a small grunt, and Dutch's footfalls heading into the family room. Daniel expelled the air he had been holding in his lungs. How could the man have missed him? Daniel looked above his hiding place, only to notice the lower door's attached shelf sticking out just above him. It must have been just enough in the dark to keep him unseen. Making every effort to keep noise to a minimum, he shifted in his cramped space. Slipping over to the opening of the bar to the room beyond, Daniel rose up slowly to see Dutch angled slightly away from his hiding spot, about halfway to the breakfast nook.

Daniel was bracing himself to gain a good shot when he felt his leg hit a bottle on the shelf below. Dutch spun around and fired, just missing Daniel's right ear, hitting a bottle of Malibu Rum on the upper shelf behind him. As he was showered in alcohol, Daniel fired at Dutch's chest, but the man was quick. Hitting him in the left shoulder, Dutch spun around firing another shot which went wide, hitting the bar's wood paneling just below Daniel's gut. Accounting for his direction and speed, Daniel fired two rounds quickly, the first taking Dutch in the upper torso, the second hitting him directly in his forehead. Dutch wobbled briefly on his feet, staring back at Daniel with a stunned expression. His weapon arm lifted, as if to take another shot, but fell to his side as Dutch dropped to the burnt-red rug on the wooden floor, lifeless.

Daniel vaulted over the bar opening, into the room. Moving as silently and fast as he could, he made his way through the nook and kitchen to check on Charlie. Sure enough, Charlie was out cold. It seemed Daniel's blind shot had only hit him in the left ear, taking off the lower portion of the lobe. He was bleeding from a gash in his forehead and must have fallen back into the chairs, hitting his head on the table.

Daniel's shoulders relaxed, and he allowed himself to lean on the table. The very same one he and Kathryn had bought together and brought to San Francisco, one of only a few items that had survived the earthquake. He brushed his hand across a repaired gouge from that day so long ago. Taking a deep breath, he headed up to his bedroom.

Opening the closet door, he threw out a few shoeboxes, spilling their contents on the bedroom floor. The space vacated by the boxes revealed a floor safe. Daniel had installed the safe back in the 1940's, made to specific dimensions. Entering his wife's birthdate, the tumblers clicked. Pulling up on the handle, he opened the safe to the smell of oil, rags, leather, and metal. Removing a long bundle from the shallow cavity, Daniel set the whole thing down on the bedroom floor, and unwrapped a museum's treasure.

Inside the well-oiled rags, held snuggly in its leather holster, was his Smith & Wesson Colt M1911 from his service in World War I. Also resting there was his Colt Army Model 1860 from his time in the Civil War and after, complete with its belted holster rig. Lastly, he pulled out his Smith & Wesson Model 66 .357 Magnum revolver. He stared momentarily at the last weapon he had ever fired, up until now. Ironically, it too had been used against the same Haig Men hired guns, at a time when he had been known as Robert Hunter. Pulling his old World War II duffle bag from the back of the closet, Daniel began throwing essentials he would need while on the run into it. Once he completed that task, he reached back into the safe pulling out several boxes of ammunition for each weapon stored there.

"Good thing I always liked to be prepared for any circumstance." Daniel smiled as he took out a wooden box of ammunition he had specifically made himself for his old Civil War Colt.

Quickly stripping off his alcohol-soaked clothes, he hurriedly dressed in a clean, black suit. Transferring everything from the pockets of the discarded clothes to his coat pockets, he took another look in the closet. His old beige duster hung in the corner, well preserved, even after a century. Grabbing the duster off its hook, he shoved it without care, into the bag. As an afterthought, he stuffed his grey suit in the bag as well. Snatching up a couple of the now empty shoe boxes, Daniel placed his guns with rigs inside, using an old belt to tie the boxes and their lids down. Tossing those into the bag, he surveyed the room in case he had missed something. He was about to leave when he instinctively reached back into the safe for the last item stored there, a small metal box.

"A hundred thousand dollars could come in handy. I believe we're looking at a downpour coming on."

As an afterthought, he picked up Abel's silenced Glock, tucking that into his belt. Slinging the duffle bag over his shoulder, Daniel hurried downstairs, past the still unconscious thug, and out the back door. He hurried back to his car, tossing the bag and Glock onto the passenger seat. Pitching the earwig to the pavement, Daniel ran around to the driver's door. He slid behind the steering wheel and took a couple of minutes to breathe in deeply, giving himself a moment to think.

With a plan set in his mind, he turned the key in the ignition, heading off the few blocks to the post office for any message left by Veronica. After that, he would collect those few personal items at his shop he couldn't leave behind and get out of there. Chances were, if his home had been invaded by the Haig Men, then his shop would also be infested. He knew he should bypass the shop altogether, but he just couldn't leave those items behind. Especially if he might never be able to come back.

●━━•

Morgan Dimico drove his car with no thought of where to go. He took the first onramp he found and just kept going, not caring about anything more than making sure Smith wouldn't be able to follow him. He was in a pickle. A real doozy of a pickle, and he had known it even before he found Smith in his office home. They wanted their files back and all the research he had accumulated on Collum/

Hunter. Why they would need the files before killing him, he didn't have a clue.

Everything seemed to hinge on something Daniel Collum had done back when he was Robert Hunter, but what? Evidently his blue-suited client and Mr. Smith had no knowledge at all about Collum's extended life. So, what was really going on? These thoughts kept rolling around in Dimico's head as he drove. Every thought kept coming back to Daniel Collum. Dimico made up his mind to go back to Orange. He needed to confront this antique dealer and hope he could get to the bottom of this from the source himself.

Getting off the freeway, Dimico stopped to put a few gallons into his car, paying with some of the cash he had. The irony was not lost on him that his former client was paying for his escape from death. He could fill the tank later, but for now, he felt it was better to be tight with the cash he had. Sliding back into his car, Dimico made the trip back to the city of Orange, and Collum's home.

His plans had come to a screeching halt upon arriving at the Victorian home. He immediately spotted a couple of men moving around the exterior of the house. Without stopping, he drove around the corner and parked, shifting his rearview mirror to get a better view. Glancing at his watch, he noted that it was 5:35 p.m. Hard to believe that his life had been turned upside down only this morning. He watched quietly as four men moved back and forth around the property, finally settling in to wait for the home's owner.

That was a good sign to Dimico. That meant Collum hadn't been home and was still out there somewhere. Making a gut decision, he put the car back into drive, and headed the few blocks to the antique shop *Yesterday's Today*. On arriving, he found it too was occupied, but not by Collum.

"Who in hell are you people?" Dimico said aloud.

It was a stroke of luck that he had chosen to park in back, otherwise he would never have known there were more people here taking up residence, the same kind of men as there had been at Collum's home. There were only three from what he could gather. By the looks of one of them, an overweight and balding older man dressed in a brown rumpled suit, this must be their boss. He was definitely not the man in blue, who had put him in the middle of all this, but must be someone of some importance, as he ordered the other two around. Eventually, they went inside the shop to wait for Collum.

Dimico was unsure what to do. Should he stay here, hoping he could warn Collum in time, or go to his home and try the same there? He decided he might be better off where he was. Driving his car around to the street in front, he crossed to the other side, parking his car on the corner. From here he should have a better view of the shop's front. This was the kind of work he was used to, waiting and surveillance. He had been in this position for about an hour when he realized he had nothing for such a stakeout. Without food or drink, this kind of work was torture, especially as he hadn't eaten since earlier that day. Setting these thoughts aside, he stayed on course, watching and guarding the front entry to the shop.

With the night came a darkening of spirit, and a drop in his resolve, as his stomach began to play a slow but growing concert of noises. His mouth became more parched with each dragging minute, and eventually his bladder started to throb. Touching the button on the side of his watch, he sighed when the readout showed him it was only just eight-thirty. His body parts decided to attack him in concert. Biting his lower lip, he managed to hold out a whole fifteen seconds longer. Grabbing the envelope of bills, he threw open the door. As quickly as his bladder would allow, he hobbled down the couple of blocks to *The Ristorante*, his familiar stakeout spot from the morning.

After relieving himself, Dimico found the hostess. Rolling his eyes at the nametag, he said "Hello Fawn, I'd like to place an order to go. If there's any chance they could rush it, I would really appreciate it. I'm late for a meeting."

Fawn looked down her nose, taking in his appearance from head to toe. Her fake smile turned down just a fraction with what she saw. He knew he appeared a mess and needed a shave. His clothes looked like he had been to here and gone, and he was sure he didn't smell like roses either, from everything that had happened today.

"I'm sorry sir, but I couldn't make that kind of promise. We'll do everything we can to accommodate you."

Reaching into his pocket and pulling out his envelope, he lifted a $100 bill, waving it in front of her smug face.

"If you can get my dinner out here in under fifteen minutes, I'll let you and Benjamin here get acquainted."

This time Fawn's face lit up, the glazed look of boredom in her eyes vanishing immediately. Suddenly she was Dimico's best friend. She made a pretense of looking at something on her podium before looking back up, spreading her smile almost further than could be possible.

"I just checked, and it appears we should be able to take care of your request after all, sir. Please take a seat and I'll have a quick word with our chef. Would you like a drink while you wait?"

This must be what it's like to have money, he thought, as he smiled back. "A cool glass of water would be nice, thanks."

Twelve minutes and twenty-two seconds later, Dimico was leaving with his dinner in a nice bag, while Fawn was making mental love to Benjamin. Both happy with what they had in hand, they smiled from ear to ear, as they waved each other goodbye. Dimico walked quickly back to his car and nestled himself back in. Throwing away money like that, especially under his present circumstances had been foolish, but he was starving. As he opened the bag, the aroma made his stomach lurch. Yes, it had been worth wiping the smirk off the girl's face.

He had never ordered dinner at his home away from home before, but the first forkful of the Italian cuisine was pure ecstasy to his taste buds. He glanced across the street to the front of the shop, making sure nothing had changed, when he noticed a brief flash from inside the shop's front windows. With fork and food halfway to his lips, he caught another brief flash, followed immediately by another. The discharge of a weapon echoed from the shop. Anyone in the area would think it was some kid setting off a firework, Dimico surmised. With one last flash of light from inside the shop, everything went back to dark.

What to do now? Dimico looked around the inside of his car but saw nothing that would help. If he only had his gun, he might have been able to do something. Collum must have come back while he was at the restaurant. *Damn it!* He tossed his meal aside and put both hands on the steering wheel, making up his mind. He may not have a weapon, but he could take the car around to the back entrance to the shop. Maybe he could see if there was anything he might be able to do there.

•⎯•

Daniel had pulled his car up to the parking lot behind his shop, deciding to park the car on the street, just a building down from the lot itself. Taking only the acquired Glock, tucked in the crook of his back waistband, he made his way through the shadows of the street lamps to the back of the buildings facing Glassell Street. He stopped for only a moment to think over his choices. Deciding on the safest course, he took a circuitous route across the small side street, then back to Glassell. Crouched low, he inched himself up beside a silver Ford Focus Sedan which had seen better days. He took just a second to be sure the owner of the vehicle was not present in the car. The inside was strewn with trash, food, and soda cans, but no occupant. Glad that no one was living in the car, he positioned himself with a good view to the front of his shop.

Yesterday's Today looked as it should after closing. The shop windows were dark, and the old-style street lights on Glassell cast an almost warm embrace over the area. He lifted his finger to turn on the earpiece, before realizing he had tossed it onto the pavement near his home.

"Not the smartest move you have made so far, but it can't be helped now."

As it was, the mercenaries the Haig Men were using, probably did not have, or need them here. The shop wasn't all that big, so it made sense, he consoled himself. He had seen no one taking positions outside his shop. That would mean they were all inside. Not an easy task to deal with. If it were him, he would probably have two men stationed near the front, and two in the back office. He would just have to assume there were four or five men to deal with, though he hoped he was wrong, and there would be fewer than that.

Easing himself back into the shadows of the building, Daniel went around to the back, entering the post office through the back door. The back room was separated from the rest of the post office by thick, dark glass walls and the single glass door. The walls were lined with various sized, postal boxes, all locked. A table with various supplies was set up near the back door, along with the familiar, blue mailbox.

Pulling the keys from his pocket, Daniel walked up to the row of medium-sized boxes and opened box 130. Daniel removed the few envelopes, sorting through them for Veronica's message. Nothing. He looked at them again, all junk mail. Tossing the mail in the trash receptacle under the table, Daniel began pacing in the small room.

"No message. That might not be bad. Maybe she didn't call before they closed." Maybe Victor forgot to put the message in his box. "He is old after all." Leaning against the table, his stomach suddenly felt sick. What if they got to her before she could get away?

Daniel took deliberate deep breaths for a few moments as he tried to think. Problem was, he kept picturing Veronica and what they might have done to her.

"Nothing I can do right now. Just go to the shop, get what I came for, and then I can figure out what to do. Maybe hole up somewhere and come back tomorrow. Talk to Victor." Yeah, that seemed logical, though reckless.

His mind made up, he backtracked his way around to the rear of the buildings connected to his shop. Hugging the wall, he skirted around the plastic-molded trashcans, ending up by the back door to his shop. He stretched on tiptoes to get a view into his back office, from the window set high next to the back door.

Inside the darkened room, someone was sitting in the chair at his desk. With only the desk lamp on for illumination, the man sitting there was none other than Frank Thomas. Wow, he has not aged well at all, Daniel thought. The bastard even had the audacity to set up a takeout dinner on his desk. Currently, he was picking at the meal with his plastic fork, pushing ravioli from one side of the plate to the other.

Daniel was happy to see that Frank was the only one in there. That would mean there were only two or three men in the shop itself, if he was lucky. He thought about unlocking the back door and using good old Frank as leverage against any others, but he would have been noticed immediately when he tried to open the door.

"Think, think. There's got to be another way to do this," he whispered under his breath.

His eyes took in the area around him. A nearly empty parking lot stared back. Just three cars sat in random slots, the backs of shops boxing in the lot itself. The street where his own car was parked was dark, and lining the back walls were a parade of trashcans. Trashcans, window. Daniel closed his eyes for a moment and sighed, then turned his sights on the smaller window to the bathroom of his store.

"I really am senile," he thought. There had been so many break-ins from that stupid window in the past - how could he have forgotten it so easily? He had lost several small, but valuable, items before he figured out how they were getting in. He had not wanted to spend the extra money it would take to burglar-proof the window, as he had done to the front and back door. Instead, he decided on another way to give his wayward visitors another chance to do right. He made it easy to get into the bathroom, but the door leading into the shop was a deadbolt. The only way into the shop was to unlock it using a key he kept on his keychain. A security alarm sticker was on obvious display on the door, though no alarm was installed. He had hoped to deter anyone stupid enough to kick in the door. Funny how a sticker was all it took to turn someone back.

Daniel reached for the black trash bin, but quickly changed his mind when he got a whiff of the contents. Quietly shifting the less fragrant green recycle bin under the bathroom window, Daniel raised himself up as silently as he could. Balancing carefully, he reached up to lift the rectangular window on its hinges. He paused for a moment, hands almost touching the frame of the window pane, wondering if it would creak and make noise. But it wasn't like there were any other choices for gaining entry to his own shop. He raised the window all the way to the locking position and grunted his way through the open window. There was a moment of near disaster when he nearly took a spill into the lavatory, but he recovered well enough so there was no distinct sound.

Daniel moved to the door and slid the key into the deadbolt. Something bothered him, so he paused. Only he had a key, right? Well, he and Andrew were the only ones with keys. Andrew's recent death hit him again, followed by a moment of panic as he realized Frank Thomas had probably used Andrew's keys to gain entrance into the shop. It was just pure luck no one had used the deadbolt key to brace the bathroom door open. Another error on his part, Daniel thought. He had really become out of practice after thirty years, or maybe just forgot how to think like his opponents.

Daniel opened the door, the silenced weapon in his hand, ready for what may come. From the dim light coming in through the windows from the street lights, Daniel spied two mercenaries, both at the front display windows. They had taken up positions on either side of the shop, their backs to him. Damn. He'd forgotten to check if the office door was closed. Nothing he could do about that now. He moved into the main shop. Daniel aimed the Glock and reluctantly pulled the trigger. The back of the first mercenary's head blew a shower of blood and brain matter on the door's windowpane.

The second mercenary heard Daniel's weapon, noticed his comrade falling, and surmised where the attack had come from, all in a fraction of a second. He pulled his weapon and turned, but the bullet hit the guy square in the center of his chest, knocking him back. His weapon arm continued its motion upward for a beat before the Glock went off, sending its silent messenger into the wall next to Daniel.

The firefight ended as quickly as it had begun. Daniel held his position for a moment, making sure he had not been hit, before turning to the office door. He came up short when he saw Frank standing in the open doorway of the office, revolver in hand. The pistol shot rang out, the flash burning into Daniel's retinae. He felt the shot graze his right shoulder as the bullet went through his coat. Pain burned in his arm, but Daniel raised his own weapon, firing back, hitting Frank in the right thigh. He almost laughed at the comical look on Frank's face when he realized he had been shot. His eyes rolled up in their sockets, the revolver fell from his now limp hand, and he face-planted onto the floor.

Daniel instinctively gripped the wound in his shoulder, then released the breath he had been holding since the shooting started. With his weapon ready, he checked on Frank, but he had only fainted from the gunshot wound. Yeah, he had not aged well at all. The Frank he had known thirty years ago wouldn't have caved so easily. He roughly grabbed Frank's arms, dragging him to a chair in the office.

CHAPTER NINE

WASHINGTON D.C., 1981

Frank could not believe it had worked as he watched the newsbreak for the umpteenth time in a small room of the White House. Nearby, the press conference room buzzed with activity as they waited on the official statement of the president's condition. John Hinckley Jr. had shot President Reagan before being taken to the ground himself, in a pile of Secret Service agents. Hinckley managed to not only hit President Reagan during his brief shooting spree, but had also shot one of the Secret Service agents, a police officer, and White House Press Secretary James Brady.

The newsfeed replayed the footage of President Reagan leaving the Washington Hilton Hotel, smiling and waving, after a luncheon address with the AFL-CIO. As the first shot rang out, Frank had been impressed with how quickly they had shuffled Reagan to the car waiting at the curb. The footage showed Reagan being shoved into the limousine as shots were fired. James Brady went down first. Police officer Thomas Delahanty fell, attempting to protect the President, while Secret Service Agent Timothy McCarthy, turning his body to shield the President from harm, was himself shot in the abdomen. Right after, a wave of agents and police swarmed over Hinckley, ending the footage.

President Reagan had been whisked away to an undisclosed hospital, and no confirmation on his condition was yet known, though the news rumored that he was unharmed. In under ten minutes, the reports changed to say Reagan had been shot, possibly twice, and it was unknown whether he would survive the wounds he received. Frank watched Deputy Press Secretary Larry Speakes pass into the press conference room and step up to the podium. As the conference started, Frank turned to see Secretary of State Alexander Haig watching the news from the doorway. As they listened to the prepared statement from Speakes, Frank planted the seeds Bennett instructed him to give to Haig, regardless of Reagan's outcome.

"Secretary of State Haig, this is a dark day."

Frank could see the genuine concern the man had for the president's life. "Yes, it is, Mr. Thomas. A dark day indeed."

"Any word on the condition of the shooter?" Frank prodded for information.

"He did it all for Jodie Foster. So she would know he loved her. What is the world coming to?" Haig shook his head.

"You may need to take over this press conference, sir. Show the people of the country that the government is still in charge. That you are in charge during this crisis."

"I don't really believe that's necessary at this point, do you?"

Frank pointed to one of the small monitors of the press conference going on, as CBS reporter Lesley Stahl asked a question.

"Can you tell us who is running the government at this time with the President in the hospital?"

Speakes stared blankly back to Stahl and responded, "I cannot answer that question at this time. Next question?"

Frank pulled out a small notepad and pen. With all the drama he could muster, he pushed Bennett's point home.

"Sir, you have to take over. Without the President and Vice President, it's up to you to take control. Tell Speakes to step down. Take control of the situation. Let the country know they're in good hands."

Haig stared at the monitor for another moment, then at the pad in Frank's hand. With another *"No comment"* answer from Speakes, he grabbed the pad and pen, scribbled a quick note ordering Speakes to vacate the podium immediately, and handed it back to Frank.

Frank passed the note to one of Bennett's loyal Secret Service men, who immediately left the room to hand Speakes the note.

"You've done the right thing, Mr. Secretary. Someone needs to take control of the White House. Show the country that, under the circumstances, it still stands strong."

Frank and Haig both watched the monitor as the note was passed to Speakes. He stood there for a moment, almost unsure of what to do, until he noticed the signature at the bottom of the note. He then excused himself and left the podium.

"Now's your chance to show the people you have control of the situation, Mr. Secretary."

Haig nodded to Frank, moved into the next room, and stepped up to the podium. Once he had silenced everyone, he took a deep breath and spoke.

"Constitutionally gentlemen, you have the President, the Vice President, and the Secretary of State, in that order, and should the President decide…"

●—·

From another room, just a short distance away, Daniel Collum stared in stunned silence at what he saw unfold on the screen before him. Secretary of State Alexander Haig was taking control of the White House? Now known as Secret Service Agent Robert Hunter, Daniel had been thrown for a loop with the attempt on Reagan's life. He had gone through the trouble of setting up his new identity specifically to stop something like this from happening, but when it had, he was in the wrong place to do anything about it. As if that wasn't bad enough, he had just watched the Secretary of State take over the press conference and simply state he was now in control. Haig did realize that in the order of things he was fifth in the line of succession. After Vice President Bush, it would fall to Speaker of the House Tip O'Neill, and then to President Pro Tempore of the Senate J. Strom Thurmond before it would fall to Haig.

Hunter pondered on these events well after Haig left the podium. He was thinking of the president when he heard voices raised in a heated argument down the hall. Following the sound of the commotion, he arrived outside the Situation Room. He could hear Secretary of Defense Casper Weinberger arguing with Secretary of State Alexander Haig. Through the door he managed to catch that Haig was angry with Weinberger for raising the military alert level without asking him first, as it now made him out to be a liar to the public. Weinberger accused Haig of exceeding his authority, to which Haig told Weinberger, "Read the Constitution. I'm not talking about succession. I know the pecking order!"

Hunter knew something was up, but he wasn't sure exactly what. What would Haig have to gain by taking control when Vice President Bush would be flying back in Air Force 2 to take over? Even without that to think about, O'Neill and Thurmond were also here in Washington D.C. to step in if needed. If the President had to leave control to either of those men, they would have to resign their current position before taking office. Hearing a voice he recognized in the opposite room, he stepped over to the half open door and peered inside. He saw a group of Secret Service men he didn't particularly know well, along with a man he had seen about the White House the last few months. It was this man who was speaking to the agents.

"Make sure no one gets to Haig. If this plan is to work, he must remain safely under our control. Bennett is taking care of Bush, O'Neill, and Thurmond, so it's up to us to make sure that our keystone is in place and safe if we're all to gain from this."

Hunter backed away from the door. What was his name? Oh yeah, Frank Thomas, the man with two first names. So, there was something going on. A takeover of the government? That was ludicrous, no one would ever attempt something like that -- would they? Was Secretary Haig involved in this as well? Hunter found it hard to believe, as he had heard many positive things about the man, but you could never be sure. He heard the Situation Room door open. Making a split-second decision, he walked briskly to Haig as he exited the room. Taking hold of his arm, Hunter whispered to him that he was in danger and needed to be moved out of the White House immediately. Haig began to protest, but Hunter raised a finger to his lips. Applying pressure to the arm, he moved Haig down the hall in the direction of the carport.

Turning a corner, he told Haig in a low tone that immediately after the press conference, a call had been made from inside the White House threatening his life. Not wanting to take any chances after the assassination attempt that had just occurred, it had been decided to move the Secretary out of the White House and to a safer location. Haig found this all a little hard to chew on, but with everything else going on, he consented. They reached the carport without issue and Hunter sat Haig in the back of one of the black sedans. Telling him to buckle up, in case anything went wrong, Hunter drove the sedan out to the main gate.

Back in the White House, Frank Thomas had excused his men. He was now waiting for John Bennett to answer his phone, when one of their loyal Secret Service agents came barging back into the room.

"He's gone, sir! Secretary Haig is gone!"

Through the phone receiver by his ear, Frank heard, "Bennett. This you Frank?"

Forgetting the phone by his ear, Frank snapped back "What do you mean gone?"

"We went to the Situation Room and he'd left with an agent, a Robert Hunter."

"Goddamn it, Frank! What the hell is going on over there?"

"John, we may have a situation. You don't have a Robert Hunter from the Secret Service on your payroll, do you?"

"What are you talking about? No, no one named Hunter is on my list, why?"

Frank's face went suddenly white. "Jesus Christ! I think he took Secretary Haig. He must have known somehow."

"Frank, there's no way he could know what we're doing. I'm putting a hold on everything until you can find Haig and bring him back under our control. Without him, the whole plan is shot to hell. You have less than a half hour before I pull the plug on the whole thing. Frank, I'm holding you responsible if the shit hits the fan." The line went dead.

Frank's heart skipped a beat with that disconnect. Turning his attention back to the worried agent, he forced himself to remain calm. "Find Haig at any cost. If Hunter gets in the way, take him out. Bring a car around for me now." Without checking to see if the agent had done as he was ordered, Frank dialed the phone again.

"Pennsylvania Gate," a voice answered.

"Do not let Secretary of State Haig leave the premises. We believe he may have been kidnapped by one of our own agents."

There was a brief pause on the other end of the phone, then a worried response. "I just let him pass out the gate right before you called, sir. He turned right, onto the street."

Oh Lord, Frank thought. His ass was grass if he didn't catch them. Getting the license plate information from the guard, he hung up and ran to the waiting car.

Hunter breathed a sigh of relief when the car passed out the gate, turning right onto Pennsylvania Avenue NW. Haig had made light conversation about Lafayette Square across from the White House North Lawn, and Hunter had played along with the 'nothing is wrong' banter, until he saw the genuine concern on Haig's face in the rearview mirror.

"Don't worry sir. This is just a precaution, what with you taking over."

"This is insane. A crazed man shoots the president, and someone in the White House threatens my life? There must be some kind of mistake."

"Some find any kind of change hard to deal with, even in the White House. I'm sure it was a veiled threat and we'll have the person under control soon. Again, just a precaution to keep you safe, sir."

Hunter had been half-watching Haig's face during the exchange. All signs showed he knew nothing about what was going on, and his own gut was feeling the same. There had to be something else happening, but what?

Hunter radioed Henrad and Stone, the two agents he knew well. Without using his name, he had them change to a rarely used channel, and told them to meet him across from the National World

War II Memorial. He made up some story about Haig's life being in danger and needing to switch cars. Told them to speak to no one else as it was some of their own Secret Service men who were after him. The two of them were the only ones he could trust. They weren't too far away to help, and friends that they were, told him they'd be there.

He looked constantly in the rearview mirror, but had not seen anyone tailing them. When he turned right onto 17th Street SW, he saw Henrad and Stone waiting for him opposite the WWII Memorial. Hunter began to think everything would be alright.

Parking behind the other black sedan, Hunter got out, ran around the car, and let his passenger out. Haig had been worried, to be sure. With the conversations they had during the drive, Hunter was pretty sure that whatever was going on was outside his purview. The two agents walked up and Hunter shook Stone's hand.

"Bit of trouble again, Bob?"

"You might say that. Would you mind taking Secretary Haig on a sightseeing trip until I call you? That reminds me, you bring the walkie-talkies?" Hunter attempted to smile back but only partly succeeded.

"No problem at all. I've changed the channel to one we don't normally use. I figured you wouldn't want anyone else listening in." Stone handed Hunter one of the black boxes, showing him the other attached to his belt.

"I'll call you as soon as I'm sure it's safe enough to take him home."

Stone nodded, got Haig into his car, and took off. With that taken care of, Hunter had a moment to think.

"Hey Henrad, how's the blonde wonder boy?"

"Seen better days, as I'm sure you have too. What's our move?" Henrad nodded at three more black sedans racing up fast in their direction.

"Take the car. Try and lose any that follow you. Meet me on the other side of Lincoln's Memorial on Ohio Drive."

Without waiting for a response, he ran across 17th, dodging traffic the whole way. Just as he made it to the other side, Hunter heard the screeching of tires, and doors slamming. Glancing over his shoulder, he could see two of the cars had stopped, and four men weaved their way across the street to follow him. Some luck he had. Only one car had decided to follow Henrad.

Making his way past the World War II Memorial, he glanced back to see the four men were making headway on him. Hunter was in great shape for a man in his forties, well, one hundred and thirties, but the men behind him had him by about one hundred years. He soon found he needed to use the tree line on the left in an attempt at dodging them.

He felt the splinter of wood right before he heard the shot hit the tree he had just dodged around. These men were not playing any games. They were firing at him out in the open, in a crowded area. Whatever he had stumbled across at the White House must have been big. He weaved his way back and forth through the trees, all the while heading straight for the Lincoln Memorial. He heard another couple of shots fired, but they must have gone wide.

Taking up a position behind one of the few remaining American elm trees, Hunter leveled his Smith & Wesson against the trunk, took careful aim, and waited. Just as he expected, one of the four was directly on his trail. Coming around an oak tree about fifty feet away, Hunter pulled the trigger. The man looked as if he had been grabbed and tossed backward off his feet. Without waiting to see if he would get back up, Hunter left the safety of the elm tree, and continued his run toward the Lincoln Memorial.

Altering his course, he moved through the trees to the second path. Taking a chance, he glanced back, not seeing his three remaining followers. Taking one man down must have given him a little headway. This second path was nearly empty of foot traffic, exactly what he was hoping for. The men following him seemed to have no compunction about shooting into a group of people, and the last thing he wanted was for some innocent tourist, or their children, taking a bullet meant for him.

The solitary sound of a bullet whizzed past his head, and he knew he needed to get back into cover. He chose to follow the south side of Lincoln Memorial Circle NW, and without stopping for cross traffic, dashed over Daniel French Drive SW. From there he dodged back into some small tree covering. Exhaustion was setting in. He would need to stall his assailants again soon or he would collapse. If he could just make it to the mass of trees near the Equestrian Statues, he would be able to use them to his advantage and get himself a few moments to breathe.

He was almost halfway across 23rd Street SW when he felt a punch in the left shoulder and the burn of the bullet that had found its objective. Hunter sprinted to the other side of the street, dodging back and forth like some insane man. Avoiding a few more shots directed at him, he managed to pass into the clump of trees by the wall bordering the statues. He hoped to have an advantage now he hadn't before. He was under the cover of trees, but the three following him would be out in the open once they crossed the street, giving him a chance to stall or take some of them down.

Unfortunately, these men were trained Secret Service men. When they ran into the clearing, they were all in crouched stances, and had spread themselves out well. They knew as well as Hunter that he wouldn't be able to hit all three before they reached him. Blinking his eyes from the sweat and pain, Hunter took aim at the lead man, fired off two rounds into the man's chest and watched him go down. He took off along the wall, using the trees for cover. The remaining two men split in opposite directions, angled to still advance toward Hunter.

His lungs were screaming at him to stop, but he knew that was suicide and pushed on. He was almost to the Arlington Bridge and Ohio Drive, and hopefully, help. At the right corner of the wall, he veered away in a straight line to the edge of the trees. From there he could see Henrad standing outside the sedan on the passenger side, parked on Ohio, just south of the Bridge overpass. Forcing his legs to push just a little longer, Hunter sprinted across the open ground to the sedan. He only had twenty feet left to go when Henrad pulled out his handgun, pointing it directly at him. With his momentum, and his oxygen-starved legs, there was nothing for Hunter to do. He continued running, waiting for the bullet that would hit him.

A shot rang out and he felt a sting as another bullet grazed his right calf, just seconds before Henrad fired his own weapon. The bullet whizzed past Hunter's head, and he heard someone scream out behind him.

"Get in the car fast!" Henrad waved and yelled as he jumped into the passenger side of the car. As Hunter reached the back of the sedan, he saw two men jump out of the third car that had followed Henrad. Using the car door as a shield, the agent fired at him, hitting the trunk of the car. The other man, Frank Thomas, wasn't as smart and had left himself in the open. Hunter swung his Smith & Wesson up, firing multiple times, as he maneuvered around the back of the car. The first shot hit Frank in the right thigh. As his leg collapsed from the bullet, Frank's body leaned away enough for the second shot to miss, but the third bullet found its mark in his right forearm, shattering bone. The weapon in his hand fell away from numb fingers, hitting the dirt roadside with a thump. Almost at the same moment, Frank himself collapsed to the ground. Another shot rang out, ricocheting off the top of the sedan, just as Hunter dove into the driver's side of the car. Through the rearview mirror, Hunter watched the two remaining agents help Frank Thomas into their car as they sped off.

Hunter and Henrad drove under Highway 50, past the John F. Kennedy Center. All the while, they were closely followed by Frank's black sedan. Hunter reached across with his good arm, grabbed the seatbelt, and locked himself in for some rocky driving.

"What have you gotten me into, Bob?" Henrad stared back at the sedan weaving through traffic to gain ground.

"I'm betting it has something to do with Reagan being shot and Haig taking over."

Turning sideways in the seat to face Hunter, Henrad asked, "Where is Haig, Bob? We can get to the bottom of this fast if we can speak to him."

Keeping his attention on the cars as he weaved through traffic, Hunter stated, "I don't know. I just told Stone to drive around until I radioed him otherwise."

"Radio him to meet us." Hal, his friend and colleague, pointed a gun at him.

"Oh Hal, not you too," Hunter said, deflated.

"Sorry buddy. I ran into some big debt with some very bad people and Bennett got me out of it. Choosing between being Bennett's man, or my wife hearing about my body floating in the Potomac, I chose this." He shrugged candidly.

"You could have come to me, Hal. I could have helped." The disappointment and hurt rolled off his tongue.

"Doesn't matter now. The radio, Bob."

Hunter glanced once more at the gun and his former friend sitting next to him. How deep did this go? He had heard the name Bennett before, in connection with Frank Thomas. He felt he should know more about the man, but the pain in his arm and leg, the gun pointed at him, the betrayal of the man holding the gun, and the car chasing him took all his faculties. He made a sharp left into an abandoned parking lot, noticing that Henrad reached out to the dash to hold himself in place. Henrad's seatbelt still hung just behind him.

"Damn it, Bob! Don't make me do something we'll both regret. Get Stone on the damn radio and let's finish this now."

The parking lot was a dead end, but Hunter knew of a bridge that ran across to *The Mole*. Due to a failed interstate highway expansion that was shelved, *The Mole* had fallen into hard times, and was now just condemned industrial buildings and wharves. He just hoped the bridge still stood, as it had been a few decades since he last heard of its existence. With Frank's sedan hard on his heels, he spun the car hard left around a tall clump of bushes. His car skidded onto the old stone bridge leading over Rock Creek River. Henrad was thrown back against the car door, his arms scrambling for some purchase. His gun flew out of his hands, bounced off the back seat, landing on the floor of the car. Hunter reached out with his right arm. Cupping Henrad's forehead, he slammed the back of Henrad's head against the passenger window, cracking the glass. Feeling Henrad go limp under his grasp, he quickly grabbed the steering wheel with both hands, recovering control of the vehicle.

Making a right onto an overgrown path, Hunter saw one of the concrete buildings looming up on him fast. Cranking hard on the steering wheel, he swerved hard left to avoid it, just clipping the right back end of the car. Glancing quickly in the rearview mirror, he noticed that Frank's sedan made the turn with ease, though it still fishtailed a little in the dirt covering the paved road. The seed of an idea came to Hunter. He veered around overgrown trees and bushes, and maneuvered just off from the decaying cold concrete structures near the Potomac River.

The car sped through the tall reed grass between the cottonwood trees. The reeds diminished Hunter's ability to see the ground so badly, he could not tell if he might drive over an object large enough to do irreparable damage to the car. Pushing the thought aside, he caught sight of what he wanted. He pulled a hard right around a tall green ash tree, and drove directly toward a small service alley between two of the abandoned buildings. Flicking his eyes to the rearview mirror, he made sure the car behind was still following on his course. Frank's car had fallen back a full car's length, which would not do.

He let up on the accelerator just enough, so the cars were practically bumper to bumper, when he reached the point of no return. Taking a sharp left turn away from the driveway, he hit the accelerator hard, taking the turn full force. The back of his sedan fishtailed, threatening to go into a spin. Using the momentum of the car, Hunter held the steering wheel steady. Letting up on the pedal just enough for the car to straighten out, he punched the accelerator. The right side of the sedan scraped the concrete building before continuing down the overgrown road.

Chancing a glance into the rearview mirror, he watched with satisfaction as Frank's car attempted to make the same maneuver full speed. It fishtailed, spinning for a moment, before losing control. The spin flipped the sedan hard over once, before slamming it directly into the concrete wall Hunter had avoided. Maintaining his course past abandoned buildings, dilapidated carts, and sun-damaged boats, Hunter took a deep breath to calm his nerves. Pulling the radio from his belt, he hit the switch, "Stone, Hunter. Take Haig to one of the safehouses. Keep a watch on him overnight, but I think whatever was going to happen has been stopped for now. You should be able to get him home safe tomorrow morning. Be careful out there. Henrad was working for whoever is running this thing."

There was a pause of static from the other side, then Stone's voice came through clearly. "I understand. You might want to lay low yourself. I'll see what I can find out on this end."

"Got it. Take care of yourself, Ezekiah." He tossed the radio to the back seat before Stone could respond to his hated first name. He hadn't wanted to tell Stone he had made up his mind to vanish. He knew the stunt he pulled today wouldn't end it. No matter what, if this Bennett knew he was alive, he would do everything he could to finish him. After all this time, it was funny he finally found someone willing to end his life. Problem was, he now wanted to live.

Up ahead, the Potomac curved slightly, the road flowing with it into a bank of crumbling buildings. Hunter caught sight of a small group of makeshift huts off to the side. A transient camp. Opposite the camp was a swath of cottonwood trees and the river. Hunter drove off the road at the curve. Keeping the car between the rows of trees, Hunter saw the Potomac looming. Undoing his seat belt, he opened the door slightly, waiting until he found an opening in the tree line, and jumped out and rolled. He heard the splash of the car dropping into the Potomac River. He got to his hands and knees, a little worse for wear. The last thing Hunter saw before he disappeared from the world was the black sedan, butt end up, sinking into the Potomac.

Frank Thomas woke briefly as he was stretchered into the back of an ambulance. The pain he felt was unbearable. The paramedic informed him he had been shot in the leg and arm, his other leg had been broken in five places. It was possible he'd broken his back as well, and they were unsure about his neck. They believed he was suffering from multiple concussions and had already given him something for the pain. Frank had groggily asked about the others and was informed they hadn't made it. They were surprised he had survived, as he hadn't been wearing a seatbelt at the time. He caught a brief glimpse of a reporter and crew as the drugs coursed through his system and knew Bennett would abort the whole plan. Years of work, planning, and gathering the right people. . . everything had gone down in flames due to Hunter. A part of Frank hoped that he would never come out of it once the drugs took hold. He didn't want to deal with the wrath Bennett would surely throw at him when he woke up.

Frank slipped into the dreamy world of the morphine, feeling himself floating, as if he were in the ocean. He couldn't quite slip all the way into dreamland though - his right thigh kept throbbing from the gunshot wound, denying him peace. Something was wrong. He tried to wave to the paramedic, but he couldn't move his arms. Why was his leg hurting so much?

"Wake up, Frank. We have to talk."

No, it wasn't possible. The paramedic sounded just like Hunter. He tried to open his eyes but could only get a blurry image of the paramedic moving his lips.

"I don't have a lot of time, Frank. Wake up."

CHAPTER TEN

YESTERDAY'S TODAY, 8:30 P.M.

The pain in Frank's right thigh grew excruciating, forcing his eyes to pop open as he screamed out. Coming fully awake, he found himself in the office of Daniel Collum's antique store. He attempted to move his limbs but found he was tied with twine to a wooden chair. His thigh throbbed.

"Well, hello Frank."

Frank turned his head to that all too familiar voice. Sitting on the edge of the desk, in the shadow of a desk lamp, was Robert Hunter. Involuntarily, Frank's bladder seized up. It took every ounce of his being not to lose control and wet himself in front of the one person he feared more than John Bennett.

"Hunter." His voice trembled.

"I see you remember me, Frank. But please, why so formal? I would think after all we've been through we'd be on a first name basis by now. Call me Daniel, or Robert if you like, seeing as you knew me as him."

"Ro . . . Ro . . . Robert."

Daniel smiled. "See, isn't that better? Now, I don't have a lot of time." He glanced at his pocketwatch for emphasis, "It's just after 8:30 p.m., and I have other business I need to attend to, so we'll have to make this quick. How many of you are there? Why are you still after me? And who killed Andrew?" That last was with a stony glare.

Frank stared at Hunter, barely hearing a word he had said. He looked hardly older than when Frank had last seen him thirty years ago. It wasn't possible. No one could look that good in his seventies. He must still be dreaming. But then he felt the hardness of the wooden chair against his back and butt. He felt the digging of the twine around his wrists and ankles, the throbbing of the bullet wound in his thigh, and realized he was awake.

Daniel snapped his fingers in Franks face. "Over here. Did you miss I'm short on time?"

"It can't be you."

Daniel sighed, glanced at the pocketwatch again, deciding. Leaning forward, he pushed down on the leg wound with his thumb. Frank screeched.

"It's me. Now, how many, why, and who killed Andrew?"

Frank caught hold of the last question and ran with it in fear. "It was a mistake. I think his heart just gave out. I told Smith to back off a little, but he said the boy could take more, and then his heart just stopped." He glanced up to see Hunter's features were granite. His jaw clamped tight, eyes as cold as ice, and Frank feared for his life.

"Who is this Smith?" The calm tone sent shivers through Frank.

"I don't know. I only know him as Mr. Smith. I don't even know if he has a real name. He's some kind of assassin Bennett hires for special jobs. That's all I know."

"We'll come back to that. You mentioned Bennett. John Bennett?"

"Yes, John Bennett. He's the one running everything."

"How many of you are there, Frank?"

"Just the three of us."

"I don't believe you." Daniel leaned forward to push on the wound.

"I'm telling the truth!" Frank blurted. "There's only three of us left! There were five of us back then, plus an army of paid men, but I'm telling you, there's only three of us left!"

Daniel sat back on the desk and folded his arms for a moment, thinking. "And the parlor soldiers?"

"The what?" Frank was confused.

Daniel nodded his head toward the shop area. "Old term, sorry. The men you brought with you."

"Bought and paid for. Mercenaries. After what you did in '81, Bennett had to give up a great deal. What you did shortened the lifespan of dozens of men and women he couldn't afford to have around anymore."

Frank knew he was spilling it all, but he didn't care. Bennett wasn't the one tied to a chair with his nightmare staring back at him.

"So, there was you and John Bennett. Who were the other three?"

"Samuel Phillips. He died of pancreatic cancer in 2000. Donald Worth went against Bennett in '85 and Bennett leaked his kiddy porn habit out. He was found in his prison cell, sodomized, and with his neck cut from ear to ear. Mark Royston is still around and still Bennett's right-hand man."

Daniel recognized all those names as influential men back when Reagan held office. So, it had only been five of them, with Bennett pulling the strings. All the rest, including Hal Henrad, had been puppets to this one man.

"Now for the important question in all this. Why? What was Bennett's plan with Haig?"

Frank paused for a moment, weighing his options. He had already spilled a great deal, but this one was on a different level altogether. If he gave Hunter what he wanted, and Bennett found out, his future would not be any brighter than when Donald Worth opposed him. He decided to hedge his bet.

"Bennett has a way of reading people. He found a way to lead Haig to his own ends without Haig ever realizing he was doing it. He figured if he could get Haig into power, he could easily manipulate the presidency the way he wanted it."

"That's ridiculous! How could he expect to put Haig into power on the spur of the moment? Even if he had made plans toward that end, the assassination attempt couldn't have been known. He would have had to . . ."

Daniel was suddenly hit by the enormity of it all, and he felt sick to his stomach. "Are you telling me that Bennett had this whole thing set up from the beginning?"

Frank didn't say anything. He had said more than he should. Anything else would completely open him up to Bennett's wrath. A thought suddenly struck him, and the realization of it almost made him laugh, despite his fear.

"You had no idea. When you took Haig from the White House, you had no idea what was going on, did you?"

Daniel shook his head in wonder. "I only knew you and Bennett were up to something and it somehow hinged on Haig. What was the full plan?"

Frank set his lips tightly, looking back with what he hoped was defiance. He was scared out of his wits. Hunter gave him the heebie-jeebies, but if Bennett learned what he was doing right now, he wondered which death would be less painful.

Glancing at his pocketwatch again, Daniel looked down to a metal case sitting on the desk next to him, then back to Frank.

"I don't have time for this." He leaned forward, applying all the pressure he could to the damaged leg. Frank nearly passed out from the pain. Daniel slapped him twice across the cheek, hard and fast, to keep him conscious. "What was the plan, Frank?"

There was a time when he might have held off. A time when he would have spit in the face of this man. Those days disappeared thirty-four years ago when Hunter had thwarted everything they had worked towards. He had never been a strong individual. Power hungry, yes. Sex starved, without saying. But strong had never truly been a part of his makeup. The excruciating pain Hunter was putting him through, in conjunction with thirty-four years of nightmares his mind had conjured of the man, wiped out all thoughts of Bennett. Frank found himself spilling everything without a care for the consequences.

"Stop! Stop! I'll tell you what you want to know!" He took but a second to catch his breath, "Bennett had something on all of us. Well, everyone but Royston who thought of himself as a patriot. His plan was to assassinate Reagan if he was voted into office, and then make sure Haig was in position to take over the presidency. From there, Bennett could nudge Haig down whatever path he decided. He figured out how to push the man's buttons in a way to have things happen how he wanted, and Haig would find agreeable."

"But, for Haig to take power, four men would have to step down. On top of that, the assassination was a fluke. A psychotic stalker's attempt to show his love for a woman who didn't even know he existed."

Frank stared back and didn't say anything.

"Are you telling me that John Hinckley was involved in this plan? He's insane! There's no way he was involved."

"That was the beauty of Bennett's plan. He found out about Hinckley's infatuation for Jodie Foster early on. I don't know how. That's where I came in. Bennett knew Hinckley would take to me. He set up for us to meet by accident. It took a year to gain his complete trust, but Bennett had other issues to work on for the plan. I was able to get Hinckley to believe that, if he killed the president, Jodie Foster would see how much he loved her, and they would be together." He shrugged.

Daniel shook his head in disbelief. "So, whether or not Hinckley succeeded in killing Reagan, there would be no one to know that anyone else was involved because of Hinckley's mental issues. Amazing. What about Bush, O'Neill, and Thurmond? Bush was on Air Force 2 when it happened, O'Neill was at the Capital, and Thurmond was driving in his car some place, if I remember correctly."

Frank nodded. With each piece of the plan he gave up, he felt liberated. It was as if a huge weight was being lifted off him, and it felt good to finally get it off his chest. "Royston was wrangling Hinckley. I told Hinckley that I knew someone who could get him close to the president, and he went along with it. My job that day was to keep tabs on Haig. Have him take over the press conference, regardless of whether Reagan had been killed or not. Samuel Phillips was to make sure Tip O'Neill had an accident going down the stairs of the Capitol building, with a little help from a syringe of something hard to trace if you weren't looking for it. Donald Worth tampered with the brake lines on Thurmond's car, so he would crash at just the right time. Think someone following the car with a kill switch. He'd also had the safety belt rigged. Bennett was ringleader. He blackmailed someone to slip a bomb aboard Air Force 2 which would go off only when Bennett gave the order. He had also set up a doctor at the hospital he knew Reagan would be taken to, in case he survived. He would find a way to make sure the president didn't make it through. Air bubble in the blood or some such. I have no idea."

Daniel Collum just stared back at Frank Thomas, dumbfounded. Only someone highly intelligent, dangerous, and completely psychotic, could ever have come up with a plan like that. To think it could work at all was pure madness, and yet it would have, if not for him removing Haig from the equation.

"So, when I took Haig out of the White House, that whole chase was to get him back, rather than to stop me."

Frank shifted uncomfortably in the hard chair. "We needed to make sure Haig was available and ready to take over. When you took him away, Bennett gave direct orders to get him back and have you killed. We didn't know what you knew, and if we didn't get Haig back within the half hour, the whole plan would have to be scrapped. We had to scramble to stop the deaths of four men, that included Reagan, who had stabilized from his wounds. With all the security at the hospital, we almost didn't get word to our man inside before he finished the job."

"Why didn't you search for me after?"

"I had been sent to the hospital. Royston was busy doing Bennett's bidding, erasing any indication of complicity to kill four men at the top of the rung. Bennett allowed the news to run with their inaccurate report of only one man in your car. That was a whole other cleanup for Bennett. The shootings, car chase, and crashes all took up a great deal of time and money. Your kidnapping of Haig started a spree of killings throughout the eastern seaboard. Bennett was cleaning up the mess, making sure there would be no one outside us five with knowledge of what really happened. Bennett greased many hands, leaving your name out of it all. Some kind of misdirection, I think, with the man found in your car. When you never surfaced, we all believed you had died in the crash, possibly drowned, and carried down the Potomac somewhere. The driver's door was open, so it was possible, though I always expected you to show up sometime."

Daniel raised his eyebrows at that. "Really? Well, I must say, it did take me some time. I was lucky the shots that hit me were through and through. I've had a great deal of experience with bullet wounds."

The phone on the desk began to ring, and both Frank, and Daniel stared at it. After the third ring, Frank asked "Aren't you going to answer that?"

Still watching the phone, Daniel responded "In a moment. I want to see who it is first. Wouldn't be good to answer if they're expecting you, would it?" He glanced at his pocketwatch again.

The answering machine clicked on and Andrew's voice said, *"You have reached Yesterday's Today. We are either busy bringing the past to someone's future, or it may be after hours and we are ourselves moving through time. If you wish to leave a message, we will respond back in a timely manner."*

The long beep of the answering machine took over, there was a brief moment of silence before the uncertain voice of Veronica came through. "Daniel? Um, Daniel, I know I was supposed to call the post office, but something came up and they were closed by the time I called. I had a feeling something bad was going to happen to you, so I hoped I'd catch you at your shop..."

Daniel snatched up the phone and turned off the answering machine, all the while looking at Frank. "Hi, Vee. I have company, but don't worry, he's a bit tied up at the moment, so we can talk. Where are you?"

"Not too far off from your neck of the woods. I knew it was getting late, and I didn't want you to worry about me, so I thought I'd call now while I'm getting gas in the car." Her voice was calm but carried just a hint of worry in it.

"No bother really. I was just having a wonderful conversation with a very old friend. I have to admit, I was a little worried when I didn't find a message from you. Have you set up a place yet?"

"Yes, about fifteen minutes ago. *Hotel Solomons* in San Diego, in the Gaslamp District. Tell them you're Daniel Kilmer when you go to the front desk." Her voice sounded very satisfied with that last comment.

"Wait, over the phone? Please tell me you didn't use your credit card."

"Oh no, I thought of that." She said smugly. "I stopped by an old friend I haven't seen in years, and they reserved it with theirs for a week. I gave them a story I'd forgotten my credit card in a coat at home, and due to an unforeseen interview, I had to get a room ASAP. I paid them with some of the money you gave me."

"And they believed that?"

"Not exactly, but he accepted it."

Daniel chuckled lightly. "How old a friend?"

"Jealous? Just someone that helped me out on a story when I first got in the business. Haven't talked to him in almost ten years."

"Good work. I'll be leaving soon, so I'll see you in a bit." He couldn't help but smile to himself.

"Be careful, Daniel. I've been worried about you."

"Had some trouble at the home and shop, but all's well. You just make sure you stay safe. Got to go now." He hung up the phone, opened the answering machine, and removed the tape inside. Putting the tape into his pocket, he turned back to Frank.

"Just to be on the safe side, I took the liberty of making sure you hadn't bugged the room or phone while you were out cold. You must be slipping, Frank. I didn't find anything."

"Let's get this over with. I'm a dead man anyway."

"You've been a dead man walking for thirty-four years Frank. You just didn't know it. One last question. What does this Mr. Smith look like?"

Frank gladly told Daniel what he wanted to know, and then with a confidence he hadn't felt since the last time they met, he said "You can kill me now."

Daniel stood up, turned, and hit the stop button on the old tape recorder that had been hiding behind the metal case the whole time. Without looking at Frank, he stepped behind the desk.

"I'm not going to kill you, Frank. I'm going to let you live. I want you to know that at any moment, in what life you have, that I can deliver this tape to the right people, and your life will be over. So, leave me alone."

He entered the four digits for each of three segments on the case's dials. Placing the tape recorder inside, he closed the case again, turning the small tumblers.

"You might want to tell Bennett the same thing. I have no doubt his reach goes far, so I'm taking a chance by letting you all off the hook. As long as you let this all die now."

Daniel picked up the silver case and walked over to unlock the back door of the office. Before he could open the door, Frank blurted out "Wait! You can't leave me tied up like this!"

"I'm sure what men you have left will be here soon enough. I don't ever want to see you again, Frank." With that, he left, closing the door behind him.

•———•

Morgan Dimico had driven around to the back of the shop, parking in the furthest spot he could find, well-hidden in the night's shadows. He watched the building for what seemed forever, before deciding to get out and move to the back entry to the shop itself. He made his way to the back door, when he heard the muffled talking of two men on the other side. The screams of a man in pain suddenly echoed, then the sound of someone being slapped a couple of times in quick succession. Looking around, he saw a small wooden fruit crate. Bringing it back to the window and, hoping it wouldn't break, stepped up and peeked through the corner of the window. Collum sat on his desk, a small lamp the only light in the room. A metal case glinted from the lamplight on the desk next to him. Tied to a wooden chair was the balding man in obvious pain.

So Collum had survived the trap set for him. He pulled away from the window, but stayed close enough to hear the story that this Frank told, leaving Dimico stunned. If it wasn't for Collum's obvious belief in what the man was saying, he would have thought it all a put on. Now he understood why Collum had disappeared when he was this Robert Hunter. The whole Collum story was already too much to believe, but this boggled his mind.

The phone inside rang. He listened to the one-sided conversation, the mention of Mr. Smith, and the tape recorder. Dimico quickly moved away from the window, taking the apple box with him. As stealthily as he could, he managed to get around the back side of his car just as Collum left the store. He watched as Collum walked casually across the lot, metal case in hand, to his car. Dimico got in his own vehicle, wondering what Collum had in that metal case. It seemed heavy in his hand. Putting that aside for the moment, he followed as far back as possible. He wanted to see this to the end, whatever that may be.

As he followed the Austin Healey, Dimico tried to put into perspective everything he had heard and found out. He was following a man who had been a boy during the Civil War. A man who had changed his identity multiple times until becoming a Secret Service Agent for President Reagan. At that point, a group of men who planned to take control of the government, by using another as a figurehead, had found their plans thwarted by this same individual. This man then hid himself from them for over thirty years, only to be found out due to a chance article in a magazine.

He wasn't sure where Collum was headed, but that didn't really make a difference. He was driving south on Interstate 5, so no problem, unless Collum planned to cross the border into Mexico. He'd wait until Collum met up with this 'V' person. Some woman, he had easily figured out, even from the one-sided conversation. Someone Collum obviously cared for. Interesting. Looking down, he remembered the take-out meal he had set aside. Pulling it across his lap, he ate it cold.

CHAPTER ELEVEN

WASHINGTON D.C., 7:00 P.M., 12:00 A.M.

Bennett fought with his tie in the mirror of their bedroom, yanked it off his neck, and cursed.

"I don't know why you insist on buying me these new ties. It always takes me five tries to get them just right, and in the end, I just want to strangle someone."

"They're all the rage. I like the way you look in them. So, shut up and put it on." Valerie's assertive voice carried from the vanity room.

"What time are we meeting Mark and Brittany at *Rosetta's Luxury*?"

"I've told you twice already. Eight o'clock."

"Why are we having dinner so late?" He wrestled with the tie, all the while picturing himself wrapping it around Valerie's throat.

"I don't understand you. For someone whose been working in D.C. for almost forty years, how is it you don't know anything about the social etiquette of the power base?"

Bennett grumbled to himself, "I've had multiple men killed, and more under my finger. I almost managed an overthrow of the government. And yet, this woman still runs circles around everything I say and do."

"Did you say something?"

"No, dear."

Putting his coat on, he turned back to the mirror, admiring himself. She was right, of course, the tie made him look good.

He walked around to the vanity, and saw Valerie touching up her makeup in the light of the three-prong mirror. He gazed at her slim, tanned body, clad only in matching dark blue silk bra and bikini combination.

"You better get dressed or we won't get there."

She glanced back at him through the mirror, and without skipping a beat said "I have plenty of time. I will need your help zipping up the dress."

The buzz of his cell phone stopped their banter. Pulling it from his coat pocket, he glanced at the name of the caller, and his face grew serious. "I have to take this."

Valerie didn't hide her disappointment. "You tell them whatever they want from you can wait."

"Don't worry, this shouldn't take long. Just get into your dress."

Bennett walked downstairs to his office and closed the door. "Well?"

"Our business with Mr. Dimico has been delayed." Smith said.

"What do you mean, delayed?"

"It would seem our private investigator is a bit more resourceful than I gave him credit for."

"I don't want to hear excuses. I just want the job done."

"Just keeping you updated, *sir*. I did not want you to think there was an issue."

There was a knock at the door.

Setting the cell phone on the desk, he opened the door. Valerie was standing on the other side, dressed to the nines in a beautiful, lightly sequined, cobalt blue dress. The fabric just touched her curves without clinging to them. The bottom of the dress fell just below her knees, and she wore matching dark blue heels. She turned her back to him, showing the open zipper. Without a hint of apology in her voice, she said "Sorry to interrupt."

He deftly zipped her dress up. Telling her he would only be a moment longer, he closed the door, not waiting for a response. He picked up the phone.

"Smith. I don't pay you the sums I do for excuses. I expect you to get the job done."

Another pause, "I understand your concern, *sir*. Rest assured, it will be done."

Looking at the small clock on his desk, Bennett said "Frank Thomas should be landing in just over an hour's time. Make sure you are there for him when he gets in."

"It will be done. Sir."

"It better be." He ended the call, and opened the door to the office. Valerie was standing on the other side, waiting.

"All taken care of. I'm all yours for the night."

She handed him his black wool overcoat to ward off the fall weather rain outside. "It better be. I don't want work ruining our dinner plans tonight. We hardly ever get to spend time with Mark and Brittany."

He put the overcoat on and helped her into hers. "Don't worry, we won't be interrupted for the rest of the evening."

•————•

The dinner with the Roystons had gone as promised. Though Bennett was not one for chit-chat, he found himself enjoying the dinner conversation. Brittany talked about her grandchildren at length, briefly asking about the Bennett's two grown kids, before switching to another subject. While the two women caught up on their gossip, the men conversed over their nominee for the coming election season. After thirty-four years, it seemed as if they were finally going through with their plans. All that would be needed was to make sure they made it through the polls to the White House.

It was midnight by the time the limousine pulled up to the Bennett's home. Bennett helped Valerie out of the car, making sure she didn't stumble, as she was more than buzzed from the evening. They had just opened the door when his cell phone rang.

"No work, John. It's late and I want you in bed." She smiled, glassy-eyed.

Glancing at the phone, he sighed. "It's Frank, dear. I have to take this."

"Don't answer it. He can talk with you tomorrow.

"I won't be very long. Get yourself a drink of water."

Without waiting for a response, he marched into his office and shut the door. "Well?"

"We have a problem, John. He got away."

Bennett gripped the cell phone tightly. His good-natured mood promptly disintegrated.

"John? Did you hear me? Hunter got away."

"I heard you just fine, Frank. What in hell happened?" He managed to keep his tone even. Raising his voice would only cause Frank to delay answering, and it wouldn't do him any good if Valerie heard him yelling through the closed door.

"He took out the men at his house. Two of them are still alive, but Dutch is dead. The two I had with me at the shop are dead as well. I've been shot, John. I need a doctor. I think it's bad." That last had a slight whimper to it.

"What about Smith? Where was he during all this?"

"He missed his chance with that detective and is searching for him. He took out Hunter's assistant. It was an accident. I think the guy had a heart attack, but Hunter wasn't happy about it at all. I thought for sure he was going to kill me."

That stopped Bennett for a moment. He took a deep breath to keep his emotions under control, then asked through his teeth, "Why didn't he kill you, Frank? You said you were shot. Were you just lucky, or is there something you aren't telling me?"

"Um, he shot me in the leg. I think the bullet is lodged in the bone. It hurts like a mother, John. I need medical attention." Again, with the whining tone.

Bennett remained silent, grinding his teeth.

"John?" A long pause. "Hunter captured me, but I didn't tell him anything he didn't already know, John. He told me if we left him alone, he wouldn't take the information he had to the authorities. I swear to you I didn't say anything! He tried to get it out of me, but I just kept giving him misinformation. You know I wouldn't cross you, John."

Bennett didn't say anything for a moment. Cracking his neck, he said calmly, "I know you wouldn't cross me, Frank. Because you know what would happen if you did. First thing I want you to do is a full cleanup of the mess you've made. Once that's done, we'll see if there's any way we can hunt our Hunter down. You've brought me a whirlwind of trouble."

"I know, John, I know. I'm sorry, I really am. I've had Abel call in a cleaning crew on the house and shop. No one will ever know we were there. He and Charlie are at the assistant's apartment right now making it look like a robbery gone bad." Frank paused. "I think Hunter has someone with him, John. While he was trying to get information out of me, the phone rang. I couldn't hear what the other person was saying, but by the way Hunter was reacting, I think it was a woman. He called her V, and it sounded like they were going to meet up somewhere, but that's all I got from it."

Through the thick wood of the office door, Bennett heard his wife calling him.

"Come to bed. John? I'm going up to bed for your surprise."

"I'm going to have to wrap this up, Frank. Valerie wants me to go to bed. It's late, and you know how she gets."

"Give her my best, John. John? What about a doctor?" The question was almost pleading in its tone.

"You know we can't send you to a hospital with a gunshot wound. I'll call Smith. Where are you now?"

"I'm at a dive called *Stars and Sleep*, just a couple miles south of Collum's shop. I think the street is Chapman."

"Good, I'll make sure you're taken care of. I'll have Smith take care of Hunter, Dimico, and whoever this woman is."

There was a sigh of relief from the other end of the receiver. "Thanks, John. I'm sorry I messed things up over here, but I'm really not cut out for this anymore. I'll make it up to you when I get back."

Bennett ended the call, briefly considering throwing the phone against the wall, but stopped himself. He checked the time. Valerie was probably passed out on the bed by now. He thought about calling Mark Royston, but decided it could wait until morning. He dialed. "Mr. Smith. I understand you've had a problem."

"Just a minor setback, sir."

"I don't need to remind you of the importance of getting those files back from Dimico."

"I'm fully aware of the issue. Sir."

Bennett heard the clipped tone in Smith's voice. He was about to respond in kind when he decided on a different tack.

"I have full confidence in you. Once you take care of Dimico, I want you to personally deal with Robert Hunter, Daniel Collum, or whoever he wants to call himself. Include anyone he may have contacted. But first, I need you to go to a place called *Stars and Sleep* off Chapman. Take care of Frank Thomas. He has become a liability."

"Consider it done."

•———•

Mr. Smith walked across the dark parking courtyard of the *Stars and Sleep Motel* in Orange as some building's clock echoed the eleventh hour. He stepped up to a door with a large gold star. In the center of the star, boldly labeled in black, was the name BOGART. Cringing at the motel's theme, he knocked once.

Frank Thomas pulled back the window curtain, fear lined his face until he registered Smith as his visitor. Smith waited patiently as the door was unlocked and the chain removed. Without saying a word, he slipped inside. "Everything taken care of, Mr. Thomas?"

"Yes. Abel and Charlie have removed any signs of us from the boy's apartment and are waiting by the phone. The cleaning crew has taken care of the other two locations."

"Good. May I have the number please, as I'll be taking control over that end of things. I'm sure I can find something for the two of them to do." He held his hand out.

Frank grabbed a piece of paper off the nightstand and handed it over to Smith. "I'm glad you're taking care of this. I'm not cut out for this kind of work."

Smith put the slip of paper in his coat pocket without looking at it, pulling his silenced Glock, he quickly placed it under Frank's chin and fired. The bullet entered Frank's head and exited out the back in a spray of blood and gray matter. He stared blankly at Smith for just a fraction of a second, before what life was left in his brown eyes went out and his body slumped into a sitting position on the floor next to the bed.

Smith stared at Frank's body for a moment. He pulled out his cell phone, calling a number from memory.

"Corpus, I have a job for you. In a short period of time, the local enforcement will be calling for a medical examiner to the *Stars and Sleep Motel* in Orange. I will need you to intercept that call when it comes in and take over the work needed. You will receive the normal amount for your attention to detail."

Smith hung up without waiting for a response. Pulling gloves from his back pocket, he casually put them on as he surveyed the room. Picking up Frank's phone on the nightstand, he pulled a piece of paper from his shirt pocket, calling the number.

"*Jacklyn's Escort Service*. How may we serve you tonight?"

"Yes, I'm alone on business and would like to have one of your girls for company. Preferably someone with that Marilyn Monroe look."

After giving her Frank's name and credit card information, Smith thanked the woman for her help and hung up the phone. Moving around the room, Smith turned out all the lights. He stood there, silently waiting.

Daniel Collum pulled up to the *Hotel Solomons*' valet parking. Pulling his old army duffel bag out of the car, he accepted the valet ticket, and walked into the main lobby of the hotel.

The lobby was a cross between modern chic and thirties retro. The dark browns of the wood contrasted nicely with the black furniture and the light beige of the walls. The ceiling was a beautiful cross pattern of black beams, and the area to the right of the entry held a living room warmth, with a large fireplace burning low in the back wall.

Daniel was greeted by the front desk agent with a smile that put him at ease. "Welcome to the *Solomons*. We try to make every visit a memorable one. Do you have a reservation?"

Daniel smiled back, glancing at her name badge as he set his duffle on the floor beside him. "Hello, Abella. That's of French origin, isn't it?"

"Why, yes, it is. How did you know that?" She sounded pleased.

"I spent some time in France, in the past. Its meaning is breath, if I'm not mistaken."

"Correct again." Her smile radiated.

"Yes, a reservation for Daniel Kilmer. I hope I'm not too late."

"Oh no, not late at all. Your wife had phoned ahead to hold the reservation. She only got here herself about a half hour ago. She's a very lovely woman. I hope you know how lucky you are."

"My wife." Daniel almost said it as a question. "Yes, she's definitely something."

"Your room key." She handed him the card. "The suite is one of our best. It's on the tenth floor on the west wing, and overlooks a great view of the harbor. It's easily accessible to our rooftop bar and pool area, just four floors above us, in the main section. Do you need any help with your luggage?"

"No thank you, I can manage. You've been very helpful, Abella. I'll make sure I let my wife know."

Daniel gathered his things, and went over to the bay of elevators leading up to the tenth floor. Wife? He knew she had a sense of humor, but she could have warned him about that one. On the way up, he caught another of her small jokes. Kilmer. He thought he had heard that name before, but it hadn't clicked until just now. Joyce Kilmer had been a writer and poet who, during World War I, had fought with the *Fighting 69th*. He had died at the age of thirty-one, the victim of a sniper's bullet in 1918.

That was why she sounded so smug when she told him the name she had given him for the reservation. He was beginning to think Veronica might be too intelligent a woman for his own good. He chuckled to himself as he watched the digital numbers count upward. He exited the elevator waiting area, turning right, down the long, empty hallway. Reaching the door at the end of the hall, he checked his electronic key to make sure he had the right room before swiping the key without knocking. Hearing the click of the release, he walked into a room the size of which nearly stunned him. The entry immediately opened to a living area with two large couches, a loveseat, and three plush chairs. The upholstery was a tan/beige, accented by the chocolate brown wood trim. There were hints of mint throughout. A simple, yet elegant, coffee table rounded out the area. Hanging from the far wall was a large fifty-inch flat screen television. The room was decked out with tall vases and small candle holders, all in white, with a retro feel. Next to the doorway to his right, inset into the wall, was an intricately carved, wood pattern of a crashing sea wave, through which he could see an office, complete with rolltop desk and chairs. To his left, a full bar setup in the style of the '30s. Just past that, near the far wall, a dining area with matching table and six chairs. There were two steps leading up to a larger area just out of sight, off from the dining area, finishing off the view.

Daniel whistled to himself as he surveyed his surroundings. Veronica had not skimped on comfort and luxury. He could easily afford places like this with the money he had hidden away, but he had never done so. He was beginning to wonder why he hadn't. The thought of Veronica brought him back to the present. Daniel could see a laptop and piles of folders on the coffee table but no sign of Veronica. He headed for the steps leading to the area beyond. This section opened to a large bedroom, filled with the same motif and color scheme as the other rooms. Loveseat, long couch, a couple of comfortable-looking chairs, and a king-size bed adorned the room. The room itself looked out on two full glass walls, a glass door leading out to a large balcony with a small bar and Jacuzzi. Against the far wall must be the connecting bathroom. Leaning against the loveseat, in contrast to its color scheme, were a couple of deep purple suitcases, but still no Veronica.

He stepped over to the bathroom door and knocked lightly, but did not receive an answer. He called out her name, but still nothing. Swinging the door open lightly, he heard the spattering of running water, and the gentle soprano hum of someone down the short hall around the corner. He found himself drawn to that voice, and it wasn't until he was next to the smoky glass artwork inset in the wall that he realized the whole glass pane was a window looking directly into the shower. Even with the steamy mist from the hot water, he could see Veronica's nude form. Her back spotted with bubbles of soap and shampoo as the water cascaded over her body from the two opposing walls. He was mesmerized by the suds flowing down the hollow of her spine over the curve of her buttocks. She was humming softly to herself, massaging the shampoo in her now darkly wet, but still lovely, red hair. Self-conscious, he tried to slip back to the door unnoticed.

"Daniel? Daniel is that you?"

"Yeah, sorry. I knocked and called, but I didn't get an answer. Seems these walls are pretty thick."

"Isn't this place wonderful?" she yelled from the shower. "I just needed a nice hot shower after that long drive. I'll be done in a minute."

"Take your time, we don't have to be anywhere. I think I'll get myself some bark juice." He said, a bit embarrassed at being caught.

She giggled at his use of an old term for liquor. "Make me one too, please. A Manhattan, if you know how."

Still flushed from the encounter in the bathroom, Daniel walked back to the living room and the long bar there. Pouring himself a whiskey, he felt the sting of the alcohol as he downed it in one, long gulp. Dropping a couple cubes of ice into the glass, he poured himself another before going through the motions of making the Manhattan for Veronica. He hadn't had whiskey since his move to San Francisco, preferring the flavor and smoothness of a good scotch. The West had been a difficult place for alcohol. Whiskey was easy to store back then, and easy to come by. For some reason, whiskey just seemed to be called for tonight.

He sat down at the loveseat, perusing the folders and files spread out haphazardly on the coffee table. Even so, he couldn't mask the image of Veronica in the shower. He knew he should stop thinking about it, but he couldn't. Truth was, he didn't want to remove the image from his mind. There was something beneath the folders that shifted his thoughts. Pushing them aside uncovered a very old journal. His curiosity peaked, he set down his drink and picked it up. He had not seen workmanship like this in a very long time. He caressed the old chocolate leather, noticing the browned indications of age as his fingers brushed over the edges. The spine was well worn but incredibly still intact. There was no title or writing on the spine, or faded cover, so he gently opened the binder to the first page. The light brown of the paper did nothing to mask the India ink set there. In a clear, cursive hand was written:

Notations of a work-in-progress dealing with the life of a man of the western frontier. All characters to be pulled from real individuals observed through the course of study of this wonderful culture.

Daniel scanned through the pages, only occasionally stopping at certain points. The writer had been very meticulous in his notes on the people he had been watching. He could almost smell and hear everything through the ink on each page, even in this informative, notational style. He had skipped through multiple pages, taking only a few moments here and there, when he came to a specific page that stopped him in his tracks. Daniel stared in stunned disbelief at the browned page. Above a section of notes, in a bold hand, was written **The Occidental Hotel, proprietor Daniel Collum.** He quickly flipped through the aged paper, making sure to hold his place, until he reached the last few pages of the journal. It was here he saw what he feared would be there.

After all my research, I have decided to write this as a piece of fiction. Borrowing to certain degrees from reality, I have decided not to give the main character a name, so as to draw interest. I will call him only by the moniker THE VIRGINIAN.

Daniel immediately went back to his place, scanning what was written there. How did this journal end up in Veronica's possession? That he was being followed by the Haig Men after thirty years was bad enough. Add to that this journal, in the hands of the woman he was on the run with, and it was all too much of a coincidence as far as he was concerned. Did she know? What was she up to? His mind raced from one possible scenario to another, completely lost in his own thoughts.

"I feel so much better."

Daniel whirled around to see Veronica entering the room in a terrycloth white robe, the name *Hotel Solomons* stenciled tastefully in mint green. She had a white towel over her head, and she was vigorously drying her hair.

Daniel gave himself that moment to calm himself by taking another pull on the glass of whiskey. "Where did you find this?" he asked casually.

Veronica removed the towel from her head, tossing the damp fabric onto the end of the bar. Spying the Manhattan on the counter, she stepped over, picking it up.

"I saw it at an auction. I got lucky. The owner didn't really know what they had, and I got it for a steal. They're the original notes of Owen Wister who wrote *The Virginian*. I've had a thought, for the past few years, of writing up something based on his notes on the subject, but projects kept getting in the way. I thought I might actually do some work on it while we're holed up here."

"I thought you had a project you were working on already."

"I do, but I'm almost done with it. I find it hard not to have something going on. Idle hands, I guess." She shrugged lightly, taking a sip of her drink. "Wow, I must say, that's probably the best Manhattan I've ever had."

"I used to bartend when I was much younger." Daniel decided the journal was just that, a story, and nothing more to her. He realized, having been around for over one hundred and sixty years, his life was bound to bump back into him at some point. He kept coming back to the vision in the bathroom and he smiled. Looking up, he noticed she was staring at him, and he began to turn red all over again.

"Why, Mr. Collum, I do believe you are blushing."

"Um, I'm just not used to a beautiful woman wearing just a robe in my presence." He felt self-conscious with her staring at him.

"So, you think me beautiful?" she said posing playfully.

"You know what I mean." He blushed again. He went back to the bar to fill himself another drink. He could feel his ears getting hot. What was it about this woman that had him on the defensive so much?

She laughed good-naturedly, leaning against her side of the bar, "I'm sorry, it's just that you look so cute when you blush. Seriously,

I think I was just letting go of some nervous energy. You sounded odd over the phone."

"Did you toss the phone after the call?"

"I've seen a TV show or two in my time. I turned it off, smashed it and tossed the parts in the trash. I even thought to remove the chip." she stated proudly.

"Good. That should take care of everything, and yes, I'm fine. Unfortunately, I wasn't wrong. They were waiting for me. They had already gotten to Andrew. That poor kid didn't deserve this."

"Daniel, I'm so sorry. I knew something wasn't right on the phone

"What's done is done. There's nothing I can do about that now. I'm just glad you are all right." He took his refilled glass, walked back to the loveseat, and sat down. "Some place you have here, Mrs. Kilmer."

Veronica giggled, "I couldn't resist." She pranced over to the loveseat and plopped herself down on the other side, folding her right leg under her robe, somehow not spilling her drink in the process.

"So . . . figure out the other surprise?" She smiled like a schoolgirl with a secret.

"Joyce Kilmer."

"Damn. I thought I might have had you on that one. You're a dangerous man, Daniel."

His smile immediately left his face. "What do you mean?"

"Intelligent men are dangerous men. Well, for me they always have been. I'm a sucker for a brain."

"You do realize I could be your father, Veronica." The slightest hint of regret entered his voice. He grinned lightly back at her.

She gave the same regretful smile back to him. "A different time maybe. Tell you what, why don't we celebrate our escape by ordering some champagne, maybe some cheese and crackers to go with it. We can jump into the Jacuzzi and talk."

"I didn't think to bring swim trunks when I was gathering things."

"I didn't either. I thought we could just dive in nude." She stared at him like a cat chasing a mouse.

Daniel felt his face and ears turn red again. He stammered to find a reply when Veronica laughed again. "You should have seen the look on your face. A girl always comes prepared, and I'm sure Abella could find us some trunks for you to wear."

"You had me there for a moment, I admit," he breathed out a sigh of relief.

"Too bad. You don't know what you're missing."

"I'm sure I do."

•—•

Morgan Dimico managed to keep himself awake the whole drive down to San Diego. He was beginning to fear that Collum might really be heading for Mexico when the Austin Healey exited the freeway, stopping at a hotel called *Solomons*. Dimico waited only long enough to see Collum enter the hotel with his bag before entering the underground parking garage.

Taking the elevator to the lobby floor, he stepped out and stopped. He instantly knew he was out of his element here. He tried to look nonchalant as he walked up to the woman with long, jet-black hair behind the check-in counter. She looked up from what she was working on, sizing him up quickly. Dimico had to give her kudos when she smiled warmly to him without any effort. He knew what he looked like.

"Welcome to the *Solomons*. We try to make every visit a memorable one. Do you have a reservation?"

"Unfortunately, no. You wouldn't happen to have anything available, would you?"

"What would you prefer? An overnight, work retreat, suite, or executive?"

Dimico stared blankly at her for a moment. He was sure she was speaking English in some way and wondered what move to make next.

"I was going to have a meeting with a man called Collum, who was supposed to stay here as well. Also, a Hunter," he added as an afterthought. "You wouldn't know which they chose, do you?"

She typed on her computer for a moment before looking back up apologetically, "I don't have anyone with those last names sir, I'm sorry."

"I could have sworn they were going to stay here. Oh well, I'll just see them at the office tomorrow then. It's been a rough set of layover flights for me." He figured that would work, considering how rumpled he appeared. Then a thought struck him. "When I came in, I saw someone I recognized. At least, I think it was someone I knew from years back, in the Service. His name is Daniel."

Abella's face lit up at the mention of that name. "Why yes, Daniel is staying here in one of our best executive suites. Very nice man, and his wife is a dream."

"His wife? Oh, yes. Last time I saw him he was engaged. Don't remember her name though, but she was quite lovely." Dimico wondered who the woman was that was with him. He knew for a fact that Collum wasn't married. It would have to be this V person he had talked to on the phone.

"Would you like one of our executive suites then?"

"My business budget is a bit limited… how much do those run?"

"Anywhere from $2,000 to $5,000 a night depending on the suite."

Dimico started to hyperventilate, and coughed to regain his composure.

"I think I'll have to settle for one of your, what was it, overnight rooms?"

"Very well sir, that will be one hundred fifty dollars for the night. What card would you like to use?" Again, no hesitation, this woman was good at her job.

Dimico pulled out the deflating envelope of money. "I don't have credit cards, don't believe in them. Any chance I could just pay in cash?" He made a point of showing her what was in the envelope.

"Normally we require a credit card in case of damages to the room, restocking of the complimentary bar," she looked him up and down, "pay-per-view movies." She paused for a moment, deciding. "Tell you what. Since you are a friend of one of our executives, I'll bypass it this once. Just add an extra day's stay in case of any purchases. We'll refund you whatever amount is not used."

Dimico nodded and sighed, handing over the required amount.

Abella speedily worked her magic behind the counter, asking him a few questions in the process, finally producing an electronic key.

"Your room is on the 7th floor of the west wing, Mr. Dimico. You can reach your room using the elevators over there." She pointed to the same batch of elevators she had directed Daniel Collum to just minutes before. "I hope you enjoy your time with us."

It was a little past 12:30 a.m., and Veronica watched Daniel sleeping on the couch. The day's events, piled on with the driving, alcohol, and the Jacuzzi, had wiped him out. Veronica moved her laptop and files to the office to work, so as not to wake him. She could see him through the artistic wave wall, and could hear his even breathing, touched with a light snore.

Smiling, she turned back to her laptop to finish the article she was working on. *The Unsung Flyers of Pearl Harbor* story had been even more interesting than she had expected. She wanted to add one specific event into her story. To add that one item, she had been forced to remove a couple of smaller pieces that were already completed, to keep her article length down to size.

Wheeler Army Airfield had been a primary target, and the site of the first attack on December 7, 1941. The Japanese attempted to prevent the numerous planes there from getting airborne. Damage to the planes had nearly been complete, and yet, a dozen planes - a mixed batch of P-36 Hawks and P-40 Warhawks, still managed to gain flight and engage the Japanese warplanes.

The interesting part of the story came about when she had talked to a few eyewitness survivors who still survived. Each one of their stories mentioned an Army Air Force Captain named Benjamin Richter, a flight instructor, there to train the young pilots in the art of warfare. He had put his own life on the line to draw fire from several Mitsubishi A6M Zeros, crashing his Warhawk into an embankment, so that his pilots could get their own planes in the air. Richter had received a medal for his bravery under fire.

Veronica was going through what pictures she wanted to use for the article. Slowly, almost meticulously, Veronica went through one after another of the photos from Wheeler Field. She was trying to find one of Richter to use with the story. There were only a handful left when one snapshot jumped out at her.

The black-and-white photo showed eleven young men. In the forefront of the photo, six men kneeled, with five standing behind. In the background, in all its majesty, was a P-40 Warhawk. She had almost set the photo aside when she noticed a man standing in the background next to the P-40 as if he had been trying not to be in the picture. She couldn't make him out and moved some of the folders around until she found the magnifying glass under the pile.

Turning the desk lamp light on, she placed the magnifier over the picture, staring hard at the face. The face came into a grainy semi-focus and suddenly she dropped the magnifying glass with an intake of breath. It couldn't be. There was no rational way it was possible. Veronica checked the number on the back of the picture, found it in the large photo file on her laptop, and zoomed in on the face. She used her photo program to clean up the slightly unfocused visage and sat back in shock.

She sat there, staring at that face with the unmistakable lazy smile. She pulled up the photo file from her Civil War story, split-screening the close-up picture of the snapshot she had taken. Captain Benjamin Richter, thirty-five years of age, was the spitting image of Daniel Collum, fifty-two years old. Veronica glanced through the window at Daniel sleeping on the couch, then searched through her notes. She passed over multiple pages to find the one showing the wounds Richter had taken. Having that in hand, she quietly tiptoed into the other room. Daniel was sleeping on his left side, facing the couch, gone to the world. She snuck over and carefully lifted the t-shirt he'd strangely worn in the Jacuzzi, revealing the scar of a bullet wound on his torso, right where Richter was shot.

She gingerly moved the trunks down, watching to make sure he wouldn't wake, until she found a bullet scar on his right buttocks.

Putting his trunks back where they belonged, she stood there staring at a man who shouldn't be. Daniel was Benjamin Richter? That couldn't be possible. She walked back to the office and sat down. If Richter had been thirty-five in 1941 he would be one hundred nine years old now. A crazy idea suddenly struck. She began a search on Daniel's relation, Robert Hunter, on her laptop. Was he an uncle? A cousin? She had little to go on and felt it would be a long night. As it was, she wasn't sure she wanted to know the answer to the questions racing through her head.

CHAPTER TWELVE

FRANCE, APRIL 1916

The mud-soaked wheels of the drab transport truck continued its journey through the war-torn towns of France, occasionally spitting its human cargo out its back at one location or another. The remaining three men sitting on the wooden benches in the flatbed were quiet. Each was lost in his own thoughts as they were jostled back and forth on failing shock absorbers along the sludge-grooved roadways.

Gazing out at the remains of a small town, Hayden McClellan compared this place to the San Francisco he had left behind so many years ago. There were tense and stressful moments, going through the system, unsure whether his forged papers would work. He had fully expected to be found out as his real self, Daniel Collum, but it never happened. He had done enough of a good job to make it all the way to Europe.

The memory of losing his wife made him feel bitter, alone, and numb. He turned to the two faces in the back of the truck with him, and though he noticed they were quiet, he could see the thrill in their eyes. Boys wanting to play at war, except this time for real. They had already begun calling him Pops, though they were all in their late twenties. He wondered what they would have thought if they had known he was sixty-eight years old.

They would be the first of some thirty-odd Americans to fly for the French, as the United States had not yet committed to declaring war on Germany. The three of them knew it was only a matter of time, each deciding individually to get in early, to gain the experience necessary. At least that's what Collum/McClellan had told them. If he had told them the truth, that he was hoping to die in the skies over France, he might not have made it into the truck he was being jostled around in now.

Bert Hall lifted his head to look at him. McClellan did not look away, so he took that as an invitation to speak.

"So, how long have you been flying, Pops? I've had about four years under my belt so far."

"Just last year for me," McClellan responded.

"How about you, Prince?"

Hearing his name, Norman Prince answered absently "For a while."

Hall glanced back to McClellan, smiled nervously, and shrugged. He was about to say something else when, without warning, the truck ground to a halt. Caught off-guard, McClellan was nearly thrown out the back of the truck. The lurch of the vehicle in the opposite direction, as it came to rest, saved him from that embarrassment. Instead, he was tossed up against Hall. Hall let out a guffaw at the surprised look on McClellan's face. Staring back at the joy in that face, McClellan knew he was not going to like this man.

A French-accented voice yelled at them from the front of the truck. "Corcieux, Lorraine, gentleman. Last stop."

Grabbing their kits, they hopped out the back into the dark mud. As the truck drove off, they surveyed their surroundings believing a joke was being played on them - only one permanent building, made of stone, the rest having been put together hastily with wood planks. McClellan figured their air base had been a farmhouse before the war. When he saw the field the planes were sitting on, his guess was confirmed. Forgotten crops ringed the airfield.

On the field were the most beautiful machines man had ever created, in McClellan's mind. The Nieuport 11 biplane, a single seat fighter aircraft. Their full-sized top wing with two spars, and a lower wing of a much narrower chord, were connected by interplane struts in the form of a 'V.' The layout of these planes offered a reduced drag and higher rate of climb, as well as a more improved view from the cockpit. McClellan had read that the narrow lower wing tended to twist under stress, especially if the pilot was moving at high speeds. Still, as far as McClellan was concerned, these white birds of the sky would eventually turn the tide against the German's might in the air.

McClellan turned in time to see an officer walking directly toward them. His uniform was crisp and clean, and as he walked, McClellan could almost swear the mud shied away from the man's boots. He stopped a good five feet away from the three Americans, and in a French accent boldly stated, "I am Lieutenant Colonel Georges Thenault, commanding officer of the Lafayette Escadrille N. 124. I welcome you on behalf of the French Government."

Thenault then stepped forward, offering his hand to Prince. "It is my pleasure to see you again. None of this would have been possible had it not been for you."

Prince accepted the hand warmly in greeting. Then Thenault bowed slightly to him. "We do not have much here, but what we do have is yours. You will all be housed in the wooden bunks we have constructed. My office, the pilot's mess, and ready room are in the chateau."

Later, McClellan would talk up Prince, finding out he had spent a year talking with the French government about having a group of American pilots under the command of the French. It had taken time, but eventually he convinced them. McClellan liked Prince and his outlook on life, much brighter than his own. Hall, on the other hand, would begin to rub the influx of pilots the wrong way. The rumor mill buzz hinted he had lied about his flight experience.

In a show of bravado, Bert Hall set out to prove his fellow pilots wrong, and jumped into a training craft. With everyone watching, he taxied down the runway field, lost control, and rolled the craft into a barn. Many of the pilots believed this would be the end to Hall, but the French commander found his tenacity endearing. Hall was kept and trained how to fly.

Such were the ups and downs of his time in the Escadrille. Their first major action had come on May 13, 1916, at the Battle of Verdun, where they flew one-handed and fired machine guns with the other.

Shortly after that, the machine guns had been mounted on the top wing of the plane. Just five days later, Kiffin Rockwell recorded their first aerial victory.

The pilots would return from a mission and raise hell; drinking heavily, singing loudly, and telling stories. All the while, McClellan sat in a dark corner, sipping his drink and dreaming of the bullet that would end his misery. There were attempts from the boys to have him join in the revelry, but he would just wave them away, a scowl on his face and eyes glazed over. It was after one of these dismissals he received his pilot nickname, from Hall of all people. As he turned back to the others clustered around the piano, Hall raised his hands in defeat. "The Black Knight wishes to be left alone."

The bullet he so longed for, wished for, unfortunately had a different name on it. Victor Chapman, only twenty-six years old, was shot down over Douaumont on June 23, 1916, becoming the first casualty of the Escadrille. Unfortunately, he would not be the last.

The Escadrille was eventually moved from the front lines, back to a place called Luxeuil-les-Bains. During a rest period where many of the pilots spent time in Paris, Raoul Lufbery had managed to attain a lion cub. The cub was dubbed "Whiskey" due to its affinity for drinking said beverage from a bowl. The pilots had found themselves a mascot.

McClellan went on his missions. Many in the group thought he was a heavy drinker, but to those few he called friends - Prince and the interesting French-American Lufbery - knew differently. They began to worry about him, but McClellan would flatly tell them it was his own business. When asked why he went on so many sorties, the response had been biting. "Well, Hall is always either sick or dizzy. Damned hospital rat!"

Then on September 23, 1916, they lost Kiffin Rockwell, killed by the gunner of a German Albatros observation plane. His life snuffed out at the age of twenty-four. McClellan's dark mood shifted to ink black after that. He would talk in low tones to himself in his usual corner. "Seven weeks was all. Supposedly the lifespan was seven weeks of active service. One casualty for every sixty-five hours of flight time, and yet, here I am."

His grumblings unnerved his fellow pilots who whispered their concerns to Prince. Prince got up and walked over to his friend. "Hayden, some of the men feel you should take some time off, get some rest."

Staring into his drink, McClellan snapped back, "I don't need rest. I need to get back up in the air."

Glancing back at the others, Prince smiled, giving a thumbs up. He turned back to McClellan, concern creasing his face. "Look. I don't know who this pilot is you're so bent on hunting down, but like all of us, we go up and we come back down. At some point you'll find him and take him down."

"Take him down? Do you really believe that's what I'm after?" McClellan swallowed hard. He'd almost spilled the real reason which would get him grounded if they knew. He took a deep breath, sipped from his glass, and smiled sheepishly back at his friend.

"Norman, I'm sorry. I think it just hit me harder than I thought with Rockwell. I'll be fine. I'll take tomorrow off and rest." He hoped his smile would allay any of Prince's concerns.

Prince scrutinized his friend for a moment. Quickly smiling back, he clapped him on the shoulder and laughed. "That's the Pops I know. One day, and you'll be right as rain."

But it turned out he didn't have one day. Hall had called in sick again and was asked to resign. So, McClellan went up. On October 12, 1916, returning with Prince from an escort run for a bombing raid on Oberndorf, Germany, Prince's landing gear struck some telegraph cables near the air base. His plane flipped over and crashed. Not a single shot had been fired on the mission, and yet Prince died of his severe injuries just three days later. McClellan held his hand in those final moments.

Eventually the United States entered the war in April of 1917. Word had come that the Escadrille would be changed over. That same April, McClellan received his fifth confirmed kill, receiving the title of Ace. None of that really mattered to him. With just a few short days before the Escadrille would become the 103rd Aero Squadron under American control, McClellan flew escort duty for an observation plane gathering information on a future bombing run.

McClellan, in his preferred Nieuport 11, along with Lufbery in his Nieuport 27, had been keeping an eye out for enemy planes. Without warning, the staccato sound of Spandau machine guns cut the air. Like a beehive hit by a stick, the planes veered off in all directions. McClellan turned to see an Albatros D.V. pulling up fast on his tail, and without thinking, he maneuvered to get away from his adversary.

The Nieuport and Albatros waltzed their way among the clouds. Turning down and to his left, attempting to get around and away from his adversary, McClellan heard the tearing and ripping of the wood of his plane, and felt the searing heat of pain in his left leg as one of the bullets found its target.

McClellan shifted his aircraft tightly right, hearing the cloth and wood of his right wing scream in agony. With no time to compensate, he watched helplessly as part of the lower wing tore away. As he worked furiously to regain control, he heard hot metal hit wood, and then his head was jarred by the impact of a bullet. He blacked out for just a moment, regaining consciousness with some difficulty.

Wiping blood from the glass of his goggles, he blinked his eyes. He found himself in a slow, circular dive. McClellan, once known as Collum, managed to level his plane out only a couple hundred feet above the scarred ground, and limped his Nieuport back to the airfield, landing safely before blacking out again.

McClellan woke up with a splitting headache. Whiskey was licking his arm while Lufbery watched over him. Seeing his eyes open, Lufbery smiled widely.

"You are lucky to be alive. The bullet hit ze curve of your head in back and followed ze skull to ze front before exiting." His thick accent heavier than usual.

Hoarsely he answered, "My leg is sore."

"Ah, yes. You did take a bullet zere as well. Whiskey was most, how shall I say, worried."

"I can see that." He responded with a wan smile, scratching the lion behind the ear.

"Rest. We will be on ze move to our new location Vauconleurs. A beautiful place I did visit once."

McClellan nodded ever so lightly and immediately fell back asleep.

CHAPTER THIRTEEN

THE HOTEL SOLOMONS, SEPTEMBER 25, 8:00 A.M.

Daniel Collum, Hayden McClellan, Robert Hunter, William Kinney. The names swirled as his brain tried to figure out who he was at this moment. Benjamin Richter, Benjamin. Captain Richter. Someone kept calling him, and with slight annoyance in his voice he responded, "What?"

Daniel slowly opened his eyes and realized he had fallen asleep on a couch. He had a splitting headache and assumed that must have been what brought the dream on.

"Captain Benjamin Richter?" a female voice asked.

"Yes, what's going on? Pilots get in trouble with hula girls again?" He blinked his eyes a few times, working to clear his vision, as he rolled over to sit up. He was not in Hawaii… he was in the *Hotel Solomons*. It was the 21st Century, not the 20th, and Veronica Jenkins was giving him a look.

"You are. You really are Benjamin Richter, aren't you?"

"I was dreaming."

Veronica tossed a photo at him "Explain that then."

He tried to focus on a blown-up picture of himself in his World War II uniform. She threw another picture at him, then another.

"And while you're at it, maybe you can explain these as well. Daniel Collum, Robert Hunter, Benjamin Richter. Who are you?" She was standing firm, but at the same time, there was a flash of fear in her eyes. "Or, what are you?"

Daniel held his head in his hands, his skull pounding from last night's overindulgence. "Aspirin, please, and some water?" He caught her stony gaze. "Look, I'll tell you everything you want to know, but please, my head is killing me."

Veronica stared at Daniel for a moment before finally getting up from the loveseat. She returned with a bottle of aspirin and filled a glass with water at the bar. She handed four pills to Daniel, which he bit first, then washed down with the cool liquid.

Veronica was still staring at him as he tried to figure out where to go with this. He decided to jump in with both feet.

"My real name is Daniel Collum, I swear to you." He glanced at the photo prints she had thrown at him. Gathering them, he placed them one at a time, left to right on the coffee table.

"So, this is me, as you know me now." He pointed to the snapshot she had taken of him for the Civil War article. "Before that, I went by the name Michael Phillips, a retired rancher. Robert Hunter was the name I went by when I was a secret service agent at the White House." He placed the photo of himself as Hunter on the coffee table next to the first.

"Normally I would never have opened myself up to the kind of scrutiny working at the White House would bring, but I saw things moving in a direction I could not allow." Daniel paused for a moment. Veronica's eyes locked on him, listening intently. "I'll give you the fast version, as I'm sure you already have many questions."

Veronica nodded.

"Before Robert, I was known as William Kinney, again a retired rancher. I found it easy to stay out of the mainstream that way. And before him, Benjamin Richter, as you guessed. A captain in the Army Air Force at Pearl Harbor." He placed that last photo next to the others.

He noticed Veronica was about to speak when he held up is hand to stop her. "I'm not finished."

Veronica's eyes widened. She sat back on the loveseat and grasped one of the decorative pillows from the couch, clutching it to her chest.

"Before Richter, I was known as Hayden McClellan. That was World War I. Under that name, I was labelled as one of the 'Untouchables' during prohibition."

He tried to gauge her reaction. She was holding it together. Far better than anyone should have been able to who had a story like this thrown at them.

"Now we come to the beginning. The first me that there was, who also happens to be the last me. My name was Daniel Collum, the son of immigrant parents from Ireland. Who fought in the Civil War as a drummer boy, became an officer in the U.S. Cavalry under Custer, before leaving to make it rich in the Gold Rush in the Black Hills. I left there to set up a store in Deadwood, eventually moving to Dodge City, then finally on to San Francisco. Until the earthquake in 1906 took my wife and nearly my soul."

With that, he stopped, watching Veronica for any reaction. The silence in the room was thick. Neither of them said anything for a few minutes, just staring into each other's eyes. She finally shifted her position, moving the protective pillow away from her.

"How? How is that even possible?" Her voice a mere whisper.

Daniel shook his head. "I wish I knew. I really do. All I know is that, at about the age of sixteen, my body just seemed to -- slow down. Call it hormones if you like, an act of God if you go in that direction, but that's about the best I've been able to come up with."

"Are you immortal?" Her face scrunched up as she said it.

Daniel chuckled a little at this. "No, no I'm not immortal by a long shot. Seems I'm just damned lucky."

With that, her questions began in earnest. She would ask one thing or another, and after his responses, she would pause a moment to take it all in. After about a half hour, she got up and went to the suite phone. She called room service, ordering the two of them a huge breakfast. They ate as they talked, Veronica asking more questions, and him answering them as best he could.

"I'm finding this very hard to believe. I want to, as I would like to think I know you, but…" She trailed off for a moment, "…I'd like some proof that this is all real."

Daniel nodded, "I understand. Bring your laptop in here and I'll give you all you'll need.

She retrieved the laptop from the office, setting it down on the coffee table.

"Let's start with Benjamin Richter. You'll find that I was shot twice during the attack on Pearl Harbor. If you check the location of --."

"I already verified those," she responded, a bit sheepishly.

"Oh, really?"

Chuckling at this, he came clean. "I guess that's only fair as I accidentally walked in on you while you were taking a shower."

It was suddenly her turn to blush. "Fair enough then." She smiled at him.

He went on to describe the various wounds he had received as different identities, allowing her to examine each one. Some had faded a bit, as they were quite old, but others were still very noticeable. The last one was the head wound he had received during the Great War. Taking her hand gently, he placed it on the entry wound scar, then lifted his hair in front so she could see where the bullet had exited.

He retrieved his metal briefcase, and set it on the coffee table. Daniel showed Veronica the medals he had been given during the two World Wars, before handing over a stack of framed photos from his past: standing in front of his store in Deadwood, at his hotel in Dodge City, Daniel and Elliot Ness posing with damaged barrels of alcohol in the background, a portrait of Daniel with his wife and two children.

Veronica handed back the pictures with tears in her eyes.

"What's under the plastic?"

"A surprise."

He pulled the plastic aside. The colors and material of the item, along with how it was folded, immediately identified it as a flag.

Daniel smiled. "Yes, it's the original. I couldn't let it go, so I had an exact duplicate made and switched them out."

Her hands went down to the fabric, hovering just inches above. "The Fighting 69th?"

"I knew you would know exactly what it was." He allowed her to stare for a few moments, before covering it again with the heavy plastic. He put all the other items back as she sat there, taking everything in. Closing the case, he shifted the combination numbers randomly.

Reaching over, he picked up the journal which Veronica had left on the coffee table.

"Another bit of proof you might find interesting is in here."

"Now you're just playing with me."

"No, seriously." He flipped through the journal. "Read the page about the *Occidental Hotel*."

Veronica read the page in question. Daniel could see her scanning through the handwritten notes until she found what he wanted her to see. She stopped, glanced up to him for a moment, then completed reading the page.

"My God," she said, "You owned the *Occidental Hotel* when Owen Wister was writing *The Virginian*?"

"I didn't know that at the time, though he was quite an affable man. How was I to know he would use my gunfight in his story?"

"I've read *The Virginian*. Are you trying to tell me the gunfight on the street was you?"

"Yes, but nothing like the way it was written. I'm not much on killing, never have been, even though my career choices might imply otherwise. But the man I shot had been a problem for a long time. I just couldn't get around it - too many eyes watching. The man was drunk, pushed the issue of my bloodline far enough, that I felt it needed to be done. Oddly, that was the first time anyone recorded a gunfight at the proverbial 'High Noon.'"

"What about family? You had a wife, children. What happened with them? Do you have any family around?"

Daniel got very quiet. He picked up his coffee cup and held it in both hands. "My wife, as I mentioned, died during the Big Quake.

But before that happened, I lost my son and his entire family to a hurricane in Galveston, Texas. His name was Nathaniel. My only other child, Mary, had one daughter. Years later, I learned my only living grandchild had died during an influenza epidemic, right after the Great War ended. My family is gone. My line is gone. It took a long time for me to come to terms with that. With my condition. Maybe it's for the best."

Veronica wiped tears from her eyes, and got up from her seat. Moving to Daniel, she kissed him with utter abandon, but he gently pushed her away.

"Vee, I'm one hundred and sixty-seven years old."

"I know. I believe it all now, but I don't care."

"Don't you realize that I'll probably outlive you too?"

"I'm twenty-seven now."

"I know that, but when I'm roughly sixty-two, you'll have aged to sixty-one. Shortly after that you'll be older."

Veronica stood, then walked over to the far side of the room near the office. "And when I'm seventy-three, you'll have only aged to sixty-five. But Daniel, life is a crapshoot to begin with. Who's to say we won't slip in a tub, or get hit by a car, well before then? We have what we have. If there's anything I've learned from my years writing about history, it's that you can't just let it slip past you."

"Okay, okay." Daniel held up his hands in mock surrender. "We can discuss this later. Believe me, I want to, but right now I need to tell you about the danger we're currently in. We may really only have today if the Haig Men find us."

Daniel told her about being around during the deaths of Lincoln, both Kennedys, and Martin Luther King. How these senseless killings had pushed him to do something he would never have thought he would do. When he heard rumors of death threats on Ronald Reagan, he could no longer stand aside. He gave the details of his last day as Robert Hunter.

"And you've been hiding from them ever since, until the picture I took for the article, somehow caused them to notice you. Daniel, I'm so sorry. I didn't know."

"How could you? It's all right. It's better that this all ends here and now. I don't know John Bennett or Mark Royston well, but I have a feeling they have not been idle the past thirty years. I get this terrible feeling Bennett may be setting himself up for something else."

"What do we do?"

Daniel glanced at his pocketwatch. It was getting on toward eleven. They had been talking for hours, and he felt just about as tired now as he had when she had woken him, though his head wasn't pounding any longer. He stood up and stretched.

"I need to get out of this room for a bit. Let's get dressed, get some sun, and discuss our options."

They got dressed and took the elevator to the main lobby. Daniel had wanted to check in with the desk, just in case to make sure they were still safe. He had learned a long time ago to listen to his hunches. They walked up to the check-in counter and found Abella working there.

"What are you doing here? Don't you take any time off?" Daniel asked with a smile.

Abella laughed lightly, "What may I do for you, Mr. and Mrs. Kilmer?"

"I have a few colleagues I'm expecting may show up, and would appreciate you letting me know if they come in." Daniel gave her the name and descriptions of Bennett, Royston, and what he could of Mr. Smith.

"No one with those names have come in yet that I know of, but I'll let you know."

They thanked her and turned to the elevator when Abella called them back.

"I'm not sure if it matters, but there was a gentleman who showed up just a few minutes after you went upstairs last night. He said he thought he knew you in the service." She turned to check her computer for a moment. "Mr. Morgan Dimico."

Daniel glanced to Veronica. "You don't say. What a small world. If you see him in the next couple of hours, would you let him know we'll be on the pool deck."

They thanked her again for her help and went on their way to the elevators. When the doors closed, Veronica turned to Daniel, "Why do you want this Dimico guy to find us? Isn't he dangerous?"

"He might be, but I don't think he's as dangerous as this Mr. Smith I've been told about. I have a feeling Mr. Dimico could be tailing us for them, so if we remove him from the equation, we'll be in better shape."

"You're not going to kill him, are you?" she said in surprise.

"No, no, not if I don't have to. I just want to talk with him. We'll find out what he knows, then we can just lock him up somewhere until we're long gone, and he can't follow us again."

•———•

Morgan Dimico had nightmares. At every turn he would find himself running from Mr. Smith, or see the blue suited man, who would turn into a nightmare vision with forked tongue and snake eyes. Those had been bad enough, but then he commenced to dream of Daniel Collum chasing him all over the world, and every face he saw became another Daniel Collum. After the fifth time he was shocked awake, he gave up on any semblance of sleep, spending the rest of the night going over the files he had on Collum. While he was working through the files, he finally nodded off for a few hours. He might have slept longer if not for the sunlight beating down on him through the open curtains of the window.

Dimico moved the stack of papers out of his way and shuffled groggily into the bathroom. He grimaced at the face gazing back at him in the mirror. He spent the next half hour leaning his head against the shower wall while the hot water massaged his stiff back and neck. When he eventually emerged from the bathroom, feeling refreshed and more like himself than he had in years, he glanced at the small clock on the nightstand by the bed. It was just after eleven o'clock. He walked over to the phone on the table and called the front desk.

"Front Desk, how may I be of service?"

"Yes, I didn't realize the time, and was wondering if I could extend my stay another day."

"No problem at all. May I have your room please?"

"One Moment." He reached into the pile of papers on his bed for the keycard. "Room 713. Dimico."

"Oh, Mr. Dimico. Mr. and Mrs. Kilmer were down here just about fifteen minutes ago. They mentioned they would be up on the pool deck, in case you wanted to reach them."

Dimico smiled with this stroke of luck. "Thank you. I think I will. I could do with a bit of food myself."

The salt breeze rustled through the fronds of the scores of palm trees in large potted planters lining the deck, colorful lounge chairs ran in long rows, empty of sun worshippers. Also empty were the cabanas facing the far end of the rooftop. A smattering of hotel guests sat at umbrella tables, eating lunch or drinking coffee. The smell of food cooking from the open walled restaurant wafted across the deck. The pool, which ran the length of the rooftop, was solely engaged by a family of four who had flown down from Oregon. Daniel and Veronica spent the next twenty minutes discussing how she felt, how she was handling his secret, did she have any other questions. He was surprised by the question she did pose.

"You've never truly mourned for her, have you?"

"Vee, I've spent an entire century mourning the loss of my wife. There's been no one else, until you, and I'm finding it difficult to come to terms with those feelings."

"That's because you never had any closure. From what you've told me, you just walked away."

"I'd lost everything. It just seemed to be the easiest way to erase myself from the world. With Kathryn gone, there was a huge hole I didn't know how to fill."

Veronica shook her head, "That's the problem Daniel. You haven't looked back. You said there's been no one since Kathryn. Don't you think there's a reason for that? You need closure."

Daniel opened his mouth to say something and stopped, choked with the love he had tried to hide for so long. Taking a deep breath, he looked back up to Veronica with moist eyes, not caring if she saw. "I…"

Daniel stiffened. "We have company."

"What do we do now?" Veronica asked, just a hint of fear creeping into her tone.

"It's me he wants. Take the back stairs, go to our room, gather your things, and get out. If I'm able, I'll find you."

She started to object but he held her hand tightly for emphasis. "Promise me. I don't know what I would do if something bad happened to you. Please."

They held each other's eyes for a minute before she finally looked down at the table and their clasped hands. "I promise. I don't like it, but I promise.

As she walked away, he heard her say, "I love you, in case I don't get another chance to say it."

Feeling a sharp pang of emotion, one he hadn't felt in over a century, Daniel watched her go, then stood to face Dimico.

Mr. Smith was not in a good mood. He had never failed a job in his life, part of why he was so good at what he did. It also happened to be why he was paid so handsomely, but this private investigator, Dimico, had become his Achilles heel.

The contract on Frank Thomas was complete but Morgan Dimico had disappeared in the wind. He looked forward to eliminating Daniel Collum who had outwitted Bennett for thirty years. With their whereabouts unknown, he had driven up to Cambria to take care of Veronica Jenkins. His mood went sour when he found her home vacated, clothes tossed about in her room, car gone.

It was six o'clock in the morning by the time he made the call to Bennett from his motel room. The call had not gone well, nor improved his disposition. He had lain on the bed stewing over Bennett when he fell asleep.

His phone rang. "Smith."

"I have a lead for you, Mr. Smith." Bennett's voice came through clearly.

"I'm ready, sir."

"It appears Mr. Dimico did not throw away the phone I gave him and left it active. According to my sources, it is currently in San Diego, at a *Hotel Solomons*. Be sure you remove anyone Dimico may have contacted, once you get down there."

"I'm on it, sir."

"Make sure you are. If I need to make a trip there it won't be pleasant."

"I'll take care of it." Smith hung up the phone with force. Four hours of sleep. He headed for San Diego, formulating a plan to remove Bennett from his worries after his contracts were done.

Daniel Collum and Morgan Dimico stared at one another from a distance. The family in the pool sloshed around, oblivious of anything. Motioning toward the cabanas, Daniel walked off, not waiting to see if Dimico followed. He was ready when the investigator rounded the corner.

"Daniel Collum, I've been looking…"

Daniel grabbed Dimico by the jacket and threw him against the brick wall. As he put him into a chokehold, he did a quick, one-handed pat down for any weapons Dimico might have hidden. He came up with nothing, which surprised him.

"Did the Haig Men send you?"

"I don't know who you're talking about. I was hired by someone wearing a blue suit, never got his name. All I know is that he sent someone to kill me once I gave him everything he wanted to know."

"And what exactly did they want to know?"

"If you were a man called Robert Hunter."

"That would explain the men I had to deal with. So, you're the reason I'm on the run again."

Daniel saw the man flush with anger as he struggled against the chokehold. Dimico looked a mess and Daniel was glad he did not smell the way he looked.

"Look, I'm not the one that started this, you did. All I was told was to find out whether you were this Hunter, and report back, that's all! Now let me go!"

Daniel released Dimico and stared into his eyes. He thought he saw something else hiding in there, "That's all. You wouldn't be holding back on me now, would you?"

Dimico spat back, "I know who you are, Collum. Or, what you are. I could have told my client about the many names you've had over the past century, but I kept them to myself. I think sending someone to kill me at my office was enough to sever any agreement I might have had with them."

Daniel shifted a few steps away from Dimico. "How did you --?"

Dimico put his hand up to his neck and massaged his muscles. With a deep breath, he responded, "You may be good, but I'm better at what I do. I have a number of questions I'd like to ask."

Daniel stood in silence for a moment, thinking, then motioned to an empty cabana. "In here. We can talk a bit more privately without being noticed."

Dimico stepped past Daniel into the cabana. Closing the flap behind him, Daniel pulled out a chair next to a small wicker table and sat. "Ask away. I think maybe you've earned it."

Dimico paced back and forth. Daniel watched him open his mouth then close it. He sat down just to stand up again. He rubbed the growth on his chin, plopped back into the chair, and stared at Daniel.

Daniel smiled. "Let me help start. I don't know why I am. No, I am not immortal. If you cut me, I do bleed. I just think I'm a bit luckier than most, though I have many scars to show for it."

"Three centuries. You've lived in three different centuries, and still managed to pass yourself off as a normal person." He absently rubbed at his neck. "The stories you could tell, what you could teach. It boggles the mind."

"The torches that would be lit, the mobs that would gather, the stake they would burn me at," Daniel added flippantly.

Dimico gazed at Daniel, shaking his head. "It's the twenty-first century, Mr. Collum. Things like that are a thing of the past. We are an enlightened species of the modern age."

Daniel laughed out loud. "We are not as enlightened, as you might think, Morgan. I'm sorry, may I call you Morgan? I feel we should be on a first name basis, considering."

The tent flap was suddenly thrown open. Veronica jumped in, clutching a circular glass candle votive holder in her hand, ready to throw. The two men, startled at her entry, just stared for a moment.

"What do you plan to do with that, Vee?"

"Damn it, Daniel! I thought you might be in trouble." She lowered her arm and set the holder on the low table before taking a third chair. "How was I to know that you two would be all buddy-buddy? I thought he was dangerous."

"Hardly dangerous. Ms. Jenkins?" Dimico asked.

"Please, call me Veronica," she sighed.

"Well then, you may call me Morgan, both of you. Nice to finally meet you in person Veronica. You had such a lovely voice on the phone when we spoke the one time. It's nice to put a face with it. And who should I call you Mr. Collum? Daniel, Robert, Hayden?"

"Daniel will be fine, as that's my real name." He then turned his attention to Veronica. "I thought I asked you not to come after me."

Veronica glanced from one man to the other in surprise. "He knows who you are? All of you?"

"Morgan here has been busy for a while, gathering information on me. For some reason, he has decided to keep that information to himself. Well, except for my personae of Robert Hunter, which is why we're all here now."

"Wait a minute. She knows about you too?" Dimico indicated Veronica.

Daniel sighed, "As of this morning she knows everything. Like you, she managed to figure it out last night. I've been diligent in hiding myself for the last one hundred and sixty-seven years, but in less than a year's time, both of you have managed to flush me out. I'm beginning to think the world has become too advanced for someone in my condition."

Dimico turned to Veronica, "And you're okay with this?"

"I'm still dealing with some of the pieces, but yes, I'm good. In some ways, it all just seems to make sense," she smiled at Daniel.

Dimico studied them. "I think I see how that would make believing easier. I came close to having a nervous breakdown once or twice myself."

Daniel and Veronica both blushed slightly. Daniel said apologetically, "I'm sorry if I've caused you any mental grief, Morgan. I know it's a lot to have to filter through."

"I'm a man who believes in hard facts. The files in my room are nothing if not facts of who you are and have been. I think that's what's kept me sane."

That brought Daniel back to their current situation. "I think we should move our conversation back to our room. It might be safer if we have Morgan move his things in with us, just in case. I think we have more than enough room for the three of us."

———

The three of them spent another few hours talking about Daniel's long life, the men that were after them, and what they should do with the files that seemed to mean so much to John Bennett.

"I still find it hard to believe that you've spent almost your entire life in the United States," Dimico said. "The countries you could have visited. The things you could have done. Hell, it boggles me that you didn't take that as an opportunity to hide from these Haig Men."

"I've never been all that interested in travel." Daniel thought about that for a moment, "The trip from Ireland to America wasn't an easy one. That kind of sticks with you as a kid. I didn't have the best of memories from the Great War. Hawaii has its own horrors in my memory from December 7th. I do admit, it was a lovely place before that day." He shrugged, as if that answered everything, his face full of regret.

"I'm starving. I haven't had a chance to eat since yesterday," Dimico said.

Daniel came out of his revere, glancing at his pocketwatch, which now showed the time at 3:50 p.m. "Let me take a quick shower and we'll head back down to the pool deck. We can grab a root then."

"Grab a root?" Dimico was confused.

"He means get some food." Veronica grinned.

While Veronica researched cemeteries in San Francisco on her computer in the office, Dimico flipped on the television. He was not looking for anything specific, just passing time, when he abruptly stopped on a news station.

"We have breaking news that has just come in. The names in the apparent murder/suicide that took place last night, in the city of Orange, have just been released. In a bizarre turn of events which led to the murder of Jessica Hardgrave at the Stars and Sleep Motel, it now appears that the man who took Ms. Hardgrave's life, and then his own, is none other than Frank Thomas, Lobbyist for the oil conglomerates in Washington, D.C. A suicide letter was left by Thomas, the details have yet to be released by the authorities. Thomas was said to be on business in California by his wife, though at this time, we have been unable to confirm this."

Dimico turned off the power, watching the screen go black. Daniel came in dressed in a grey suit. "Ready?"

Dimico replied, "We're in even more trouble than we thought."

CHAPTER FOURTEEN

HOTEL SOLOMONS, SEPTEMBER 25, 4:00 P.M.

They argued over what to do. Dimico wanted to take the files he had to a news station or newspaper, but Daniel had stopped that plan quickly. The files Dimico had accumulated left Daniel open and naked to the world. He couldn't risk that.

Veronica wanted them to go into hiding, change their names and lives if necessary. She theorized that Daniel had done it before and had been safe from these Haig Men, but he had turned that down as well. Now that Bennett knew he was alive, he would stop at nothing to finish them all to save his own worthless skin. He had already killed members of his own team. Daniel saw no reason for him to shift gears now if they attempted to disappear again.

The real argument came when Daniel wanted to confront Bennett and put an end to it all in one fell swoop.

"You can't do that," Veronica said. "These men… these Haig Men… will kill you."

"I guess we're at an impasse…" Dimico said.

"A compromise then. We'll leave here first thing in the morning. Vee, why don't you take your luggage down to Dimico's car now just to be safe. I'll take mine down after we figure out a safe location for us."

"All the way at the end from the elevators on level two. Sorry about the mess." Dimico gave her the keys.

Veronica rolled her luggage down to Dimico's car, walking back to the elevators in deep thought. She vaguely heard the screech of a car's tires as she went over cemetery locations in her head. She waited so long, she almost decided to take the stairs when the elevator opened. She hardly noticed someone entered the elevator with her until he cleared his throat.

"Excuse me. This is my exit."

She absently shifted out of the way, letting the man exit on the lobby floor. As the doors closed she glanced up just long enough to recognize Daniel's description of Mr. Smith. She had recovered from her shock by the time she arrived at their suite.

"Smith is here! He got on the elevator with me and got off at the lobby. I don't think he knew who I was."

Daniel stared at Dimico. "Did you use cash or credit when you got here?"

"Cash, I wasn't going to take any chances – Oh, shit! The phone!"

"What phone?"

"Bennett gave me a phone he could use to call me when he wanted an update. I threw the damn thing on the passenger seat of my car the last time we talked. I forgot all about it."

"We have to get out of here." Daniel took his .357 Magnum from the duffel and strapped it on. Grabbing the Glock with silencer, he shoved it into Dimico's hand. Pulling his duster out of the duffle, he donned the coat, hiding the weapon.

Veronica disappeared into the office, returning with her laptop case and bag.

"I'll meet you at the car," Dimico said, gathering his files strewn about the coffee table.

Daniel grabbed the metal case and duffle bag, Veronica's hand with the other, and they ran.

The two of them exited the elevator on the second, sub-floor parking structure. They walked down the underground driveway toward the car, when Daniel noticed someone toss a lit cigarette from behind the pillar next to Dimico's car. He stopped and gestured

"Shh" to Veronica. Daniel checked the mirrors of the cars around them and spotted a man with a white bandage covering one side of his head behind a pillar halfway down. Two men. Hiding.

Daniel quickly shifted their direction, moving Veronica up against a black Pontiac. She was shocked when he unexpectedly grabbed her in an embrace, kissing her fully on the lips. Keeping their faces very close, he whispered, "Two men. They're set up so anyone going to the car will get caught in a crossfire."

"What about Morgan?"

Smith marched across the vacant lobby, stepped around the check-in counter behind the manager working there, and hit him in the back of the head. He quickly dragged the man into the manager's office, took his master key, and searched the computer for his contract's room.

Dimico scooped up the last of the files, threw them into a folder, and raced for the elevators.

Abella returned to the lobby to see a man vault over the counter and run to the elevators. Running to the manager's office, she saw his unconscious body on the floor, his computer screen facing her. Grabbing the phone, she called security.

While Veronica continued to kiss him, Daniel deftly pulled his Magnum from its holster, eyeing the pillar just four cars down, on the opposite side.

The elevator doors opened. Smith strode to Dimico's room, pulling his silenced Glock. He swiped the master key and pushed open the door.

•———•

The elevator door opened to the parking garage and Dimico stepped out.

"What are you two doing? We have to get out of here."

The Magnum rang out, sounding like a Howitzer in the underground parking structure. Concrete shrapnel exploded from the pillar.

"Son of a Bitch!" The merc hugged the pillar.

Dimico froze, confused by the sudden change of events.

"Morgan, get over here!" Daniel yelled as he and Veronica ducked behind the Pontiac.

Dimico was about to sprint to them when he caught sight of a man taking aim at him from the pillar by his car. Shifting gears mid-stride, his shoes slid on the cement floor for a terrifying moment, before gaining purchase. He launched himself behind a nearby Saturn opposite from where his new friends were, almost spilling the files in the process.

The shot hit the pavement just inches from where his heel had been before he jumped. From the pillar near his car, he heard someone yell, "He's got the files, Charlie!"

"I'm a little more worried about the guy with the cannon right now, Abel!" Charlie darted around the pillar, just long enough to take a shot with his silenced Glock, the bullet hitting the black Pontiac. Not waiting to see the result of his shot, he pulled back behind the pillar.

Daniel glimpsed Abel through the passenger window of the Pontiac. He rose up and took another loud shot. The metal bullet hit the pillar, spraying Abel with concrete shards.

"Holy shit! It's Hunter!" Abel exclaimed, as he dove behind his own pillar.

Daniel motioned at Dimico, hoping Dimico would figure out what he meant to do. He told Veronica to count to ten, then follow him between the wall and the cars.

Taking a blind shot at Abel, Dimico crouched down and moved away from the open driveway, turning between the front of the car and the wall.

Shifting around the Pontiac, Daniel took another shot at Charlie, forcing him to pull back behind the pillar again. He then wasted no time advancing behind the back of the next vehicle.

"I got bullets with your name on 'em, Hunter! You shot off half my ear, you son of a bitch!" Charlie jumped out long enough to take another shot, hitting the Pontiac again.

Daniel positioned himself on the far side of the next car, briefly checking his position against Abel. He had been correct in his estimate that, unless Abel came fully around his pillar on the one side, Daniel couldn't be seen. He took aim at the pillar Charlie was hiding behind and waited.

As he expected, Charlie jumped out for another shot. Daniel fired, shearing off Charlie's right ear, at the top. Screaming in pain, Charlie pulled back instinctively, firing wild into the parking structure's wall.

"Now you have a matching set, Charlie!" Daniel taunted, hoping the man would do something stupid.

"Charlie! Where's Dimico?! I haven't seen him since he dove behind that Saturn!"

"Motherfucker shot off my other ear!"

Dimico found Charlie sitting on the pavement, the left side of his head covered in bandages. Blood poured through his fingers as he held his damaged ear. His weapon, forgotten for the moment, on the ground next to him.

"Don't move, Charlie, you're done," Dimico said with satisfaction.

Charlie glanced at Dimico, then down to his Glock. With a guttural growl, he reached for his weapon. Dimico hesitated for only a fraction of a second, before firing multiple times, hitting Charlie in the chest with each shot. The grimace forever frozen on his face, Charlie toppled over, eyes vacant.

"One down, Daniel!" Dimico yelled.

Dimico and Daniel leapfrogged forward, avoiding the shots Abel fired at random intervals. Each time, Veronica held back until they had secured their new position.

Daniel made it to the last car across from the pillar Abel was using for cover. Seeing Dimico take up position on the opposite side from him, he took a shot at the pillar corner. The concrete exploded. Abel jumped out on the opposite side of the pillar from Daniel. Dimico popped up and fired. The bullet hit Abel in the neck, taking him down in a spray of blood.

Daniel ran to the damaged pillar. Gun at the ready, he rounded the cement column to see Abel stretched out on the ground, writhing in pain. He gurgled something Daniel couldn't understand. With a sense of remorse at the waste, he watched what life Abel had left bleed out.

Veronica ran up with their things, dumping them in the trunk.

"You sure make things exciting." Dimico grinned.

The crash of the stairwell door echoed in the structure. Daniel saw Smith rounding the pillar near the elevators.

"Morgan, down!"

Daniel reached for him, but it was too late. Dimico glanced at him quizzically, pulling a bloodied hand from his back from one of two bullet wounds.

Dimico dropped to his knees and shoved the files at Daniel.

"Go. I've got this. Get her out of here," he said through clenched teeth.

Daniel grabbed the files. With a nod of regret, Daniel made a break for the car, firing as he went.

Dimico angled his body, firing at Smith standing at the far end of the structure. His vision was fuzzy, so just kept up a barrage to cover his friend's escape. As his shots grew muffled in his ears, he smelled burning rubber as his car peeled in reverse. His body involuntarily forced him to the ground from a bullet to his chest. The sedan slid sideways, almost running into him. His fading vision caught a flashing red light attached to the underside of his car and he spat blood out in an attempt to warn Daniel. They had escaped Smith with his help. Wheezing with satisfaction, Morgan Dimico closed his eyes.

•——•

Smith heard the firefight in his earwig, ran out the room and down the stairwell. As he crashed through the door, he saw Hunter and Dimico at the far end with the files he needed. His first shots got Dimico out of the way, but Hunter ran to the sedan. His shots, added with Dimico's, forced him behind a pillar. He managed to hit Dimico once more before he heard an unfamiliar voice to his right.

"Put the gun down!"

Without waiting, Smith wheeled around and fired, killing a security guard who had come out from the stairwell. He saw Dimico's car peal out of the garage, almost hitting Dimico in its escape. He sprinted to take a deadly shot at Hunter, but his chance was gone. He toed Dimico's dead body. At least this pain in the ass was no longer a problem. He pulled out his cell.

"Mr. Corpus. Your services are needed again, ASAP. I'll text you the address."

He surveyed the battle area, shaking his head. There was a good chance they wouldn't be able to hide this one from the public eye. It really depended on how long it took Corpus's men to get here, and how well he could stall. He walked with purpose to the black BMW rental car. Opening the trunk, he threw off an army surplus blanket, which covered some sports bags. Unzipping the one on the right end, he shifted items around inside, until he found what he was looking for.

Taking the **DO NOT CROSS** yellow tape, he walked over to the passenger side of the car. He leaned in to release the catch on the glovebox. Taking up most of the compartment was a bulging manila envelope, which he took out and opened. Smith pulled one badge after another, until he found the detective's badge for San Diego. Clipping the badge to his belt, he began the process of cordoning off the entire area.

Morgan Dimico's sedan was just one of many cars making its way north on the Interstate 5 freeway. The only sound in the car, Veronica's crying from their loss of Dimico. She dabbed away the last of her tears as she pulled the battery from Dimico's cell and stuffed it into the glovebox.

"Good idea," Daniel said, feeling numb himself. "You never know when we might find ourselves in need of the thing."

"Where are we going?" Veronica asked.

"San Francisco. We need to get far away from any place they might think to find us, and I feel I should… it's time I said goodbye to my wife." His crooked smile waned a little at this, touched with melancholy, and he turned back to the road ahead. "How are you doing finding her location?"

"Nothing yet. I'm sorry," she sighed.

"I have complete confidence that you'll find where she's laid to rest by the time we get to San Francisco." An idea struck him, and he glanced back to her. "Have you tried searching for both Kathryn and Daniel Collum? It's possible they may have put up a marker for me as well, when they put one up for her."

"I'll try that. For now, I just want to look at the scenery." She gently placed her left hand on his right thigh. Without another word, she turned to look out the window, at the hills of scrub and browning grass.

CHAPTER FIFTEEN

WASHINGTON D.C., SEPTEMBER 25, 8:00 P.M.

"May I get anyone another drink?" Valerie Bennett asked of her husband and the Royston's.

"You haven't finished your first one yet, darling." John Bennett said as she stood up.

"You know I've never been much of a drinker. I'm just trying to be a good hostess."

Brittany interrupted, "Valerie, did you happen to catch the news? It's horrible. Who would have thought Frank was capable of murder? I feel so sorry for Irene and the kids."

"I know exactly what you mean. I called Irene earlier today and she was a mess. I wish there was something we could do. John, what do you think?"

The office phone rang from across the hallway. Bennett and Royston both excused themselves.

"One of these days we'll actually have a dinner party where he doesn't run off for work." Valerie sighed with defeat, downing the rest of her drink in one swallow.

Royston closed the door to the office as Bennett answered the phone. "Bennett."

"This is Smith."

Bennett sat in the office chair, set the receiver on the desk, and motioned to Royston. Locking the door, Royston moved to one of the chairs opposite the desk, settling himself in. Bennet put the phone on speaker.

"What news do you have, Mr. Smith?"

"Partial success. Morgan Dimico is no longer an issue. Unfortunately, the information he was carrying still is."

Bennett and Royston locked glances as Bennett responded, "I thought I had made it clear that you were not to fire Mr. Dimico until you had the files he was working on."

"I know exactly where the files are. There was an issue. The information was transferred before I could collect it."

Royston stood straight up in his seat. Bennett leaned forward toward the phone. "An issue? What kind of issue, Smith?"

"It was Hunter and the woman. They were with Dimico. He was able to transfer the files to Hunter."

Bennett leaned even closer, his nose nearly touching the phone base. Through clenched teeth he spat, "Are you telling me that you allowed Hunter to go freely on his way? With the files that I explicitly stated I wanted back?"

"It could not be avoided," Smith's voice sounded strained.

Royston shook his head. "Damn it, Smith. Where were your men when all this was happening?"

"Their service had been terminated by the time I was able to confront Hunter and Dimico."

Royston stared at the phone, while Bennett slouched in his chair. The silence was interrupted by Smith's voice mumbling to someone. Bennett leaned forward, "What the hell is going on there?"

"Containing the mess until Corpus shows with his team."

Bennett pushed his chair violently against the wall. "And Hunter is off to God knows where while you sit on your ass?"

"It is taken care of. Sir." Smith's tone was clipped. "The car has a tracker attached. Once I am done here, I will follow them and finish the job. As I always do."

Bennett placed both hands on his desk and leaned forward. He took a deep breath to calm himself. "Mr. Smith, as always, you will receive your pay for Dimico. As to Hunter, when you ascertain their destination, I want you to immediately inform me. Do absolutely nothing but watch them until we get there. Is that clear?"

There was a long pause on the other end. "Crystal."

"We will be in touch." Bennett slammed down the receiver, then paced across the room. "I'm done with hired men fucking this up. More than half a dozen men at their disposal, yet Hunter is still alive, and now he has the files. Those files put us in the hangman's noose. Smith is the best there is, yet he's failed time and again on this contract."

Bennett glared at Royston. "Mark, get my private jet ready."

"I'll make sure it gets done. Location?"

"We'll know that once Smith calls. That's another issue. This must end where it all began, with the two of us. Once Hunter is taken care of, I want Smith terminated.

The trip up Interstate 5 had been uneventful, which hadn't been good for Daniel. The day's activities, the night driving, and the odd quirks of Dimico's old sedan, were wearing him down. Their only stop had been to get gas and some food at a gas station in San Juan Capistrano. He had not wanted to get back in the car for the long drive. Veronica was busy on her laptop, and he had stalled continuing their drive until he felt they couldn't wait any longer.

Daniel's thoughts drifted. Smith. Now there was a problem. Smith was not a run-of-the-mill hired gun, but a professional assassin, currently under the payroll of Bennett. Daniel could not be sure if Smith would stop, if somehow Bennett were out of the way. Men like Smith were inclined to finish the job they were given. It was a point of pride to them, almost a personal code. At some point, regardless of anything else, he was sure he would have to go up against Smith. That was an encounter he was not looking forward to.

That brought his thoughts to the Haig Men themselves. John Bennett and Mark Royston. Royston might beg off the whole thing if Bennett were out of the picture, but Bennett would never stop. Especially now that he knew Daniel was alive. He knew Bennett's type. There was only one way to deal with a megalomaniac such as him. It reviled Daniel to think it had to come to that. He should have done something about Bennett and his cohorts decades ago, but had let them go unchecked to play their little games. What was it to him, who lived so long, for these men to play at being God? He had disrupted their plans, content that it would be the last he would see of them. Well, as long as they had no knowledge he still existed. It had almost worked, except for one error in his judgement.

"For crying out loud!" Daniel exclaimed as his eyes watched a gauge needle slip into the red.

"The radiator?"

"Yeah, got lulled by the driving."

He took the next exit, happy to see the lights of a gas station. Daniel managed to roll the car up to the water pump. They stretched their stiff muscles before braving opening the hood of the car. A cloud of steam escaped from under the hood.

"I don't see any water running out of the radiator." He checked under the car.

"Doesn't look like a break or leak. I think it just overheated," she said.

Daniel wiped his hands as he got up, seeing Veronica leaning over the radiator at a safe distance. He glanced at his pocketwatch, just after ten.

"I'm starving." Veronica stated.

"And I could use a restroom about now."

"That too." She shivered.

"It's getting chilly." He took note of the summer dress she was wearing. "You should put something on. Think I'll put my coat and rig back on."

"Is that necessary? You said no one was following." She opened the trunk, pulling out a retro Bolero and shrugged into the black sweater.

Glancing around, Daniel quickly donned his rig and duster. "Better to be cautious."

"Cautious?"

"You know what I meant, and don't give me that look." He stared at her, "Wow, you look amazing."

"Thank you. I like to come prepared. Take me to dinner?"

She crooked an arm for him to take and they walked arm-in-arm into the *24/7 All-Night* station. They laughed to themselves at the look the attendant gave them from behind the counter when they strolled up to him and asked to use the restroom. The shaggy-haired kid of twenty handed Veronica a large piece of driftwood with RETURN scribbled in red on the side, then went back to watching his small black-and-white TV. She returned shortly, and they exchanged the key.

Veronica stepped from one item to another along the back wall wondering what was worth eating. She was surprised at how calm she was. They were on the run from people wanting them dead, and yet, she felt Daniel had things under control. There was something about him other than all his years. Something about that crooked smile that made her tingle. Nothing about him made sense and she did not care.

"I must be out of my mind." She said aloud, staring absently at the shriveled hot dogs turning in front of her.

"Excuse me?"

The attendant was looking at her. She must have said that louder than she thought. "Sorry, just commenting on the selection."

"Stay away from the dogs. The owner won't throw them out. The sandwiches are almost expired too. If it was me, I'd go for the nachos and cheese, but the tamales are fresh so those shouldn't be too bad."

"Thank you."

"Ken. Kenny to my friends. You two are pretty dressed up for around here. You and your husband going someplace?"

"Oh, we're not married," she said and saw the glint of hope in the boy's face, "Not yet anyway. We're on our way to San Francisco. Unexpected death in the family." That should curtail any further conversation.

Daniel returned, handing the driftwood back to Kenny. "What's the verdict?"

"Kenny was telling me that if we don't want to get poisoned, we should go with the tamales."

"Good to know. Tamales it is then."

They talked as they gathered supplies for the drive.

"You said you found the cemetery?"

Veronica smiled. "Yes, *Hillside Cemetery*. It's somewhere in the Marina District overlooking the bay. They're transferring everything out to other cemeteries, seems some big land developer bought up the land. I wrote the address down."

"We won't have to worry about it until tomorrow, if the car decides to work."

They paid for their supplies and walked back to the car. Daniel glanced at Veronica.

"I think that boy has a crush on you."

"Jealous?"

"Maybe. He is much younger than I am."

She laughed out loud. "Daniel, everyone is younger than you are."

"Very funny," he chuckled.

•—•

The black BMW rolled up to the *24/7 All-Night* station and Smith stepped out. Other than an old, beat up lime-green Pinto and a midnight-blue Saturn SL, the place was empty. No sign of Dimico's car, not that he expected to see it. The tracking device showed them further up the road, about a half hour if he kept to the same pace.

He walked up to the non-attentive kid at the TV, taking note of the one camera facing the counter above the entry doors, another hiding between racks of cigarettes behind the counter. He cleared his throat but only received a mumble back.

"Yeah?"

"I'd like to ask you a few questions regarding some patrons that passed this way about a half hour ago."

"Whatever floats your boat." Ken responded, not looking up.

Smith tried not to show his annoyance with this kid. "There was a couple, man and woman, who stopped here. What can you tell me about them?"

"Who are you, her father?" Ken glanced up, "Sorry pal, old boyfriend?"

Smith tossed the badge on the countertop. "Official business, smart ass."

Ken sat up straight. "Whoa! Who are they? Some new age Bonnie and Clyde or something?"

"Something like that. What can you tell me about them?"

"Well, they were dressed nice, don't usually see that here," he eyed Smith, "Well, mostly don't see it here. They used the restroom. He let her go first, I thought that was nice of him."

Smith's patience was running out. "Did you catch where they were going?"

"Didn't pay much attention. Look man, she was hot! My attention was elsewhere if you know what I mean."

"That's it? Nothing else? You didn't hear anything?"

"What's your issue anyway?" Smith's mood was not helping Ken's.

This line of questioning wasn't getting Smith anywhere and he had lost his patience. He pointed to the two cameras, "These things work?"

"The one above the door is on the fritz, the other one doesn't have a tape in it." Ken stood up, "Not that you could look at them without a warrant anyway."

Smith grabbed the front of Ken's shirt, yanking him halfway over the counter, near his face. "I've had about enough of your sniveling attitude. What did they say while they were here? Give me that and I'll let you keep breathing."

"Wait, wait, wait! I don't know! I didn't pay much attention to anything but how she looked!"

Smith gripped the kid's shirt tighter.

"Wait a minute! She said something! Something about a death in the family!"

Smith was inches from Ken's face. He clenched his teeth and barked, "Who?"

"I don't know, they didn't say!" Ken's knees connected with the countertop as Smith pulled him against his face. "No, no wait! She said something about a cemetery!"

"What cemetery?"

"Umm, uh, H – H – Hill…Hillside! I think that was it! Yes, it was *Hillside Cemetery* in San Francisco!"

A different voice called out. "Hey, what are you doing to that boy?"

Smith turned to see a black man in is forties, well-muscled in his designer clothes, stride toward him with a piece of driftwood held like a club.

"This doesn't concern you."

"I don't think so." The man raised the makeshift club to strike and advanced.

Smith released Ken's shirt roughly, causing him to fall behind the counter. Reaching out with his right hand, he caught the club hand and twisted, snapping bone. Pulling his pistol with his left, he smashed the grip into the man's right temple, silencing his screams of pain. Smith stepped to the counter and pointed his Glock at the kid's face.

"Think very hard. When the police arrive, you were being robbed. The man back there interrupted, causing the thief to flee. Leave it at that and you live your pathetic life. Tell them why I was here, and I'll put a bullet between your eyes. You won't know where, you won't know when, but I will find you.

Smith saw the kid's pants suddenly go wet. He read the nametag on the kid's shirt, "You understand me Ken?"

Ken nodded very carefully, his eyes never leaving the silencer pointed at him. "My friends call me K – K – Kenny."

Smith took the badge and left. "See you around, Ken." Halfway to the BMW he made the call.

"Well?"

"They're headed to San Francisco, supposedly a death in the family."

"We'll fly in and meet you. Neither of them has any living family. Inform me of any changes when you get to San Francisco."

"As you wish."

CHAPTER SIXTEEN

SAN FRANCISCO, SEPTEMBER 26, 2:00 A.M.

Daniel nudged Veronica awake. They were parked in front of a motel off the beaten path in San Francisco. They dragged their worn-out bodies into the manager's office of the *Seagull Motel*. Cheap paintings of seagulls and the bay, possibly paint-by-numbers, adorned the walls. The smell of decay assailed their nostrils, a layer of film covered everything. He caught a look from her but rang the tinny bell before unconsciously wiping his hand on his pants.

They were greeted by the manager - stained wife-beater, boxers, even his tufts of matted hair seemed oily. Wreaking of non-filter cigarettes, he shuffled out of the back room.

"Suppose you'd be wanting a room?" He grumbled while lighting a cigarette.

"If it wouldn't be much trouble." Daniel tried a polite approach.

"After one in the morning, it's always trouble. Suppose you two don't want your significants knowing you're bangin' each other hard and long." He laughed with a nicotine rasp.

Daniel took Veronica's arm, shifting slightly in front of her to block the manager's view. "Look, we need a room. One with two beds and a kitchen. It would behoove you to keep a civil tongue in your head."

The Popeye-looking man shrugged, "Fifty bucks for the night, or any portion of the night. You slide the beds together, make sure you put 'em back after juicin' her."

Daniel avoided arguing, paying with cash and taking the key. They drove the car to the end unit, gathered their things and went inside. They were relieved to find the room free of grime, though it still smelled moldy. The small kitchen seemed clean enough, even the fake seagull paintings looked better.

After putting their things by the small table, Daniel pulled the sheets down from the closer bed. A thorough examination came up with nothing but a clean bed, no other occupants. He excused himself, returning from the car with two bags of groceries.

"You were asleep. Found a store that was open, so got us a few things."

He filled the refrigerator, finally taking a seat on the bed and stretching his worn muscles.

"You look tired, you should sleep." Veronica told him from the table where she had set up her laptop.

"I'm played out, but I'll be all right. I need to clean my weapon, check the others. We still need to figure out where this cemetery is."

"Where exactly are we anyway?"

"Marina District. Not too far away from Pier 39, if that helps," he said through a yawn.

He missed what she said after that. Without realizing it, he had laid down, passing out from exhaustion.

•━━•

Less than a half hour after Daniel Collum passed out on the bed, the black BMW pulled up on the street by the *Seagull Motel*. Smith turned off the car's engine, flicked off the lights, and took a quick recon of the motel. There were only two cars in the lot. The one down at the far end was Dimico's silver sedan. The other, an old AMC gold Gremlin, rusted and ill-kept, was parked near the manager's office.

Pulling out his cell phone as he sat back in the car, he punched in a number and waited. It only took one ring before he was connected.

"Well?"

"We're all in San Francisco. They're at a small motel called the *Seagull*, not far from Pier 39."

"Good," Bennett said coldly. "We're at a hotel near the cemetery. I'm betting Hunter is planning to bury the files there. We'll take them out tomorrow."

"Why wait until the cemetery? The motel is out of the way, no one else but the manager. I can take care of all three, get the files, and hand everything over within the hour."

"Absolutely not. You will wait until they go to the cemetery. We will meet there and take them out together."

"Why take the chance, sir? The cemetery is in the open, it will be daylight, possible witnesses, why expose yourself?"

"The cemetery is shut down. It's a Saturday, so no one will be working. They know we're after them, and yet, they risk this detour. Hunter is planning to use the files as a bargaining chip by hiding them there. Until then, we don't know for sure where the files are. We stick with my plan!" Bennett's tone left no argument.

"Understood. I will call when they leave the motel." There was a click, ending the call.

"Smith good with the plan?" Royston asked gingerly.

"He'll do as he's told. That's what he's paid for."

Bennett threw the phone at the bed, satisfied with the sound it made on the plush pillow. His face was three shades of red from talking with Smith. He caught Royston picking up the bottle of rum from the bar. This would not do.

"No drinking until this is done. Take a bottle of water if you need to quench your thirst."

"Sorry, I wasn't thinking."

Bennett began pacing, "I can't figure out what Hunter is up to. It has me at a loss."

"Why would he hide something in a cemetery that's being torn up? Maybe there's another reason to go there."

"That's what has me stymied. He must know something we don't about the location. I'm missing a piece of the puzzle and it's pissing me off."

"What's the plan for tomorrow?"

Bennett turned his cobra smile to Royston. "Hunter won't expect to see us at the cemetery, that's where he'll be at his weakest. We put Smith in the middle as bait. As soon as you see Hunter drop, take the kill shot on Smith."

"What if Hunter takes Smith out first?"

"Then you take out the girl and I'll have the pleasure of killing Hunter myself."

"Are you sure you want to eliminate Smith? He's been an asset, he's also dangerous."

"Then you better not miss." Bennett answered cold-blooded.

CHAPTER SEVENTEEN

SAN FRANCISCO, SEPTEMBER 26, 9:00 A.M.

Daniel woke to the sunlight streaming in through the slit in the curtains of the motel room. Pushing away the fog of sleep, he breathed in deeply, and felt Veronica's arm on his chest. She was on her left side, facing him, her right arm over him as she slept. She had comfortably melded her body to his. Emotions welled inside him. He gently ran his hand through her lush, red hair. When he looked at her face, he saw her eyes were open.

"I'm sorry. I didn't mean to wake you."

"That's all right. It felt nice," she smiled.

"You know there was another bed you could have slept on."

"But that one didn't have you in it."

Daniel gazed into her eyes, forgetting everything else. With his hand still caressing her hair, he impulsively leaned to her, softly kissing her lips.

"That was nice too." she said. "I knew I could fall asleep if I was with you. It just felt safer."

Daniel's eyes traveled down her body. He took in the contours of her curves, and how her simple white bra and underwear hugged them. Feeling his own body heating up, he sat upright. Partly to get a little distance between them, partly to regain his composure.

Daniel made his way to the bathroom before turning back to face her. "I'm going to take a shower, maybe a cold one," he smiled at her.

When Daniel came out of the bathroom, Veronica held up the pad with her notes, "I found it. The cemetery is near *Lands End*, overlooking South Bay, so it's not too far off from here. I wrote down the location of the two graves, so it shouldn't be hard to find."

Daniel began removing everything from the duffle bag. "Why don't you take a shower? I'll see if I can iron the wrinkles out of this suit."

Veronica headed for the bathroom. "I'll fix us something when I get out, you still have to clean your things."

"If there's time. I really want to see her. That's not odd, is it?"

"Not at all. This is something you've been needing to do for a long time." With that, she closed the door.

Daniel shifted his service revolver from the Great War slightly on the left side of his waist. He drew it a few times, checking the feel. Finally satisfied, he gazed down at his Colt wrapped in the leather belt. He ran his fingers over the well-oiled leather lovingly.

"How I've tried to get you to do that to my body." Veronica said playfully.

Daniel noticed she had changed into a high waist Vivian swing skirt. Its black contrasted well with her white blouse. She had also put on ankle strap black heels. "I've known this woman a lot longer than you. Give me time," he winked.

Daniel opened the old wooden box and began filling the belt loops with the bullets he had made for his old Colt. That done, he donned the rig at his right hip, taking a few practice draws for good measure.

"I am officially turned on by that and I don't know why. Are you sure you're going to need all that firepower?" Veronica asked.

"With everything that's happened so far, I'm not going to take any more chances." Putting his coat on, he then added the duster, feeling the weight distribution. He checked himself in the one mirror opposite the bed to make sure the weapons were concealed.

"I really have fallen for a cowboy. How do I look?" she asked, "I wanted to look my best for your wife. That's not silly, is it?"

He crossed to her, kissing her lightly on the cheek. "Not silly at all. Thank you. We better get out of here," Daniel said. "We've pushed our luck long enough."

CHAPTER EIGHTEEN

HILLSIDE CEMETERY, SEPTEMBER 26, 10:15 A.M.

The short drive to the cemetery had been noticeably quiet. They parked just outside the cemetery as bulldozers blocked the entry. Before they left the car, Daniel asked Veronica if she had enough room inside her Oxford briefbag for the files Dimico had given him.

"I think I can fit it all in there."

Daniel put his Magnum inside the glove compartment. Wouldn't hurt to have it close, just in case. He grabbed his metal case and they walked without a word into the *Hillside Cemetery*.

The entire front section of the cemetery had been torn up by heavy machinery. The graves that had been there for over fifty years, had long been removed to their new homes at other locations. The landscape reminded Daniel of France during the war; also the great earthquake which had taken his wife. Fitting that that thought would come to his mind, as they were now here to pay their respects to that very woman.

As they drew closer to the headstones, tombs, crypts, and statues that were all that was left of the cemetery, Daniel unconsciously took Veronica's hand. She squeezed it lightly to let him know she was there for him.

There was the feeling of death and loss in the smell wafting in on the breeze from the bay. It did not seem to matter if it was a lake, beachside, or harbor area. That smell of decay, nature's decay, was always there. The few remaining trees that still stood, showed the signs of age and slow death themselves. As they weaved their way through the tall headstones without saying a word, they noticed many had been worn away, by time and lack of care. So many were hardly readable from the constant barrage of the harbor weather over time. They felt regret, and a little shame, for the forgotten.

Reaching an area overlooking South Bay, Veronica whispered, "We're here."

Daniel stopped and stared at the headstone on the right. It leaned slightly to the left, almost as if it were reaching to touch the headstone next to it. He could make out enough on the headstone to read. It sent a chill down his spine.

DANIEL CALLOM
???? – 1906
SAN FRANCISCO EARTHQUAKE

Veronica had also been staring at his headstone and involuntarily squeezed his hand again.

"This would have creeped me out more if they hadn't spelled your name incorrectly."

Daniel nodded, "Still pretty creepy. I wonder why they even bothered. It's not like they found a body." That statement hung in the air for a moment before he looked at her, "Or did they? My God, what if they found someone and thought it was me?"

"Don't think that way Daniel. It will only drive you insane." She nodded to the headstone next to his. "Forget about that. This is what you came here for."

Daniel turned his attention to the headstone his was tilting to, apt as he always felt a pull when thinking of her.

KATHRYN CALLOM
1852 – 1906
SAN FRANCISCO EARTHQUAKE
IN LOVING MEMORY

Daniel released his grip on Veronica's hand. Kneeling on one knee, he reached out to touch the top of his wife's headstone. The cold of the stone went through his fingertips. His duster whipped slightly from the chill of the early fall breeze working its way to them from the bay. He felt none of it as his fingers slowly traced their way down across the indented letters on the face of the headstone.

He knelt there for some time, just feeling the letters of her name. He did not know why someone had added the extra sentiment, but was very happy it was there, as it was true. He had not stopped thinking about Kathryn since he had left her that day. Everything he had done from then until now, in some small part, had been because of her.

Another breeze passed through the stone markers. Feeling the chill on his face, Daniel turned to Veronica. "I'm sorry, what was I thinking? You're cold."

She shook her head, "I'll be fine. You've waited a long time for this. Take all the time you need."

He smiled that crooked smile of his. "Thank you. Would you mind if I have a moment alone?"

"Absolutely, I understand." She smiled reassuringly, walking just a couple of feet away to give him some privacy.

Daniel turned back to Kathryn's headstone. Standing over it, he thought for a moment before talking softly to it. "My love. I am so sorry that I left you the way I did. I keep thinking back to that day and wish that I had been the one to stop long enough for the picture. If I had, you would still have been alive, and I might have made it through. Yes, I know I'm not indestructible, but I've always had luck on my side. Especially when I wished for nothing else but a swift end."

He turned his head briefly to look at the back of Veronica. Smiling gently, he turned back to the headstone.

"I want you to know that I will always love you, but I have come to feel for another woman. She's like you in so many ways, and yet nothing like you in so many others. She wanted to look her best for you today. I think if you could have met her you would have liked her. She makes me feel alive again, Kathryn. Something I have not felt since you left me. I hope you will give me your blessing to move on. She can help me be the man I want to be again. The man that will also honor your memory. I will always love you, Kathryn."

Daniel brought his right hand to his lips, kissed his fingers, then placed them gently on top of his wife's headstone.

Veronica caught snippets of Daniel's one-sided conversation. She felt her own emotions swell, and was close to tearing up herself, when she thought she saw movement headed in their direction through the headstones.

She turned to see him kiss his hand, placing it on the headstone. She took a step toward him, hating to interrupt his moment. "Daniel?"

She heard a puffing noise, then felt something punch her in the back, the pain knocking the wind out of her lungs. The force of the blow threw her into Daniel's arms.

On the right of the couple's position, Bennett was not advancing as quickly as the others. The crouched stance put a strain on his aged knees. Smith had already taken up position against a statue of a fallen angel. Royston just about at a gnarled tree on the left position. He smiled to himself when he saw the metal case in Hunter's left hand. A puff sound, followed by another went off, and he watched as both Hunter and Jenkins fell in a spray of blood.

Royston saw both Hunter and the woman go down to the ground. Following Bennett's plan, he turned his sights on Smith. Aiming quickly, he fired, hitting the left wing of the statue next to Smith's head. Smith turned immediately with his lightning reflexes, firing back. His shot hit the bark of the tree, showering splinters into Royston's face. The dislodged pellets of wood forced him to hide behind the gnarled trunk.

"Shit! I knew this was a bad idea."

Knowing Smith would not stop until he was dead, Royston positioned himself behind the tree, taking the occasional blind shot. He could feel his heart thumping furiously in his chest.

•—•

Veronica slammed into Daniel, taking them both down to the ground. He had the air taken out of him momentarily when they fell, as he had fallen flat on his back, with Veronica landing directly on top of him. He could tell she was in pain. "Daniel?"

"Vee, don't move. You've been shot."

"It's hard to breath. Felt like someone punched me in the back." Her voice just above a whisper.

Daniel got to his knees. "Hold on, Vee. I'll get you out of here."

He felt in his pockets for anything he could use as a makeshift bandage, when his hands felt something inside his coat pockets - firecrackers, matches, and two rubber bands from his assault at his home. He had forgotten he had transferred them to his gray coat. Now, how to use them.

"Daniel, I love you." Veronica's voice was beginning to slur. He glanced down, seeing a slight pink foam on her lips.

"Veronica, stay with me." He glanced above his wife's headstone to see Smith and Royston exchanging shots at each other. Out of the corner of his left eye, he saw Bennett, low to the ground. His path would eventually put Bennett perpendicular to where they were hiding. "You have to stay awake."

"I'm tired. Jus wanna sleep." Her eyes blinked slowly, taking on a glassy luster.

"No, don't sleep. You're in shock. You have to stay awake, understand?"

Daniel saw Bennett was inching closer, too close. An idea suddenly came to him. He pulled his S&W revolver, firing at Bennett, the man went down in a shower of shards from the headstone in front of him. Quickly scooping up a small rock, Daniel took a large portion of the firecrackers, securing them to the stone with the good rubber band.

Gauging the distance to Royston, Daniel thought he could throw it far enough. He struck a match on the back side of his headstone. Lighting the fuse of the firecrackers, he threw the package as far as he could. The projectile soared over Royston's position, going off just before impacting the ground. The firecrackers went off in a cacophony of mini bursts. Royston whirled around, firing blindly at what he assumed was a threat.

Daniel watched as Smith took three quick shots at Royston who had left himself open. Royston went down from the hail of bullets. Daniel fired his Smith & Wesson, catching Smith twice in the chest. Smith went down, his body still.

Daniel had just enough time to hear the familiar register of the Glock as the bullet entered his left thigh. The impact caused him to lose his balance, and he fell against Kathryn's headstone. Hearing another shot, he thought the end had finally come, but the impact of the bullet took a chip out of his own headstone, missing him. Instinctively, Daniel fired while leaning against the headstone, hitting Bennett squarely in the gut with his shot. Bennett's gun flew out of his hand, his body falling behind a low stone tomb.

Returning his attention back to Veronica, Daniel saw her eyes were closed. He struggled to wake her but to no avail. Shifting her body less than gently, he noted no exit wound. The bullet must have lodged inside her. Rolling her on her stomach, he tore open her bloodied shirt, using the hole from the bullet for purchase. He examined the wound, still bleeding from her back, just above her bloodied bra. Her breath was coming out in wheezing gasps. Daniel feared Veronica might have been hit in her left lung, though the height of the wound could also mean something far worse.

Reaching back into his pocket, he pulled out the useless, broken rubber band, shoving it into the wound as best he could. Breaking open the remaining firecrackers, he dumped the contents into the wound. Lighting a match off his own headstone, he brought it down to her wound. There was a moment, before the lit match reached her back, when it began to flicker. Daniel held his breath and the flame did likewise. The black powder flashed quickly, causing Veronica to gasp in pain, waking her briefly.

"Vee, I have to get you to the hospital. Just stay with me a little longer."

"Can't keep... sleep... cold."

He shoved his pistol back into its holster. He strapped the leather bag over his head, reached down, and picked Veronica up in his arms. The metal case caught his eye and his heart fell with regret. There was no way he would be able to carry that and Veronica at the same time. Maybe this was as it should be, his past back together again. Without another thought, he ran as best he could on his bad leg, through the cemetery to their car.

Veronica lay heavy in his arms. He tried not to think of the term 'dead weight' as he laid her in the back of the sedan. Jumping in, he worked his way around the rental cars, to the road.

"Vee, you awake?" No answer. "Veronica, don't you dare leave me, I love you." Still no answer.

Daniel drove, all the while, cursing Bennett as he had never cursed before. Bennett. He should have made sure the shot had killed him, but he didn't have time if he wanted to keep Veronica alive. He knew he had hit the ringleader of the Haig Men in the gut. He remembered how that kind of wound was fatal, back in the days when men wore guns on their hip. At least he would no longer have to worry about Royston and Smith. Those pages had closed. Once he could be sure Veronica was safe, and in good care at the hospital, he would drive back and make sure Bennett was done.

Daniel could hear Veronica's labored breathing getting worse. Skidding the sedan into the emergency vehicle access lane, he pulled to a stop in front of the automatic door entrance.

Daniel winced in pain from the gunshot to his thigh. Paying no heed to the injury, he opened the back door of the sedan. Roughly pulling Veronica out of the car, and into his arms, he noticed the pink foam at her lips had turned to a red trickle. He ran through the sliding doors, yelling for help.

Veronica was quickly taken from him by multiple people in scrubs. As they moved her to one of the emergency stations, a nurse pulled him aside. Daniel couldn't take his eyes off Veronica as they turned her on her back, going to work on her wound.

"Sir, can you tell me what happened?" the nurse asked.

"We were visiting an old family grave at the *Hillside Cemetery*, before they move the remains, and these men just started shooting at each other from nowhere. She was caught in the crossfire. I managed to get her out of there, and here, as fast as I could. I tried to plug the wound, but I don't know if it helped."

"Were you injured at all?"

Daniel glanced down, noticing his duster covered the wound to his leg. The blood coming from the wound was not noticeable, yet.

"No, no, I'm fine. Just take care of her.

"What is her name?"

"Veronica Jenkins. She's a freelance writer."

"Are you her husband?" the nurse asked.

"No, just a friend. She doesn't have any living family."

"Please stay over there." She pointed to an area with three uncomfortable wooden chairs off to one side. "The police will want to speak with you."

"I understand. Let me move my car out of the way and I'll be right back."

The nurse nodded, and Daniel limped back outside. Getting back into the car, he drove it to the back section of the emergency parking lot, where the visitor parking slots were located. Removing the holster carrying his Smith & Wesson, he placed the rig in his duffle in the trunk, then sat for a moment to decide on his next course of action. With everything that had happened, he didn't feel safe being unarmed, so made the decision to leave the Colt strapped to his leg. He should leave while he had the chance, but he needed to tend to his leg wound. Instinctively, he returned through the sliding doors. Making sure the nurse saw him, he walked to the spot she had indicated, and sat.

Daniel heard them feverishly working on Veronica behind the curtains. *I can't protect her if I stay here.* Forcing the logical side of his mind to take control, he stood up, and walked over to the drinking fountain. He knew the fountain was still within eyeshot of the nurse, so waited for a moment when she was preoccupied. When that moment came, he walked around the corner, and out of her vision. He needed to find a storage room, and bandage his leg as best he could, out from under prying eyes.

John Bennett leaned against the tomb where he had fallen. How could this have gone so wrong? Everything had been planned out to perfection. They had done everything as he was sure it would happen, and yet, he was laying here bleeding, gutshot. He had tried to get up, more than once, but the pain was excruciating. Also, he was having difficulty getting his legs to do what he wanted. He needed to find a way back to the car, and to a hospital, or he might bleed out.

Hunter had beaten him at every turn and gotten away. Bennett had seen him carry the Jenkins woman in his arms. He had a clear shot at Hunter's back, but had been unable to take the shot. He couldn't reach the gun that had flown out of his hand when he was hit. He cursed himself for his inability.

He grimaced as another spasm of pain wracked his body. Gripping his arms around his stomach, he attempted to quell some of the pain. Make the long crawl back to the car? He better do that, and soon.

His thoughts were interrupted by the sound of footfalls headed in his direction, crunching on the dried, brown grass. He wondered if the woman had died and Hunter had come back to finish him. He made another attempt to reach for the gun, but it was just too far away, and every motion sent white hot spasms of pain through his body.

"Hello, Bennett," the voice that addressed him was jovial.

"Smith?" Bennett couldn't believe his ears. He saw Smith come around the blind side of the tomb. Easily noticeable were two bullet holes in his shirt at chest level, but no blood. His forehead crinkled in confusion. "I don't understand."

Smith tore open his shirt to show the Kevlar vest underneath, the two bullets lodged into the weave.

"I figured you and Royston would try and take me out after Hunter was dead. I decided on a little insurance. Good thing I had, otherwise Hunter would have finished me off."

"I don't know what you're talking about." Bennett felt himself go cold inside when he spied the silenced Glock hanging loosely in Smith's left hand.

Smith turned his head in the direction of Royston's body, smiled, and turned back to Bennett.

"Well, I'd ask him about it, but I don't think he'll be able to answer any questions. Having worked with you, on quite a few contracts, I'm familiar with your tactics."

Bennett feigned shock, sputtering a protest, but Smith cut him off.

"Please don't insult my intelligence. I may only be a hired gunman to you, but I'm a professional assassin. As such, I didn't get to where I am without using my brain."

Smith set his gun on top of the tomb lid, above and out of reach of Bennett. He took off his coat and shirt, before removing the damaged vest.

"I'm going to have some pretty deep bruises for a little while, but they'll heal," he said, rubbing his T-shirt over his chest, while looking at the bloodied area of Bennett's shirt. "Unlike you. Gut wounds can be quite a bitch."

Bennett eyed the silencer end of the Glock above him. He knew he couldn't reach it, and he knew he was in trouble.

Smith squatted beside Bennett, "So tell me, what's in those files you want so badly, John?"

"Nothing that would interest you, really. Just something from the past." He could feel beads of sweat trickle down his temple.

"Hmm, interesting. I may have to look into that."

Smith stepped around the tomb and returned with a metal case in his hand.

"This thing has one heck of a combination lock on it. I suppose I could shoot the thing open, but I'd be afraid to ruin what's inside that's so important to you. No bother. I know where to find the man who holds the combination."

"Look, Smith. You get me to a hospital, and I'll give you double. No hard feelings." Sweat dripped into his eyes and he swiped it away.

"I don't need any more of your money, John. I'm good."

Smith turned his head in the direction the cars were parked, his gaze a mile away.

"This has become personal between Hunter and I now. Killing him will be a pleasure." A rare smile crossed his face as he said the last.

"At least call for an ambulance. I don't know how long I can hold out here."

Smith returned his attention back to the tomb Bennett was leaning against. He caressed the head of the small statue which adorned the top of the tomb. He took in the kneeling angel, its hands clasped together as it gazed up to the heavens.

Chuckling softly, he said, "You know, John, I was also standing next to an angel today. Mine must have been an Angel of Mercy, as it took pity on me, causing Royston to miss his target."

He picked up his pistol, pointing it directly at Bennett.

"You, on the other hand, are lying at the feet of the Angel of Death."

"Smith, NO!" Bennett raised his bloodied hands in a pitiful attempt to defend himself as Smith fired, the puff of the weapon and Bennett's cry the only sounds as the bullet entered between his eyes.

CHAPTER NINETEEN

THE HOSPITAL, SEPTEMBER 26, 11:02 A.M.

Daniel managed to bandage his leg well enough to stop the bleeding. Now he had to find a way to slip past the police and out of the hospital.

Daniel moved through the hospital corridors, stepping into random rooms to avoid the uniforms. Eventually, he found his way out of the hospital, on the opposite side of the building from where he was parked. He knew he stood out wearing his duster, but that could not be avoided. His makeshift job bandaging his leg was enough to attract attention, and unless California's laws had changed recently, the gun he wore at his hip would be enough to draw the interest of anyone.

Taking the long route around the parking area, back to where the sedan was located, he turned his sights back to the emergency entrance. He desperately wanted to go back in, knowing he could not. He could only hope Veronica would make it through okay. As he stared at the entry, he noticed a man, and thought he saw a ghost. Smith was walking directly toward the sliding doors. He was moving too casually for someone who should have been shot. Worse, Smith was carrying his metal case.

Daniel ran back to the sedan on his bad leg, as best he could. His mind raced, wondering how Smith had found them, when he caught the flash of something reflected in a small pool of radiator fluid next to the car. In that watery mirror, he saw the red pulse of a tracking device. *Damn them all!*

Throwing open the passenger door, he tore open the glove compartment. He pulled out the cell phone and its battery, which Veronica had tossed there earlier, and shoved the battery back in.

He dialed Information and had them put the call through. He agonized as the seconds ticked away with each ring of the phone. Finally, he heard the familiar voice of the nurse he had spoken to earlier.

"*St. Michael's Emergency.*"

"Yes, I need you to do something for me. There is a man who just walked into your emergency room. Tall, with sandy blonde hair, carrying a metal case. His name is Smith. He is currently working with the federal government on a case involving the woman who was recently brought in with a gunshot wound."

"I see him."

"I need you to call him over. Tell him that Special Agent Robert Hunter is on the phone. I need to speak to him urgently."

There was a pause on the other end of the line. Daniel crossed his fingers, hoping this would work.

Daniel heard the nurse's muffled voice on the phone. After what seemed an eternity, Smith's smugly confident voice answered.

"Special Agent Hunter, so good to hear your voice. I do hope you are doing well."

"Smith, leave Veronica Jenkins alone. You want me, not her."

"Correct on both counts, though I do have an outstanding agreement about Ms. Jenkins."

"Smith, I'm warning you, leave her alone."

There was a pause on the other end. They both knew Smith had the upper hand. "Truth be told, Hunter, I doubt I'll have to worry about Ms. Jenkins. I can see them working on her as we speak, and it's not looking all that good right now. They've had to zap her once already while we've been talking."

Daniel steeled himself. What Smith said could be true, but it could also be a ruse to make him do something reckless. "What do you want, Smith?"

"I thought that was abundantly clear, Special Agent Hunter. What I want is you. We have some unfinished business to attend to. There's also the matter of those files Bennett wanted."

"Wanted?" Did his bullet kill Bennett?

"John was in desperate need of medical attention when I found him. Consider his demise a gift of good faith from me. I think we're allowed to bend the rules a little."

"I'm not sure I understand." Daniel was quite sure what Smith was up to, but the longer he could keep him away from Veronica the better.

"Please. Don't insult my intelligence, Hunter. Bennett did that." His voice came through, cold and biting.

"I'll make you a deal. I'll give you the files and a chance at me. In return, you leave Miss Jenkins to live out her life without your interference."

"I knew you were a man of honor, Hunter." Smith's voice sounded satisfied and pleased. "How do you propose we conclude this transaction?"

Daniel thought for a moment. He needed some time, and a place away from the hospital, but close enough to keep Smith from changing his mind about Veronica.

"We meet at the end of Pier 31. It's out of the way and should work for what I think you want. It's not too far away either." Daniel looked at his pocketwatch and was surprised it was only 11:15 a.m. It had felt like hours since he had brought Veronica to the hospital.

"And what time would you propose we meet?"

Daniel almost laughed for a second as the thought struck him. The irony of it rolled off his tongue. "High noon."

"How apropos. One of my favorite films. We meet at the agreed time, and regardless of the outcome, Ms. Jenkins can live out whatever life she may have left, without my interference. You have my professional word."

"Agreed. I know you have a tracking device on the car, so you can use that as proof that I'm keeping my word."

"Noon it is then." Smith hung up.

Daniel waited, watching the sliding doors of the emergency entrance, until he saw Smith exit. With that assurance he got into the car and headed for Pier 31.

Daniel spent the short drive trying to clear his mind of Veronica, focusing on what he had learned about Smith. The man was too fast. There had to be something he could use to his advantage against him. There just had to be.

●———•

The black BMW rolled up slowly to the end of Pier 31, coming to a stop, twenty feet from the silver sedan. The two stared at each other briefly through their windshields, before opening their doors. The brisk air of the harbor met them as they stepped out.

Daniel waited behind the door of his car for protection. Smith might be a man of his word, but Daniel wasn't going to take any chances. He did not have long to wait to find out. Smith stepped around his own door, taking up a position in front of the BMW, metal case in hand. Setting the case down, he carefully opened his coat, showing the silenced Glock in its specially-made holster. Smith raised his eyebrows, waiting for Daniel's approval, before taking off his coat. Folding it neatly on the hood of the BMW, he turned back to face Daniel.

Daniel saw the two bullet holes in Smith's shirt. "Bulletproof vest?"

Smith unbuttoned the damaged shirt, showing his T-shirt for inspection. "It had its use when it was needed."

Daniel stepped back to the passenger door to retrieve the bag holding the files. Moving around to the front of the sedan, he tossed the bag about halfway between them.

"It would seem you are not completely unharmed yourself," Smith indicated Daniel's left leg.

Daniel shrugged. "Nothing that will affect our meeting, I assure you."

Smith smiled slightly at this before glancing briefly at the bag between them. "What have we here?"

Daniel cocked his head in confusion. "The files you wanted."

It was now Smith's turn to look confused as he pointed to the metal case next to him. "And this? I thought these were the files in question. I just didn't want to ruin what was inside trying to bypass your intricate combination lock."

"Just some personal items of mine. The files you want are in the bag."

Smith stood there, pondering for a moment. "I must admit, I'm curious about those files. I'm not normally prone to that feeling, but with everything that has happened, my interest is piqued. I can't help but wonder what Bennett was so worried about that he not only wanted you dead, but also wanted those files back."

"There's nothing in there except information on me."

Smith cocked his head slightly.

"Seriously," Daniel stalled, still trying to find something he could use against Smith. "Oh, there's information in there that might cause someone to reopen a closed file, if they read between the lines. If Bennett had taken the time to talk to Morgan Dimico about what he'd found out, those files would have been more damaging to me in the long run."

"Again, you've piqued my curiosity. Without me reading through it all, could you expand on that?"

Daniel considered this request for a moment, deciding there was no harm in telling this man who he was. After this was over, Smith would either have the files in hand, or be dead.

"My real name is not Robert Hunter. It's Daniel Collum." Smith's eyebrow raised only slightly to this. "I infiltrated the Secret Service with the sole purpose of protecting President Reagan from assassination."

Smith's face turned to a frown in disappointment. "If you're going to make up a story, it would be best if you made up one a bit more believable. I don't see the Secret Service hiring teenaged boys."

That gave Daniel an idea he hadn't thought of before. Possibly the only thing that might give him an edge.

"You wanted to know what was in the files, I'm telling you. My name is Daniel Collum, born 1848, in Ireland. I immigrated to America with my parents, joining the Union army as a drummer boy." He could see he was angering Smith, so laid it out with the confidence of someone with nothing to lose.

"I've fought in the Civil War, the Indian Wars, World War I, and World War II. I've survived through them all. The files are proof of this. Pictures, falsified birth certificates, death certificates. It's all in there. I have spent over a century changing my identity to keep myself safe." The anger in Smith's face faltered as Daniel told his story.

"I have been shot a number of times, and yet, I still live. I have even tried to end my life, to no avail. Oh, I can feel pain. I'm sure I've been through more pain than you will ever know or can conceive of. The files will prove all this. Did you not wonder why we were at that cemetery?"

Concern began to show on Smith's face as all this information was thrown at him. "We assumed you were there to hide the files, though I had my own doubts. Why hide something in a location that was being torn up?"

"We were there to see my wife."

"That's not possible. That cemetery has been closed for over fifty years. What information I do have on you, no record shows you having been married." Smith couldn't hide the quiver in his voice, nor the confusion on his face.

"It's true. Other than Ms. Jenkins, you are now the only other living person to know the truth about me. My wife was Kathryn Collum. She died during the Quake of 1906. My son's family died in the Galveston hurricane in 1900, and my daughter eventually died of old age in Boston. I had the privilege to stand alongside the men of the Fighting 69th against the Confederate States. I rode with Custer. Have flown a biplane and been shot down by a German pilot. At Pearl Harbor, I never made it off the ground when the Japanese attacked. I was once one of Elliott Ness' Untouchables, and survived Bennett's Haig Men when they tried to take over the government in 1981." Now for the kicker, and he'd better try and sell this as best he could, if he had any hope of living through this.

"I -- am -- immortal."

Smith stood there, staring at him, for what seemed a long time. Even though that stare sent shivers through him, Daniel stood his ground, giving his own stony glare right back. There was no emotion on his adversary's face that he could see, but there was a hint of doubt that he caught in the eyes. Doubt was good. Doubt might make the difference.

Smith's face suddenly cracked, and he let out a booming laugh. "I must admit, you had me going there. High noon, the long duster you're wearing. Such good touches. If you had been wearing a Stetson, the picture would have been complete."

Motioning to the bag between them, Smith said, "What you say sounds more like fable than reality – but I'm willing to believe you on one condition. Allow me one moment to peruse the files. No gunplay or trickery while I inspect them."

"My word of honor," Daniel stated with conviction. It might not be the smartest move, and would probably get him killed, but he was still a man of his word.

Smith nodded with satisfaction, moving the short distance to the bag. Kneeling beside it, he pulled the files out. He began going through the pictures, paperwork, and documents inside. In the beginning, he only glanced at the information in the files, but as each page was turned, he began to flip through the contents more quickly. He had hardly made a real dent in them before he threw everything back inside the bag. Standing up, he pointed an accusing finger down at the bag holding the files.

"Do you take me for a fool? A well-developed piece of fiction, written by Ms. Jenkins. I'm disappointed in you, Mr. Hunter, or whoever you are. I showed up in good faith to this meeting, and all you give in return is a bag full of junk."

Daniel could see he was losing the edge he had, but he had one last chance.

"The metal case behind you. You wanted to know what was in it. I'll tell you the combination and you can have a look before we finish this."

Smith opened his mouth to say something, but instead stepped back to the metal case. Glancing at his watch, he nodded. "All right,

Hunter. We still have some time before noon. I'll give you those last few moments to humor me."

"The combination happens to be the birth years of my wife, my son, and my daughter."

"For someone who seems quite intelligent, that's not the brightest password you could use."

"That's if anyone knew of my family." He pointed to the metal case number combinations. "Ready?"

Smith put the metal case on the hood of the BMW, "Ready."

"1852 . . . 1870 . . . 1873."

Smith entered each number sequence in turn, a frown creasing his brow. When he entered the last digit, there was the unmistakable click of the lock mechanism releasing. He reached to open the lid but paused.

"What's wrong, Smith? I thought you wanted to know what was inside."

The color of his face changed to a bright red, from anger or embarrassment, Daniel couldn't tell. Forcefully opening the case, Daniel gave him instructions.

"The journal on top you should leave 'til the last. The tape recorder is Frank Thomas' confession. You might want to take a close look at the photographs I have there first. After that, give a look at the flag. From what I can gather, you might know what it is. Then we can talk about the journal."

Smith gave a sidelong glance to Daniel but did as he was instructed. Placing the journal and recorder on the hood of the car, he began going through the pictures. He scrutinized each photograph as it brought forth Daniel's life. He looked up once, to stare at his adversary, before moving to the flag. Without removing it from its protective cover he uttered, "This can't be what I think it is."

"It can, and it is."

Smith's hand hovered over the plastic, as if afraid to touch it. Suddenly he came out of his reverie.

"It's not possible! These are the things of fairytales and boogeymen, not reality!"

Daniel watched as Smith shifted away from the case, a slight falter in his otherwise methodical step. He felt a moment of pity for the man.

"I'm sorry, Smith. It is possible, and it's definitely no fairytale. From what I have been able to gather, I look to be about fifty-three years of age. In reality, I am now one hundred and sixty-seven years old."

"How is this even conceivable?"

Daniel could hardly hear Smith's voice on the bay breeze and assumed he was talking to himself, but he went ahead and answered.

"I don't know. All I can tell you is that I'm standing here in front of you. You saw the files, the photographs, the flag." He glanced up at the sun briefly, seeing it was almost above them. Slowly taking out his pocketwatch, he confirmed there were just a few minutes left. Smiling, in spite of the situation, he said "Our time for jawing is up. You have the files if you want them, but you'll have to draw against me to keep them."

Daniel drew back his duster to reveal the Colt sitting on his right thigh. Putting away the pocketwatch, he took hold of the flap with his left hand behind his back, so it would not get in the way when he had to draw the weapon.

Smith took one look at the sight of Daniel in that pose and began to laugh uncontrollably, almost maniacally. He held up his left hand, palm out to Daniel, signaling for time to compose himself.

"I must say, you look every part the gunslinger, Collum, or Hunter, or whoever you are. Are you seriously inviting me to a duel?" He glanced to the sky and back to Daniel, "at 'High Noon' as you put it?"

"Yes, in a nutshell. Poetic, wouldn't you say?"

Smith regained control, nodding consent to Daniel. "I accept your terms, but may I first remove the silencer from my weapon?"

"You may."

As Smith removed his weapon from its holster, unscrewing the silencer from the end, Daniel noticed a familiar steeple from his past in the distance. Pointing to the landmark, he laid out the rules casually.

"When the last bell rings, we draw and shoot. Until one of us lives and one of us dies."

Smith set the silencer down, shaking his head in wonder.

"I cannot believe I'm about to do this, but what a story to tell." The distant church bell chimed off the twelve o'clock hour. Smiling, he said "Do not ask for whom the bell . . ."

Daniel watched Smith's stance and face. He realized, with a sinking feeling, he was still in trouble. Even with everything Smith had learned, there was still disbelief. Smith was a black and white kind of man, and the shade of grey Daniel had tried to force on him just did not fit into the man's psyche. With the chiming of the bell he knew he was about out of time. He needed to throw one last bit of doubt in his opponent's mind before the last chime rang out.

"I've got to admit, you've got grit. Are you a well-read man, Smith?"

"Odd time to bring that up, but yes, I would like to think so. Funny thing is, my favorites have always been the westerns. Louis L'Amour, Forrest Carter, Zane Grey, and such." Smith looked calmly back to Daniel.

"Good. Then I'm sure you've heard of, and possibly have read, *The Virginian*?"

"Owen Wister. Yes, more than once. Why?" The bell rang out the second chime.

"Wister was a frequent guest in my hotel in Dodge City. Back in the day. I think I gave him a few ideas for his book."

"Interesting. Wister give you any credit in the novel?" That same lack of belief in his voice as the wind kicked up a little with the third chime.

"Humor me. Take a quick look, about the middle of the journal. It deals with the *Occidental Hotel*."

Smith grabbed up the journal, carelessly flipping through the pages as the bells rang six. Finding the few pages Daniel mentioned, he read through them quickly, then jumped back to the beginning to read the owner's name again.

"Now read the last page but remember those photographs you saw."

As the ninth chime finished, Smith turned directly to the last page with the author's comment on the main character. Tossing the journal into the metal case, Smith whirled to face his adversary.

"I'm the Virginian," Daniel revealed over the eleventh chime.

Smith's face registered fear at that statement. Daniel's duster blew back from the wind at exactly the twelfth chime, and time crawled. He reached with his right hand for the Colt at his side. Halfway from clearing the holster, he could see Smith's lightning reflexes at work. Smith reached up with his left hand to the shoulder rig, pulling his Glock. He was just a hair faster than Daniel, and as he tried to aim his Colt from his hip, he heard the register of the Glock as it fired.

CHAPTER TWENTY

ST. MICHAELS HOSPITAL, TEN DAYS LATER

It had been touch-and-go when Daniel brought Veronica to the emergency room. She had flat-lined twice before the medical staff eventually managed to stabilize her. The bullet that entered through her back had nicked her left lung before tearing its way to her ribcage. Its energy expended, it lodged itself against the bone. The surgeons had worked painstakingly, taking many hours to remove the bullet. Against all hope, they had closed the wound and kept her stable.

She had spent a week in the I.C.U. before being moved to a private room with a police guard at her door. During this time, she had not regained consciousness. Her only visitors, inspectors and federal officers hoping to gain information on what had happened at the cemetery.

Due to the high-profile nature surrounding the incident, word eventually leaked out. Newspapers, television, conspiracy theorists, and fans of her work, all converged on the hospital. By the time her eyes did open, ten days after entering the E.R., Veronica Jenkins had become famous.

She awoke to a room she did not recognize. Panic built up, ready to take over, when a nurse entered, looked at her, and left. Veronica surveyed the room she was in. It was the usual sparse accommodations of a hospital room, but the table near the window was overflowing with cards, flowers, balloons, and the like.

Veronica gasped when she caught site of a small flowerpot containing a single yellow daisy. A doctor walked in. With him were two men, dressed in very neat, dark suits.

"You were beginning to give us a little worry, Ms. Jenkins," he smiled as he checked her vital signs.

One of the suits took a step forward but was held back by the doctor's raised hand.

"Just a moment." The doctor turned back to his patient, his smile returning. "How do you feel?"

Switching her attention from the doctor to the men and back, she stated weakly, "Confused . . . scared."

The doctor smiled and nodded. "That's to be expected. You received a gunshot wound to your back that damaged your lung. You're a very lucky woman. We had a hell of a time keeping you among the living."

Veronica glanced at the two men standing behind the doctor.

"These men would like to ask you a few questions about what happened, but don't worry. I'll be right here to make sure they don't overstress you."

Taking this as an invitation, the two men stepped forward. The one in front spoke.

Hello, Ms. Jenkins. My name is Agent Kendall. This is Agent Weathers." He pointed back with his thumb to the other suited individual. "We'd like to ask you some questions regarding what happened in the cemetery."

With that, Veronica found herself answering a string of questions over the next few days. They began with federal agents and ended with the local inspectors helping on the case. From the first moment she had seen the two men by her bed, she knew she needed to protect Daniel and keep her story straight. One thing she had learned in her years of writing was how to weave a story.

When asked why she had been at the cemetery, she had told them a tale about wanting to write a piece on those lost during the 1906 earthquake. With the bulldozing of *Hillside Cemetery*, she thought it would make for a great interest story. When asked if she had seen her assailants, she responded that she had been intent on gathering information on some of the names still there when she had found herself in the middle of a shooting. She told them she had thought it was just another gang-related attack, as she had not seen anything when she was hit.

When asked about her friend, Veronica had informed them she had been alone. As she lay there gasping to breathe, a man had come up to her and saved her. She didn't know who he was. Agent Kendall had shown her a sketch of Daniel, taken from the nurse's memory.

"I don't remember," she said, and refused to say more.

Eventually, she was left to rest. The constant guard at her door was removed, and she was finally allowed access to information from the outside world. Through it all, she would occasionally glance over to the potted daisy, wondering where Daniel was.

She turned on the television, partly to find out what was going on in the world, and partly just to have some noise in the now quiet room. No sooner had the screen come on then she was confronted by a news story on the cemetery shooting. The top story of the day was still on the deaths of Kingmaker, John Bennett, and Senior Political Analyst, Mark Royston at the *Hillside Cemetery* in San Francisco. It now appeared Bennett had been executed by the same gunman who killed Royston. There was speculation as to whether the recent deaths of the two men were connected to the murder/suicide of Frank Thomas. All three men worked in Washington D.C., and in a short span of time, all three had been found dead in California. No information on the shooter had surfaced yet, and no connection with Frank Thomas had been verified.

Veronica was not paying much attention to the news, as her thoughts were on Daniel. Where was he? For that matter, where was this Smith? It seemed as if both had disappeared since the shooting. She had been glad to have the guard posted outside her door, as she was afraid Smith might come after her. Now that so much time had gone by, she wondered if Daniel had done something to keep Smith away.

The day before being released from the hospital, Veronica was on the phone with the editor for her Pearl Harbor story. She called to apologize for not turning in the piece, but he had seen the news. No apology was necessary. Just get better and turn in the story when she could. The television had been droning on as white noise during the conversation, and as she hung up the phone, she happened to look up.

Footage of a burning car at the end of Pier 31 filled the screen. The female anchor was giving a breaking news update on the story.

"*In a twist of events, the burned-out car found on Pier 31 weeks ago, is registered to Morgan Dimico. You may remember, private investigator Dimico lost his life in the parking garage of the Hotel Solomons, in San Diego. While the body found in the car is obviously not that of Mr. Dimico, no fingerprints, or dental records have been matched to any known individual, due to the body having been burned beyond recognition. The investigation has uncovered the charred remains of a handgun, which we have been told belonged to a Robert Hunter. Robert Hunter, a secret service agent for the White House, went missing on the same day as the assassination attempt on then president, Ronald Reagan. We have also been informed that the body, who may be that of Robert Hunter, died from a gunshot wound before the body was burned.*"

Veronica felt struck by the bullet all over again. She stared at the small flowerpot holding the daisy. Lifting herself up from the bed with difficulty, she shakily walked over to the table. The daisy did not have a card attached, and she was unable to find one that may have fallen from it. "But still…" she whispered, hoping against hope that she was right.

A couple of days later, she was released from the hospital. She should have been happy to hear the news, but all she could think about was Daniel. She had heard nothing from him. Her heart ached for him. Where was he?

"Ready to go?" An orderly asked, walking in with a wheelchair.

She sat on the bed, wearing the outfit she had on when Daniel brought her in. The only exception was her shirt, which had been ruined. She had been given a top with canaries, stenciled here and there on it, from the lost and found. Veronica knew she looked ridiculous wearing it, but she hadn't cared.

"Yes, I'm ready."

"You have anyone waiting to pick you up?" the orderly asked, helping her into the wheelchair.

"I've called for a cab. They can take me to the airport." She felt numb. The orderly could have left her at the curb and it wouldn't have mattered to her. Problem was, something inside told her to go home. Daniel would not have wanted her to waste away pining over him. He had done everything he could to save her. She might be alone now, but she was alive.

They walked past the nurse's station, just reaching the elevators, when someone called for them to stop.

A young, blonde nurse hustled up to them. Smiling, she handed Veronica the small pot holding the single daisy.

"I thought you might want this. I saw you water it every chance you could. It was the only one you really paid any attention to."

Veronica stared at the daisy in her hands for a long moment. "Thank you. It's my favorite flower." She smiled for the first time in days. She felt her eyes mist with emotion. "It reminds me of someone very dear to me. Thank you very much."

Smiling back, the nurse nodded before heading back to her station. The elevator doors opened, and the orderly wheeled her in.

"It is a nice flower," the orderly added.

"Yes, the prettiest thing I've ever seen." A tear trickled down her cheek. The orderly stared at her from above, not saying a word.

Two months later, Veronica sat in the kitchen of her Cambria home staring at the laptop screen in front of her. She hadn't written a single word since coming home from the hospital. Her mind just wouldn't focus on any new story ideas. There had been many job offers, but she just brushed them off, claiming she was still recovering from her ordeal.

Other than the potted daisy that had been there when she woke at the hospital, there had been no indication Daniel was alive. She began to wonder if he had sent the potted plant to her in the first place. She had waited a few days after the hospital before calling his home numerous times, to no answer. When she finally thought to try his antique shop, she found the number disconnected. On a whim, she looked up the number of the post office across from his business. She remembered to ask for Victor, and when he answered, she asked him about the shop. She was shocked when he told her the store had been vacated. Everything had been removed, including the sign.

"Craziest thing I've seen in all my days."

She asked about Daniel's post office box, but Victor said it hadn't been touched in some time. Veronica wondered if it was all for the better. There was a possibility he had gone back into hiding. She preferred that thought to him no longer living. She didn't know either way, but hoped he had found peace, whichever path took him.

"I'm better off this way," she said to herself for the umpteenth time without believing it. She wanted so much for him to be alive, even if it wasn't with her. If she could only be assured of that, she could live with never seeing him again, no matter how much her heart would break.

A sudden knock at the door made her jump. She had been so deep in thought she hadn't heard a car come up the driveway. A vision of Smith on the other side of the door flashed across her mind. Her heart fell into her stomach until she realized he wouldn't have knocked. If he had still been a threat, he would have come for her months ago. Veronica stood up slowly from the chair. She mentally knew she was healed from her injury, but part of her still expected to feel that twinge of pain hit every time she got up.

There was another solid knock at the door, and a muffled voice said "Delivery." She wished the driver would just leave it on her doorstep. All she wanted was to be left alone. She didn't feel like talking to anyone. She had not decorated for any of the holidays either. She just did not feel in the spirit to do so.

She glanced at her reflection in the full-length wall mirror. She was wearing a plum-colored sweater, faded blue jeans, her hair running wild. She decided she didn't care how she looked. Padding across the hardwood floor in her bare feet, she opened the door. She was greeted by a familiar, crooked smile.

"Hello, Vee."

With an intake of breath, Veronica launched herself into Daniel's arms. Wrapping her own around him tightly, she planted her lips to his in a long, passionate kiss. Kissing his face over and over, she locked her teary eyes on his. "I thought you were dead. The news. The car. The body."

"Smith. I needed to be sure it was really over before I contacted you. I'm sorry if I worried you." His face went from concern to playful. "I did leave you a message."

"The daisy!" She held him tightly again, tears flowing with abandon. "I'm just glad you're alive."

Daniel wiped away a tear from her cheek and smiled wanly.

"I love you, Veronica Jenkins. If there's anything I've learned from all this, it's that. For the past century, I've walked the Earth numb, a shadow of the man I once was."

He gazed deeply into her eyes. "The two months I've spent without you have been torture. This very moment, I feel more alive than I've been for a very long time. I want you to spend the rest of your life with me, whatever that may be."

"I will," she smiled. "I can move to Orange County. My work can be done anywhere."

"No. I've decided to retire. I've closed the shop and sold, or stored, everything – well, most things. I was thinking I might move here to Cambria. If you'll have me."

Veronica kissed him again, gently, taking her time. She eventually glanced up at him questioningly, "Retire?"

"Well, semi-retire." That smile again. "I was thinking I could find a writer of history. Have her help me pen some historical pieces from a first-person perspective, when she doesn't have projects of her own to do. What do you think?"

"Stories like that could be very lucrative."

Veronica pulled away from him for the first time since opening the door. Without a word, she turned to go back inside. As she crossed the entry's threshold, she looked over her shoulder to him. With a glint in her eyes, she raised her left eyebrow. "He would have to convince me." With that, she seductively walked into the house.

Daniel stood there, watching her disappear out of the winter sun, into the darker interior of the house. The warmth from her home invited him to come in. Standing by the door, he felt a calm wash over him. A cold breeze ran through the trees surrounding the cottage, flapping his duster away from his body for a moment. His thoughts turned pensive, and he found himself drifting on that breeze.

•—•

Daniel's duster blew back from the wind at exactly the twelfth chime, and time crawled. He reached for the Colt. Even in fear, Smith's quicksilver reflexes were fast. He pulled his Glock before Daniel's Colt had cleared half of its holster. Knowing he was losing the draw, Daniel tried to aim his Colt from his hip, just as he heard the register of the Glock fire.

He felt the all-too-familiar burning sensation as the 9mm round pierced the right side of his body, entering his kidney. In the millisecond that it took for the bullet to travel its path, Daniel fired his own Colt from his hip.

Daniel dropped to the wooden floorboards on the knee of his bad leg, his left hand impulsively moving to the entry wound in his side. His eyes never left Smith, still standing opposite him those twenty feet. Pulling the smoking Colt back up, the strength in his right arm weakened, he hoped he could get another shot off before Smith did the same.

Smith's weapon was still pointed directly at him, and he waited for the register of the gun which would signal the end of his life. That ominous sound never came. Daniel watched Smith's knees quiver for a moment before buckling, sending him into a kneeling position, almost as if he were about to pray. The hand holding the Glock fell to his side. Smith's shirt, near his heart, grew red with blood. "You were telling the truth. You are immortal."

"Hardly, I embellished. I needed you to think you couldn't beat me at the opening of the ball."

Smith coughed lightly once. "I don't understand."

Daniel clarified, "I meant to say start of the battle."

Smith's eyes turned glassy and he toppled forward onto the splintered, hardwood planks of the pier.

Daniel holstered his Colt. Turning his body with difficulty, he eased himself into a sitting position. Wincing from the pain, he examined the blood flowing between his left hand's fingers.

"Not good."

He couldn't go to a hospital, too many questions would come up, not to mention the ones already waiting for him. Problem was, the last time he had needed this kind of work done was thirty years ago, and that doctor was no longer with the living. He pulled Dimico's cell phone from the pocket of his duster and tried to remember a number from his past.

He had kept tabs on this individual through the years but had not thought to check on him in the last five. Moving his thumb over the numbered studs on the phone, he forced his poor memory of numbers to remember the rhythm. Thinking he had the sequence correct, he punched the numbers in, and hit the send button. All he could think to do was pray that the man still lived at the number and was still alive. He also hoped he remembered the number correctly.

"Stone residence." A very young boy's voice answered after one ring.

"I'm trying to get hold of Zeke."

"My name is Hunter. Who are you?"

Daniel paused at that. He hadn't expected to hear one of his own names tossed back at him, especially by a boy, and he faltered in his response.

"Umm, I'm Robert."

"Hi, Robert. My Granpa knows a Robert. I was named after him."

From further off, Daniel heard another voice getting closer.

"Who is it, Hunter?"

"It's Robert, Granpa!"

There was another pause on the other end as the phone changed hands. An aged man's voice, still strong, responded angrily.

"Who is this? I don't find it funny you using an old, dead friend's name."

Daniel winced again from the pain his wound was causing him. He noted the blood was a darker shade than it should be. It was possible Smith may have finished him after all.

"Ezekiah, it's me, Robert Hunter. Sorry to spring this on you buddy, but I'm alive – for the moment."

"Look, I don't know who you are, but I do know how to find people. So, I'd suggest you hang up now before you get my anger up."

Daniel couldn't help but smile, even with the pain. "You were always a stubborn old coot. The next thing you know, you'll want me to tell you about hoopsnakes and tripoderos."

There was a moment of silence on the phone. Daniel thought he had lost the connection, but he could hear breathing from the other end. Then Stone's deep voice came through, faltering just slightly. "Bob, is it really you?"

"Sorry I haven't kept in touch, but I've been on the run for thirty years. I could use your help."

"You son-of-a-bitch! I knew it! Something told me you made it out of that car. Bad thing about Hal though."

"Ezekiah, Hal was part of a plot against Reagan. He held a gun on me. Some big plan by John Bennett to take over the government somehow."

Daniel winced in pain. "Look, I'll have to tell you what happened later. Right now, I'm in a bit of a bad fix. Seems I took a dose of cold lead."

"Whatever you need, old friend." Stone's tone turned all business.

"I'm not sure if you still have connections, but I was wondering if you knew of someone who could deal with a few bullet wounds without any questions."

Daniel's vision filled with the occasional black spots dancing around. He blinked slowly a few times to clear them out. He had some cleaning up he needed to get done, here on the dock, and he didn't want to pass out before he could complete them.

"I may be retired and seventy-four, but I still keep my hand in things. Where are you now?"

"San Francisco."

"Shit, don't say." There was a pause, "Not sure if he's still in the area, but I think Doc Brewer would do in a pinch."

"Thanks, Zeke. Any chance you could have him come to me? I have a couple of things I need to clean up, and I'm not sure I'll be capable of making the drive after that." Daniel carefully laid down on the dock. Sitting was taking too much energy.

"Damn it, Bob. You were always trouble, but yeah, I'll have him come to you. Where exactly?"

"The end of Pier 31. There will be a black BMW and a silver sedan. I'll be the one bleeding and breathing." Daniel stared up at the sky. This position was helping.

Stone laughed, "Got it. I'll make sure the Doc gets to you."

Daniel heard the connection cut off as Stone hung up, and he put the cell phone back in his duster. Taking a couple of breaths, he worked himself to his feet. Collecting the Glock, he put it back in its holster, then began the business of moving Smith's body to the silver sedan.

It took him awhile to get Smith's body across the twenty feet or so, as Daniel needed to stop every few steps to regain his breath. Eventually, he managed to position Smith's body behind the wheel of the sedan. Then, making the slow trek to the bag holding his files, he dragged them by the straps back to the car. He took another few precious moments to rest before pulling the paperwork out of the bag, tossing the files holding his life on the seat behind Smith. With that done, he allowed his body to slip down the side of the car, back into a sitting position. He was having trouble with his breathing, and it took longer to catch his breath this time. With as much strength as he could muster, he tore a long section off his shirt. Twisting it like a long fuse, Daniel managed to lift himself with his bloodied hand long enough to stuff it into the gas tank, before sliding back down to the planked floor of the pier.

He blinked his eyes for a moment, or so he thought, but he must have dozed off. He woke to the sound of a van headed in his direction. It stopped next to the BMW and a man of about sixty years of age stepped out. He was bald as a cue ball, wearing worn blue jeans, and a white polo shirt. He caught sight of Daniel leaning against the sedan, and strode over to survey the situation.

"Hunter, I assume." It was not a question. "We'll have to get you in the van and away from here before anyone notices." He signaled to a second man who jogged over to help.

Daniel shook his head. "I have one thing left to do, and I'll need that BMW after you're finished with me."

"Randall can drive it." Brewer gave Daniel a trained once over, not liking what he saw. "You're hit in the kidney son, and been bleeding for a while. Your body is going into shock."

"I need the things from the trunk, the metal case, and this bag."

"Randall, take care of it and follow us in the car."

Randall went to work without a word.

"Help me up."

Daniel reached out and Brewer sighed with resignation before grabbing the proffered hand, helping him up. Daniel used the last of his matches to light the wad of cloth from his shirt stuffed down into the gas tank.

With the help of the doctor, he managed to get into the van. Randall, in the BMW, followed the van off the pier as Dimico's sedan exploded behind them.

They traveled a short distance on *The Embarcadero* before turning left into a large parking area on Pier 29. The two vehicles drove down the empty pier to a spot void of any prying eyes, and stopped. Randall jumped out and helped Brewer get Daniel into the back of the van.

The inside of the van was decked out like a mobile E.R. His body felt fuzzy, and Daniel gladly allowed the doctor to lay him down on the low operating table bolted to the inside. The last thing he recalled was the doctor telling him to count backwards from one hundred before everything went dark.

Daniel woke to the sounds of seagulls. He was still somewhere on the docks by the harbor. The seagulls were a dead giveaway, along with the sloshing sound of water hitting the wooden pylons. Cautious not to move too much, he turned his head around to take in his immediate surroundings. He was stretched out on the back seat of the BMW, his bloodied shirt cut open. Shifting his body just a little, he could make out his blood-stained left pant leg, in the same reckless condition as his shirt, but otherwise he appeared whole. Taking a deep breath, Daniel braced himself and slowly moved into a semi-sitting position. There was a slight twinge from his upper body, but not too bad.

He spent a few moments examining the bandages covering his wounds, and a note safety- pinned to his duster. It was a list of instructions on what Daniel needed to do for the next few days, in order for his body to heal quickly and correctly. He pulled out his pocketwatch, reading the time at just after four in the evening. Question was whether it was still the same day.

Daniel transferred himself to the driver's seat. From the front windshield, he could see a black plume of smoke a few blocks away. He knew it was the silver sedan, finishing off any clues as to who was in the car. As a bonus, the files of his extended life would also have been destroyed.

He had many things to consider. Close the shop? Clear out his home? Should he sell everything he was willing to part with, and store what he could not part with? It would all take time. He also needed to be sure that he was finally safe. And get a message to Veronica.

Daniel blinked to clear his mind. Turning, he looked down at the rows of daisies lining the walkway to the front door. He turned back to the open doorway of Veronica's home. Yes, there were many stories he would need to tell her. The time for secrets was over, at least where she was concerned.

"Daniel, come unwrap your Christmas present." Her sing-song voice carried out to him.

A crooked smile filled his face. "Yes, my love."

AUTHOR'S NOTE

Daniel Collum's life takes him through many historical settings. On these travels, he meets, or is involved in, the lives of people read of in history books. While I have made every attempt to keep certain locations and names true to history, there may have been a certain amount of altering, so that places and names would fit the imaginative efforts of this writer.

With that having been said, some sites may have had their names changed. I leave it to those faithful few to figure out which have been changed, and which are truly a work of fiction. The breath bringing life to these "larger than life" figures, was gleaned from information taken from historical accounts. Again, it is up to you to distinguish what is fact and fiction, in regards to the weaving of the life of Daniel Collum.

History has always been a fascination of mine, and with Daniel Collum, I hope to convey some of that passion to you, the reader. If even one person takes the time to research something in this novel on their computer, or for goodness sake, an actual history book, then I have done my job well. There is such a treasure trove of stories to find, so imagine what you could find on subjects that span centuries. All it takes is spending just an infinitesimal amount of energy to do so.

I do hope you enjoyed the journey, and the characters herein, as I have enjoyed giving them to you. I look forward to our next meeting, whether it is sitting in a comfortable chair by the fire, or on a blanket by the lake. Until then, may your own history be full of adventure.

Eldon Callaway

ACKNOWLEDGMENTS

This story could not have been told without the help of a few people. My first thanks to Valerie Sherf and Brittany Cabral, my two test subjects who read every page I tossed at them weekly. Thank you to Devon Johnson, who's interest in the story made her say yes to reading it while still unedited. To my very dear friend Jose Alvarez, who's energy, positive attitude, help beyond imagine, and sheer wish to see me succeed, got me through many a panic attack. Robin Casares, thank you for saying yes when I asked if you would design the cover for the novel. I could not be more overjoyed with what your creative mind came up with. To the many friends who have supported me on this endeavor and put up with me talking about it endlessly. My editor, Kristy Boyd Johnson. Without you, I would probably be rambling on in pages. I have learned so much from you in a short period of time. To the faithful few who have waited patiently, thank you. Lastly, to my family. I am who I am because of you. Cindy, Cheryl, Theresa and Emily, your support in this endeavor is not lost on me. Brianna, you kept my insanity in check. Jennifer, your success as a poet and support of my work will never be lost on me. To Wendy, my best friend, partner, and wife. You put up with my first draft errors, hours upon hours of working through the processes, and proofing my final work. Through it all, your support, exuberance, and love helped me through all the difficult times leading up to the finished story. Thank you, my love.

CPSIA information can be obtained
at www.ICGtesting.com
Printed in the USA
BVHW080145260319
543630BV00014B/185/P